I0614631

When We Were Flowers

by

Catori Sarmiento

This is a work of fiction. Names, characters, places, and incidents are either the product of the author's imagination or are used fictitiously, and any resemblance to actual persons living or dead, business establishments, events, or locales, is entirely coincidental.

When We Were Flowers

COPYRIGHT © 2022 by Catori Sarmiento

All rights reserved. No part of this book may be used or reproduced in any manner whatsoever without written permission of the author or The Wild Rose Press, Inc. except in the case of brief quotations embodied in critical articles or reviews.
Contact Information: info@thewildrosepress.com

Cover Art by *Debbie Taylor*

The Wild Rose Press, Inc.
PO Box 708
Adams Basin, NY 14410-0708
Visit us at www.thewildrosepress.com

Publishing History
First Edition, 2023
Trade Paperback ISBN 978-1-5092-4788-2
Digital ISBN 978-1-5092-4789-9

Published in the United States of America

Then I stopped. In one of them was a small figure of the Frog character from *Chrono Trigger*. He was in a fighting stance with his sword drawn and his shield raised.

"Ami," I said and held up what I'd found. "From *Chrono Trigger*."

"Yatta!" She held up three bags of her own, all filled with tiny mushrooms. "Me too."

We paid and then left to return to the station. By then it was dark and all the neon lights lit up the sidewalk. All of a sudden, a young woman in a maid costume said something in fast Japanese.

"*Ano*," Ami said and looked at me with her eyebrows raised, "Do you want to go to a maid café?"

I looked at the young woman who wore a performative smile.

"I'm not sure what I'm agreeing to."

Ami chuckled.

"Let's find out."

So, we both followed the overly cheerful maid to a narrow elevator inside a building. The elevator door opened to loud pop music and the strong smell of cigarette smoke. The tiny room was filled with older men sitting at tables and young girls dressed in pink maid costumes. There was a small front desk with a cash register where one of the maids stood.

"*Irrashaimase,* she said.

Ami and I looked at each other and she visibly cringed.

"I didn't think it was like this," she said.

I looked behind me and the other maid was still in the elevator, waiting for us to walk forward. "Too late now," I said.

Dedication

This book is dedicated to my Japanese friends who I will never forget, my family, my husband and daughter, and to my Grandma S. whose bedroom bookshelves were filled with romance novels.

Chapter 1

February 2011

When I think about the first moment I fell in love with Japan, I remember the taste of my first bowl of hot, Japanese *udon*. It was just after I landed in Narita airport. I was a long way from the Midwestern plains of Minot, North Dakota, a place where I had lived my entire life and, up until almost a year ago, where I thought I would spend the rest of my life.

I was a Middle School English Language Arts teacher and, though I still consider myself an English teacher, I hadn't been in a classroom for a year. I had spent six years in college, sure of my decision to be a teacher and to do it well. I worked my way through college, first as a preschool teacher and then—once I finished my Bachelor's degree—as a reading tutor for the school district. Then when I finally finished my Master of Arts, I interviewed for a teaching position at one of the only middle schools in my small town and could not have been more elated when they hired me. That was until an eventual deterioration and a non-renewal notice one brisk, snow-flurry filled morning in May.

"Despondent" would be the word that described me for months afterward. I wanted to be nowhere near a school. I took a job in retail, but all the time I was looking for a way to teach again. I went to interviews at any school that would *ask* me to interview. Each time I was told that "we're going in a different direction" so I gave up. I decided that I would not be hired by any of the schools in such a small town where gossip had no doubt black-listed me from a teaching position.

So, after applying for a few jobs I found online, I got an email from a school in a place called Tachikawa in Tokyo, Japan. After a phone call interview, they offered me a contract for a year to be an ALT, an English Assistant Language Teacher at Tachikawa Toritsu Chugakko. I wanted to get as far away from that small North Dakotan town as possible.

That far-away place turned out to be Tokyo.

I moved all my belongings to a storage unit, gave up my apartment, said my goodbyes to my family and friends, and flew halfway around the world, to land in Narita. I walked around the airport where there were gift shops, cafés, and a food court. Every food counter had a line from the passengers who had already disembarked and were similarly hungry.

I chose one with the shorter line, a noodle place. When it was my turn in line, I pointed to the picture on the menu of a bowl of thick noodles with a glistening soft-boiled egg on top. At first, I tried to pay by handing the money to the young man at the register, but he shook his head and pointed to a short wooden tray on the counter. I placed my money there and only then did he take it and place it in the register. He counted out my change and put it back on the tray. I took it and he motioned for me to go to the pick up counter farther down.

In a few minutes, I had a large bowl of *udon* noodles.

I had a pair of chopsticks with me, which I knew how to use from practicing at Chinese restaurants before I came here. I picked up a portion of the noodles, blew on the steam, and put it in my mouth. With one taste, I realized that every Japanese restaurant I had ever been to before was not *actual* Japanese food.

There was a restaurant in my town that claimed to be Japanese dining and tasted nothing like what I was eating. I had eaten noodles there that claimed to be authentic, but thinking about it and looking at the smooth noodles in the succulent broth, what I had been told was Japanese food was likely nothing more than Top Ramen in some house sauce.

I had been hoodwinked.

Everything I had assumed as normal in my small town was not normal at all. If I had been ignorant about something as scrupulous as the taste of noodles, what else had I been ignorant about? I was excited to find out.

****

Before I left the airport, I bought an inexpensive cell phone plan.

The signs and exits were clearly marked, so it was easy to find where the main train terminal was so that I could go to my hotel. I found the terminal and the automated ticket counter. Luckily, there was a button to select English, which I used to buy a ticket to Tachikawa.

I was excited to go on a train. I'd only been on a train three times in my life and they had all been Amtrak trains to Minnesota.

When the train at the terminal lurched quietly to a stop at the exact time it was expected, I was surprised at the precision and the lack of squeaking wheels or lumbering cars. I stepped inside the train car. There were a few open seats so I took one. The train doors closed, and it began to move. A voice from the speakers said something in Japanese and then spoke the translation in English. There was a screen placed above the doors which showed the train line, which car I was in, and the destination. It stated where the train was going and included a message that I should set my phone to silent. There was also a sign on the door window that told me to silence my phone and to keep quiet. Everyone except for the small children in the yellow painted reserved section of the train followed that rule.

It was nothing like the crowded, noisy buses I took from home to school. It was pleasant. I noticed that most, if not all, of the passengers wore a type of medical mask over their faces. It struck me as a little odd, but maybe *I* was the odd one for not wearing one.

Fiddling with my new phone, I put it on silent. The woman from Softbank had configured it to display English, so it was easy to navigate to the settings and set the mode. I had also found that my phone contained a basic English to Japanese dictionary. Had I known, I might have forgone the Japanese to English dictionary that I bought before I left America.

I chose a seat by the door and watched the scenery pass. It was green, and there were hills and mountains in the distance and in between those spots were homes, buildings, and people. It was a change from the sparse, flat farmlands of which I was accustomed to. It was beginning to set in that I was in a new place and I couldn't wait to get started.

The train speakers startled me when it spoke in Japanese and then announced, "The next station is Nippori. The doors on the left side will open."

4

I took out my portable MP3 player from my backpack and I placed it on shuffle. I continued to search through my phone, getting accustomed to it, before falling asleep at some point. I woke when my head bobbed downwards and I jerked to keep it upright. Soon, the train stopped at Tokyo station, and I had to change lines.

I got off the train and followed where everyone else was going, which was a large staircase. Everyone stayed to the left as they walked up. Seeing a clearing, I started walking on the right side until I was nearly bumped into by a man descending the stairs. I moved back over to the left to stay with the crowd. As I walked up, careful of my footing, I then saw that there were yellow arrows pointing upwards and arrows on the right pointing downwards.

I must have been too tired to notice it before.

After ascending the steps, I walked into one of the busiest areas I had ever been to in my life. There were so many people and noises that I had to step off to the side, away from the bustle, to keep my composure. I'd never seen so many people in one place. I knew that Tokyo was crowded, but to know a thing and to see it with my own eyes were two very different concepts. I stood there for a while, waiting for my nerves to calm down.

Looking around, watching to see all the people, I waited for a lull. Eventually, some of the crowds thinned out and I walked towards a train line map that was spread out above some automated ticket machines. Staring at it made me even more confused as there were colored lines circling other lines and spreading out every which way. The writing was a mix of the three writing systems that were used in Japan: *hiragana*, *katakana*, and *kanji*.

I had gone as far as memorizing the first two, but still had trouble with *kanji*. Even though I memorized the characters and how they should be pronounced, that was very different than comprehending them in real-time.

Though I had studied Japanese months before, I was not prepared for the speed in which people spoke. When I wavered my attention for even a moment, someone would ask me a question so quickly that would miss what they were trying to tell me, and we would stare at each other dumbfounded. I must have had the proficiency of a preschooler. Every symbol jumbled in my head as I read the signs as fluently as I could.

After trying to make sense of the map for longer than I intended, I had to give up and ask for help from one of the information booths. The older gentleman there was nice and spoke in slow English that was a little broken, but I appreciated his help. He provided me with a crisp map of the train line and pointed at 立川.

"Miruku-shyei-ki ando furenchi-fur-ai," he said and pointed again.

It took me a second or two to understand what he was trying to say: milkshake and french fry. I looked at the *kanji* again and laughed. The first *kanji* did indeed resemble a simple cup with a straw and the second looked like three lines, or three discarded french fries at the bottom of a paper bag.

I thanked him and went on my way. I wandered slowly through the station until I found the sign and platform number. The platform had a few dozen people waiting for the train. In the center of the platform were clean, white vending machines with all different kinds of drinks. I had some change, so I bought what was labeled as "Lemon Tea".

As I stood drinking my tea, I kept looking at the vending machine. Along the side was a giant portrait of an older American actor whose name I couldn't remember but I knew I had watched him in a movie about aliens. I thought about the vending machines we had at my school which had to be placed in wire cages because they would be vandalized or broken into.

I finished drinking and deposited the empty bottle in a nearby trash can that was vertical and had separate holes for plastic or canned bottles. That was convenient.

The train towards my destination arrived and was largely empty and I was able to sit. I fell asleep until the train stopped and a nice elderly lady dressed in a formal pastel blue suit with a hat to match nudged me awake before getting off the train herself.

Following exit signs outside, the first thing I noticed was all the tall buildings and the noise of cars, buses, music coming from inside shops, the sounds of shoes stepping on the street. I had students with special needs in my classes who would talk to me about "sensory overload". I hadn't fully understood what they meant until I stood in the center of Tachikawa. I wasn't used to so many people, so many sounds, in one place. Until now, I hadn't realized how quiet and sparse my hometown had been.

My heart beat rapidly and I desperately wanted to be somewhere by myself. I had booked a hotel room at the Hotel Nikko Tachikawa for a week until I could find a more permanent place to stay. It was a little more expensive but they had more amenities.

By the time I got there, I was exhausted. The jet lag seemed to have caught up with me. Once I got into my room, I barely managed to take off my pants before crawling into bed and falling asleep. I didn't wake up until evening and even then it was my stomach which woke me. The bedside table had a notice that there was a restaurant in the building. I showered, changed, took my backpack that held all my personal items, and went downstairs.

The restaurant was sparsely occupied. The floors were wood and there were white tables and chairs. Wooden panel separated the main room from some private rooms. I sat on my own and a waitress handed me a menu. I was thankful that it was in both Japanese and English. The food looked so delicious that I nearly ordered the entire menu. Instead, I opted for a steak and a chocolate cake for dessert. For a drink, I wanted to try *sake*, their rice wine.

As I waited for my food, I looked around the room, at the people having their dinners, speaking in low tones. Although I didn't understand everything, I listened, trying to pick up words that I knew.

"Mind if I sit with you?" a voice asked.

I looked to where the voice was coming from and saw a woman standing just ahead of me. Her eyes caught my attention first. They were a light brown like the color of a sandy beach stone wetted by the waves. She was stunning. I had wanted to be alone after being around so many people all day, but seeing her changed my mind.

"Yes," I said, "I mean, no, uhm, I don't mind."

"Oh, good. It looked like you needed some company, and it turns out that I do, too."

She sat down in the empty seat in front of me and leaned to the side to put her purse down beside her seat. When she looked back at me, she swept a lock of brunette hair over her ear that had come loose. Her hair had been tied up in a messy bun and kept in place by a large silver hair clip. She wore no earrings or jewelry of any kind, but did have a pair of thin-rimmed red glasses. The woman wore a white blouse with gold buttons and left the top three unbuttoned so that the lace top of her undershirt showed.

She leaned back on the chair and placed one hand on the table. I noticed her long fingers with the nails clipped short and polished with a pastel pink lacquer. I resisted the urge to reach out to touch those fingers, to feel how it was to hold her hand.

"Ami," she said.

"Tara."

"Are you here for the *sakura*?" she asked.

I recognized the word but couldn't remember what it meant. The jet lag and hunger were making it hard to focus.

"For what?"

"Most tourists come to see the cherry blossom trees, but I guess it's early, so are you looking for plum blossoms?"

"Oh, no. I'm here for a teaching job. I just got in this morning."

"ALT or JET?"

"ALT. What's JET?"

"Japan Exchange and Teaching Program. Most English teachers are one or the other."

"Oh," I said. I didn't really care about the difference between them. I wanted to know more about her. "How about you? Are you here on vacation?"

"In a way," she said. "I had a bad day at work and decided to treat myself to a nice dinner to perk up my mood."

"Is it working?"

She smiled at me.

"It is now."

The waitress brought me my food. In the center of the pristine white plate was a thick round of steak topped with a glistening brown sauce and a twig of rosemary. The waitress then turned to Ami and asked her a question. I understood one of the words to be *nomimono*: "drink". Ami spoke perfect Japanese to the woman. The waitress gave a little bow and walked away.

"So, you work here?" I asked and cut into the steak.

I took a bite and let it melt on my tongue. No sooner had I eaten one bite that I had to have another.

"At a drug research lab here in Tachikawa."

My mouth was full, so I nodded once so she knew I heard her. When I finished swallowing, I said, "What is it you do there?"

The waitress brought Ami her drink, which was a glass of what looked like red wine.

"I wouldn't want you to lose your appetite."

I finished the meal and drank the rice wine. I was starting to feel better and my head wasn't as fuzzy.

"Anyway, I'm tired of speaking Japanese today, especially using all the damn *keigo*," she said. "Honorifics. Japanese has seven different ways to say "sir" or "ma'am" and I can't take it anymore today. Sometimes English is just easier."

"Is it your first language?" I asked.

"Which one?" she said and then giggled. "Actually, they both are. My dad's Japanese and my mom was American."

I noted that she used "was" when she mentioned her mother. I thought it would be too personal to ask her about it. Most people didn't like to talk about death with someone they'd just met. Instead, I changed the subject.

"Want to share?" I offered as I brought my dessert plate towards me.

She shook her head and drank her wine. "I don't like chocolate very much."

I shot her a look of surprise.

"I know," she said. "No one ever believes me, but it's true." She smiled. "So this is your first night in Tokyo."

"Yes."

"Then you'll need an introduction. I know a place we can go." She stood up. "Good thing it's Friday," she said.

I had to think. I was still thinking it was Thursday, forgetting the time difference.

"Have you heard about Gold Finger?" she asked.

"The James Bond movie?"

"No, the lesbian bar." She laughed. "I'll let you guess why it's called that."

I eyed her quizzically. I then chuckled when I realized that in the movie *Goldfinger*, there was a woman called Pussy Galore. Maybe that's what I would find when she took me there.

"How do you know I'm a lesbian?" I wondered aloud.

She smirked and looked down at my right hand where the nails on my two forefingers had been clipped short and the others left to grow out a little longer, covered with chipped red nail polish.

"Lucky guess," she said.

Chapter 2

We walked out of the hotel into the late evening. Normally, I was hesitant to walk anywhere at night. It was something that wasn't often done outside of special events like the State Fair. I was taught to avoid going out after dark, especially as a young woman; nefarious things happened at night. Here, there were so many people out and walking around that being out after dark didn't seem to be an issue. Maybe it was all the street cameras and station cameras I noticed as we walked that deterred them. Or maybe it was just safer.

"It's safe to walk at night?" I finally asked Ami.

"Yes," she answered directly, then said, "Ah!" in a moment of understanding. "You're from America?"

"Yeah."

"Yes, I remember when I visited, many other ladies told me not to walk at night alone. In Japan, so, it's usually fine. I don't think I've heard about any bad things happening. Except if you bother the *yakuza*."

I knew about the infamous *yakuza*, the Japanese mafia. Even in the States, the *yakuza* were seen in movies and video games. I didn't plan on disturbing them.

"I don't think I'll mess with the *yakuza*."

"Good. They're like bees; leave them alone and they leave you alone. Of course, they're not all bad." She chuckled humorlessly. "At the *Tanabata matsuri* in Fussa, they run a fried chicken food stand."

All of what she said was interesting, but I focused on the new word she said.

"What's *'matsuri'*?"

"Oh, like a festival."

We went to the nearest platform and to the automatic ticket terminal. The walk was a whirl of colors, sounds, and shapes. I was prepared to buy a ticket when Ami stopped me.

"Don't bother with the paper tickets if you're going to be here awhile. You get one of these," she noted and took out her black leather wallet and pulled out a slim card from the back pocket. It was worn at the corners where it was silver and green and had a friendly penguin mascot on it. "It's a Suica. A rechargeable train pass."

She then pressed some buttons on the screen for me, asked for my full name, and then told me to insert a certain amount of *yen* into the machine. Once I did, a silver and green card spat out at me.

"Very cool," I said.

Ami charged her card and we continued to the platform. It was bustling with people, some workers who looked like they finished their day while others were uniformed students. We continued to the platform where people stood in lines waiting for the next train to arrive. I was going to take the shortest line, but Ami told me to keep walking.

"We'll go on the women's only car," she said.

"There's a women's only car?"

"Oh, yes. Too many *chikans* on the train so there's a women's only section in the mornings and at night."

I understood everything but the term she used. *Chikan.*

"What's a *chikan*?"

"A guy who gropes women."

"Gross."

"Yeah, well, it's easy for them to do it on a crowded train."

We walked to an area near the end of the platform where only women stood with the exception of some young boys who were clearly with a female relative. The train arrived with a slow roil; the doors opened to release the passengers. Since everyone waiting stood to the left, the passengers disembarking flowed out easily to let those of us waiting inside. There were no seats open, so we stood and held onto the hanging hand rails.

"I always preferred the trains here," Ami said.

The doors shut and the train lurched to a start, causing me to lose balance for a moment.

"I took the train when I was in Seattle before. It wasn't bad, but people like to talk a lot when they're on the train. That's nice sometimes, but I like the quiet."

"It is different," I said. "I think where I'm from you'd just put headphones on so people would ignore you."

Ami nodded. "I'd worry that they'd think I was anti-social."

I smiled, thinking about all the teenagers I'd seen at the mall or in the school hallways with their ear buds on.

"That'd just be normal in America."

"To be anti-social?"

"Sometimes."

The train stopped and more passengers got on, causing bodies to begin pushing against each other. Some woman was wearing strong fruity perfume but it did not cover the smell of body odor that hovered in the air. Ami and I stood shoulder-to-shoulder, her skin against mine so that we were close. While she didn't seem bothered by her personal space being encroached upon, I was averse to it. I wasn't used to being so close to so many people at once. I took a deep breath, closed my eyes, and let myself relax.

"Are you alright?" Ami asked.

"There's a lot of people," I said.

"That's Tokyo," she said. "You'll get used to it."

"You think so?"

"It just takes time." She paused. "Maybe we shouldn't have gone out."

I opened my eyes and turned to her. I hadn't realized how close we were. When I turned my head, our cheeks touched for a moment until I backed away.

"No, it's not that. It's just, that, everything is so new."

Ami seemed to consider that.

"I do remember that most Americans like to have more personal space." She glanced at me and I felt suddenly warm. "It's not as sexy, though."

I smiled.

"Is that why there are women's only cars?" I asked wryly.

"Think of being where you are but instead of a purse shoving into your back, it's some guy's dick."

I didn't like that imagery. I couldn't think of anyone who would want an unsolicited penis.

"And," she added. "Look at how easy it is for some guy to put his hand up your legs and before you can turn around, he's crept off the train."

I frowned at that.

"I guess there are creeps everywhere," I said. "Maybe I should keep a taser down there," I added to lighten the mood.

Ami laughed. She had a wonderful, deep laugh. When she smiled, her cheeks became fuller, allowing the few freckles to stand out more as her eyes squinted.

The train slowed to a stop. I followed Ami as she led me through changing trains and winding corridors. I couldn't imagine I would ever get the hang of maneuvering the train stations.

****

When we arrived in Shinjuku, I excused myself to the bathroom that was near the exit. When I washed my hands I looked around for a paper towel dispenser but there wasn't one. I wiped my hands on my pants. I noticed the woman at the sink next to me drying her hands with a small teal hand towel.

We were in a crowd of people all crossing the same street. I followed Ami down a flashy street that had two red arches, one right-side up and the other upside down, crossing at the corners, and a sign in the center of *kanji* I couldn't read. The street there was busy with people.

"This is Kabukicho," Ami said. "The Red Light District."

That usually meant that all the most unscrupulous activities happened in the area. "So it's shady," I said.

Ami tilted her head. "*Chotto*. Do you want to go look?"

I looked at the bars, the storefronts, at the older gentlemen walking with much younger women.

"Not really," I said.

She laughed. "Good choice. Not that anything bad happens there, well, not often, anyway."

I followed her, since one look at the colorful lights and the crowded streets ensured that I would likely get lost, to a bar on the corner. The sign in the front said, "Bar Gold Finger: Women Only." It was a little relieving to see that it was women only. I'd had bad experiences when going to bars and finding men there. There was something odd that happened to some straight men when they saw a woman in a bar. I became an object for them to touch, to talk to, to try to win over, even, and *especially,* if I explained that I didn't like men. They had trouble understanding that I wasn't there for them, but for myself.

Ami opened the door. A plastic curtain hung from the doorframe. It did nothing to contain the noise. Inside was small, cramped, and full of women.

The noise startled me at first and it took a minute to realize that it was because of a few women singing along to the karaoke on the television screens that were set just below the ceiling. Overhead was a disco ball. If I stood on my tip-toes I could touch the bottom of it. Along the walls on every surface were white pages with *kanji* written on them, pictures of attractive women, and various movie posters of gay-friendly films.

The bartop took up one long wall, and was filled with women trying to get drinks. Ami led me to the bar and we waited a turn. A woman next to us, older, with a short, cropped haircut and a lock of gray hair, held a microphone and sang to a RedFoo song playing on the screen. Others in the bar sang along with her, all in various states of blissful drunkenness.

"What do you want to drink?" Ami shouted.

I had no preference, so I shrugged.

She turned to the bartender and ordered something. After a minute or two, the bartender passed her two glass mugs of what looked like beer. When Ami backed away,

I noticed that the place where the bartender was placing drinks had a ceramic statue of realistic breasts. One of the neon signs on the wall read, "TRUST ME, LOVE ME, FUCK ME," and I laughed. Ami tapped my shoulder and passed me the mug. We then slinked our way through the crowd to find a place to stand in one of the unoccupied corners.

"It's Kirin beer," she said, handing the mug to me.

She lifted her own, tapped it against mine, and said, "*Kampai.*"

"*Kampai,*" I said.

I wasn't much of a beer drinker, but I drank it anyway. Contrary to some American beers that I'd had before, this one was light and somewhat sweet.

"Do you come here a lot?" I asked. I had to raise my voice because of the constant singing and conversations happening in such a small place.

She shook her head. "Not anymore. When I was in college, I'd come here every weekend. It was the only lesbian bar that I knew about, back then."

"I would've loved a place like this when I was in college," I said.

The only bars around back in my college years were the gruff kind where people went to drink to get drunk, not to have fun. There were always house parties of one kind or another that I sometimes went to, but usually I was too busy with my schoolwork to consider partying. I always had an essay to write or a book to read

"Where'd you go to college?" she asked, taking a sip from her beer.

"In Minot,"

"Where's that?"

"North Dakota."

"Midwest?" she guessed.

I nodded. Minot was a small town in the upper Midwest, close to the Canadian border. With a population of about 50,000, Minot was one of the bigger towns in the area. It wasn't until I visited Minneapolis in High School that I realized how small my hometown was.

"How'd you know?"

"My father always tells a story about a time he went to South Dakota. Isn't it cold in the winter?"

I scoffed. "Cold is an understatement. In winter it's below freezing nearly everyday. That's how I got this," I said, flicking the spot on my earlobe where there was a chunk of skin missing. "I was shoveling snow out of my parking spot and I stayed out for a little too long."

Ami grimaced. "That sounds awful."

I still remembered that frigid day in February when it was negative thirty degrees Fahrenheit and my car refused to start despite the engine being plugged in to keep it warm.

"It is. I never liked the cold. You just deal with it."

"Well, now you're here."

"Now I'm here." We both took a sip from our beers. After a moment, I asked, "How about you? Where'd you go to college?"

"Here at Tokyo University and then I went to University of Washington for a semester to learn about drug testing on primates."

"Really? So is that what you do for work?"

She took a a longer drink. "It is. I work at a drug research laboratory. We test on animals. We start with mice and then move on up until human trials." She looked down at her drink and said, "It's depressing some days."

The loudness in the room drastically increased when the bartender started singing. Since it was hard to hear, I kept quiet, sipping my beer, and watching the crowds revel in the night. After a few minutes, the volume in the room became a low rumble. Ami looked down at the table.

"Want to dance?" I asked.

Ami smiled, put her drink down on the table and headed towards the center of the room where there were other ladies dancing to the music. With the flashing lights and the alcohol, I was feeling a little more relaxed and not as anxious about the crowd.

We danced together under the lights. With so many people, it was impossible not to touch another body and I often felt Ami rub against me or touch some part of my body.

When I got tired of dancing, I decided that I wanted to try the karaoke and tapped the shoulder of the lady who had just finished. She smiled and passed the mic to me. The song that came up was in Japanese, but there was the English *romanji* phoenetic pronunciation with it. I didn't know the song, but did my best to attempt it. Then, Ami stood close next to me and started singing into the mic. We were so close that our lips nearly touched. I'd make a mistake and laugh, and she would laugh along with me. When the song ended, there was applause, and we returned to our drinks.

"This place is great," I said.

I meant it. There were few places so celebratory of difference where I was from. Ami finished her drink, and I did the same.

"Another?" I asked.

Ami smiled and got up, but I stopped her.

"I'll get the next round," I offered, both out of courtesy and to practice the little Japanese that I knew.

I went up, ready to order in Japanese but to my surprise the woman spoke English so it was easier than I expected to pay for drinks. I brought two full mugs back to the table.

"So, how's this for a first night in Tokyo?" Ami asked.

"Better than great," I said. "I was expecting to hole myself up in the hotel room."

"Oh yeah?"

"Well, my parents weren't happy that I left. Even when they dropped me off at the airport, they kept telling me to change my mind."

Ami furrowed her eyebrows. "Why would they do that?"

I shrugged. "I gave up on understanding my parents a long time ago."

Ami nodded.

"Well, I'm here now," I said lightly.

Though I was enjoying being at the bar, the loud music and the small, crowded space was beginning to bother me; I felt my heart begin racing.

"Sorry," I said. "Is it alright if we go somewhere a little quieter?"

Ami smiled. "It is loud in here," she said. "I know a place we could go."

We both finished our drinks and weaved through the crowds to exit the bar. The farther away we walked, the calmer I became until I completely relaxed. We didn't talk very much as we walked together. I was in awe as we passed through the streets of the metropolis and stopped when we were on a bridge that neared a park. I was having trouble with the scale of things. I knew that people lived in big cities, that skyscrapers and gargantuan architecture existed, but it was another thing entirely to stand in the middle of it and see it with my own eyes.

"Nice view, *desu ne*?" Ami said. She stood next to me and rested her hands on the rail.

"It's all so…" I struggled to find the correct word to use that would describe what I saw and settled on saying, "monumental."

I glanced at Ami briefly who was looking at the same scene I was but without the same awe.

"The tallest building in my hometown is an empty eight story tower we call the 'M' building." I imagined that the old Midwest Federal Savings Bank with its spinning M sign at the very top of the roof would look insignificant compared to the glimmering Tokyo cityscape. "After graduating junior high, my friends and I snuck in the building on Halloween as a dare. Kids said the place was haunted since a guy fell and got impaled when it was being built."

"*Kimochiwarui*," Ami whispered.

"So on Halloween, a few friends and I found a way in through the basement. We walked around in there until my friends started getting freaked out because they said they were hearing voices and it started snowing."

"Was the snow because of the ghost?" She asked.

I didn't believe in ghosts, so I dismissed the idea.

"Nah. It usually snows in October. I guess I'd prefer to deal with ghosts than snow."

Ami laughed.

We decided to walk about the park which was

sparsely populated. There were a few people strolling around and one or two homeless elderly people, but mostly it was a quiet scenic park with lampposts lighting the walkway. It was difficult for me to feel safe walking at night. It wasn't something I was used to, but Ami seemed confident.

"It's kind of weird walking around at night," I admitted.

She nodded. "Mm. I remember you asked about if it was safe."

"Yeah, I only walk at night if it's somewhere with security, like the fair, and even then it's iffy."

"I know. My first week in the States was a little crazy," she said. "I wanted to go to Seattle and I didn't know why one of my classmates was so worried about staying out late. I didn't know there were drug problems and homeless people. Mostly it was fine but it was kind of *kimochiwarui*."

"You said that before. What does it mean?"

"Oh, *ano*, like a bad feeling." Then she continued, "So, bad things happen here, too, in Japan, but I think it's not so common. Once a homeless person followed me asking for money and kept telling me that there were spiders on my face. I don't think that would happen here." She laughed sardonically.

"At least I wouldn't understand them if they did that to me."

Ami chuckled. I enjoyed her laughter. She smiled in a soft way that showed her topmost teeth but she would place her three middle finger tips over her lips as she did.

"You know," I said, thinking about how surreal it was for me to be in the middle of a metropolis standing so close to a woman I just met. "I think I've done more today than I've done in the past year."

"Good," she said. "I had a nice time, too."

"Yeah, me, too." I nervously took out my *keitai*. "Could I get your number?"

She smiled widely.

"I hoped you'd ask." She took out her smartphone. It had a clear case decorated with all different types of mushroom stickers, some were realistic and others cartoonish. Dangling from the top was a plastic mushroom charm that had a tiny golden bell on it. She gave me her number. "Try calling and I'll save your number in my phone."

I did and her phone chimed. She tapped the keys and then put her phone in her purse. She took a deep inhale and smiled at me.

"So, I'll see you again?" Ami stepped a little closer to me so that she was in front of the vending machine. "Could I kiss you?"

My heart leapt. My words stopped in my throat so that all I could do was nod. She leaned forward and gave me a soft, gentle kiss. Her lips were smooth against mine. I had the impulse to pull her towards me. I hesitated at first, preferring to put my hand on her waist. I let myself relax into her touch and soon found that my arms were around her as our bodies connected.

Chapter 3

The night before I would arrive at the school, I took out my clothes from my luggage to iron my suit. When I accepted the job, the interviewers told me that there was a dress code for teachers. I had to wear black trousers, a white blouse, and a black blazer. That was a little difficult for me to find at the local mall and had to make a trip to the city of Bismarck to buy from a formal wear shop. I bought two decent suits which I thought would last me each week.

On Monday morning, I dressed in my black suit, took the train, and arrived at the school where I would be teaching for the rest of the year. It was a large, square building, with many windows. I had been instructed to go to the teacher's entrance, at the west side of the school.

I walked around the main entrance, passing the windows where some students stopped to look at me in awe. At the nondescript door, I opened it and was inside a small room with tiny lockers and a worn wooden floor. The inside smelled of warm wood and there was a light scent of coffee.

In my preparation for coming to Japan, I had read about certain customs to be aware of. One of them was that I should not wear my outside shoes inside and that most places used the tiny lockers to store the outside shoes. I opened one locker and then another until I found an empty one and deposited my shoes. I wondered if I had made too much noise, for soon there were footsteps and I was startled by a short, quick exclamation. I turned to where the noise came from and saw a woman there.

"*Konnichiwa*," she said and then briefly checked the red-banded watch on her wrist. "Tara-*sensei*?"

I nodded and said, "*Hai*."

She bowed to me and when she spoke it was with a soft, suggestive, tone. The woman must have been Haruyo, the teacher I had been communicating with about the job. She was a short, slim woman, who wore a pair of thin, silver-rimmed glasses. She wore her hair short and tucked her locks behind each ear.

"Please wear the ones, there," she said, pointing to a line of green plastic slippers. I did so. I stepped up into the main hallway where the woman stood.

"*Sumimasen*, I was supposed to be here early, but there was a problem," she explained hastily.

"It's no problem,"

"How was your travel?"

"It was great. It was the first time I've been on such a long flight."

"Yes, it is long. You are from Nor-su Dakota?"

She said the name of the state like it was the first time she had said it out loud.

"Oh, yes."

"Hm. So, first I will bring you into the main office to review the papers."

Haruyo guided me to one of the offices where we sat down with one of the front desk workers. He was a thin man who used a wheelchair.

"This is Mr. Oyabi," she said. "He will give you the paperwork to sign."

He explained everything in Japanese, which Haruyo translated for me, though I felt sorry for Mr. Oyabi, who stumbled when having to pronounce my last name: Larson. It was a common name where I was from, but here it seemed to be precisely uncommon. So, Haruyo was patient in her time and shared what each document said. It was a teaching contract that explained that I would complete a certain number of classes and hours for the school year. My first class would begin on April 1st and end the next year on March 31st. I signed it.

"We will make you a copy so you can open a bank account. Are you busy this week? I can go to help you."

I didn't know that I needed help to open a bank account, but it would be useful to have someone who was proficient in the language. All I could manage so far were the general pleasantries and a few words I could pick out in conversations.

"Anytime is good for me."

Haruyo took out her smart phone and looked at her calendar. "Wednesday at four, is that alright?"

I nodded.

"I think the MUFG is the bank that is used, so I will meet you there. Oh, and you must buy a *hanko*, like this," Haruyo took a small wooden case out of her pencil bag and opened it. Inside was a black cylinder and a tiny spot of red ink. She picked up the cylinder and showed me the end, which had *kanji* engraved into it. "It has my family name on it. To open the bank account, you must have one. I think any stationary store will carry them."

Haruyo replaced the *hanko*. Mr. Oyabi brought a copy of papers in a clear file. He passed them to me.

"Do not lose those," Haruyo said.

She stood up, bowed briefly to the man and then

said, "I will show you the school."

Haruyo led me down the hallways, showing me each door and each classroom, and then up a flight of stairs to another hallway, and on and on until we reached the fourth floor.

"Most of the hallways look the same," she said, "So, here, there are different colors." She gestured an open palm to the stairwell walls which had a colored stripe on either side. "Don't worry," she added. "I still become lost."

We walked down one of the hallways to a room at the far end.

"This is the teacher's room," she said. "You will come here each day before classes start."

"A teacher's room? The teachers don't have their own classrooms?"

"This school uses a teacher's room and we go to each classroom that the students are in. Some schools have a teacher in each class, but this school is a little different."

"Oh," I said. That seemed a bad idea to me. If I left a classroom of kids alone, there was no telling what kind of mischief or violence they would get up to. The principal had even told me directly when I first started to never leave the students alone. Most of the students were good, kind people, but it was those one or two who made it difficult for everyone.

"I'd worry that the students would do something bad," I said. "There was one math teacher who stepped out of the room once to refill her water bottle and while she was gone one student stabbed another one with a sharp pencil."

Haruyo looked at me in horror. "*Maji-de*," she said.

I got the gist of her meaning by the look on her face and her tone. I shrugged. "It happens. That's why I never left my students alone."

"I think that must be hard for teachers." She nodded once. "So, I will see you at the bank. I can show you back to the door." She started walking and I followed her back to the teacher's entrance, which I was thankful for since I was turned around.

"Then if you can start to teach classes, are you available?"

I smiled and nodded quickly. I was eager to start working as soon as I could.

"Ok. I have to go to teach a class. I am so happy you are here."

She bowed briefly and then walked back down the hallway. I changed my shoes and left the school. It was afternoon by the time I headed back. School must have been out since I was joined on the train by several small elementary school students, all in their uniforms and their leather book bags. What surprised me was that they were traveling alone. They couldn't be older than six or seven and yet they had waited on the platform, gotten on the train, and rode it all on their own. I couldn't imagine that happening in America. Parents would be too scared to let such young children out on their own, and for good reason. There were too many news stories about abducted children or accidents that happened if they were alone. I knew I wouldn't risk that if it were my own child.

****

On my way back to the hotel, I stopped at one of the shopping areas to find a stationary store. It took an hour of wandering and walking around but I finally found a little shop that had *hanko* displayed on a rack. I didn't think I could find my last name, "Larson", anywhere. I took out my *keitai* and used the dictionary to find a Japanese equivalent of my last name. The *katakana* appeared but nothing else. I had to ask the shopkeeper for help. She was a young woman of what I would guess was in her twenties, and she wore her sleek black hair in a low bun. She had a white blouse and a black pencil skirt. I showed her my phone and said, "*Hanko*". She replied in a soft voice and stepped from behind the counter to the hanko display. She looked at the display, turned it, and then removed one of them.

"Thi-su izu, *okay?*"

I was relieved that she spoke some English. I said it was okay, not that it mattered since I couldn't read the *kanji*. I would have to ask someone later about what it meant. I checked out and the woman said, "Sankyu."

I looked around more and noticed all the hand towels on display. Remembering what happened in the bathroom when I didn't have a towel. I bought an orange towel with an image of a small smiling dog embroidered on it.

My shopping done, I went back to my room. I was still at the hotel and looking for an apartment, which proved more difficult than I thought it would be. I had made contact with a Gregory Findle, a housing agent who was an expatriate from the UK.

"It can be hard for foreigners to find apartments," he warned. "Japanese like to rent to people who they think will stay here for longer than a one-year visa."

"Oh," I answered.

"Where are you looking?"

"Around Tachikawa."

"Okay," he said, his voice perking up, "that makes it a little easier."

I heard him clicking his computer mouse. A dog yipped in the background and he shushed it.

"So, there are some outside the area but close to the stations: Fussa, Hachioji, Akishima. Did you have a price range?"

"The cheapest," I said.

"Ah, be careful there. The cheapest would be a single room only with no kitchen and no bath. It's likely that you'll want something like a studio apartment. They're less costly but still have the basics."

He paused and clicked some more.

"There's one in Akishima that could be good. It's a few minutes from the station and will get you to Tachikawa in ten minutes. Should I set up a time with the landlord?"

"Yeah."

"Great," he said. "I'll contact them and will get back to you."

I spent the rest of the day walking around Tachikawa. I was getting used to the noises. I walked to the expensive department stores to gawk at the fashion and jewelry and swiftly walked out when I noticed people were staring at me. I went to a restaurant whose name I couldn't read but which served a delicious vegetable omelette. At another store called Daiso, everything cost one hundred *yen*. It had more in it than any dollar store I had ever been to. I took a plastic basket and tossed in whatever I needed or found cute. I bought necessary amenities, a toothbrush, toothpaste, a hairbrush, and more unnecessary things that I plucked from the shelves, like cute notebooks, colorful pens, erasers shaped like food items, soft blue slippers, and a dozen other tiny toys or decorations, or snacks.

When I checked out, the woman at the register took my money and I started placing all the items in the bag myself since there was no bagger. I started to walk away when the lady said something to me. I turned around and she held change in her hand and was holding it out for me. I had forgotten to take it from the money tray.

I took it and thanked her. All the way back to the hotel, I thought about how the woman gave me my change back and was unsure if that would have happened in my town, outside of a few small shops whose owners knew me by name.

I returned to my hotel room with my three bags of merchandise. When I sat down, I turned on the television and started eating some of the snacks I bought, one of which was a bag of chocolate cookies. Every channel was in Japanese, but I left it on one which was a kind of talk show. I had no idea what they were saying, but immersion would help me understand the language faster.

When I'd learned that I was accepted to teach in Japan, I started studying Japanese as much as I could. I bought language books, watched videos on learning Japanese, and tried free language exchange chats. After a few months, I knew a general amount of Japanese, but not as much as I wanted to know. While I learned the basic *hiragana* and *katakana*, *kanji* was difficult for me to grasp, and I even had to sound out the basic *kana* when reading, as if I were a child learning words for the first time. Listening to the Japanese in the background, I could pick out certain words that I understood but not the concepts that were being discussed. I would have to trust that I would learn it eventually.

I thought about sending Ami a message. Would that be too soon? I did it anyway, thanking her for the night before. Then, I regretted sending it. I may have been jumping into things. I'd done that before on dates, inevitably turning the other person off before we were even on. Pleasantly, I received a message back.

Ami—楽しむ. *We should go again. I forgot to say my full name: Kishiguchi Ami.*—

The last name came first, as I recalled. I returned the message with the same method, half-jokingly.

Ami—はじめまして(*^‿^*).—

That meant "Nice to meet you". But, it took me a few seconds to understand the emoji. I thought it was cute. I decided to try to use some of the little Japanese I knew to ask where we would be going.

Me—どこ行く?—

I didn't receive a response for several minutes, so I turned on my laptop and checked my emails. I had one from my new workplace, telling me when to arrive. I answered it. The others were from some friends and my parents.

I then loaded the game *Chrono Trigger* on my emulator on my laptop that I had been trying to finish playing for the better part of two years. I hadn't gotten far during my first year of teaching as I'd always had papers to grade, lessons to plan, parents, staff, or students to email, or any other paperwork that was required. It was nice to not have to think about any of that for once and to focus on something I enjoyed.

There hadn't been much for me to do in my hometown. I wasn't interested in many sports and I wasn't interested in church, so that limited the activities that most took part in. I did join a gaming club and we would play together. Eventually, I started by playing rudimentary text-based adventure games and over time I became interested in simple 2D games. There was something comforting about the simplicity of 2D games. It was always fun to share that with students. It gave us a kind of camaraderie, that I wasn't some old teacher who didn't understand them.

I took a break to go and get some dinner, also checking my phone.

Ami—*I have an idea. Let me know the next time you're free.*—

I hopped a little out of excitement. It had been some time since I actually had someone interested in me. My one significant past relationship had fizzled and in the last year I had one or two dates that I had to drive hours to get to that went well but distance made it difficult. I was finding the appeal of the quaintness that I had been so used to was fading, eaten up by the glamor and connectedness of a big city that was Tokyo. I decided to take a walk. That was when I discovered the Seven Eleven.

There was a stark difference between the convenience stores that I had been to in my hometown of Minot, with packaged sugary snacks, fatty food, and soda machines, to a shop that may as well have been a small grocery store. The white lights glowed against the white tile floors. The air smelled of fried bread coming from the items resting in the heated display: Corn dogs, steamed buns, and some items that I didn't recognize but which smelled delicious.

I picked up a basket by the entrance and walked around the store several times, looking around, picking up brightly colored packages, some nail polish, putting whatever I could find in the basket, then taking drinks from the cooler. There was Coca-Cola and other brands that I didn't know but had English written on them. I took a can of coffee, a bottle of lemon tea, and a bottle with a white substance in it labeled Calpis, which sounded to me like "cow piss" and made me curious to try it.

Along the outer wall was a cooled section with ready-made packaged meals that looked so appetizing that I wanted to buy them all. I took two of them, one with steamed white rice and a thick meat patty covered in a brown sauce, and another was an omelette over rice with ketchup on top and a garnish.

There were other people waiting next to me, trying to decide what to pick. A man who smelled strongly of cigarette smoke came close to me and grabbed a packaged meal without hesitation.

I thought I should also get something for breakfast, so I turned around, walked around the line that was forming in front of the register, and chose some pre-packaged sandwiches. Finally, I got in line behind the last person. I decided to try out some of my Japanese on the cashier. I ran over the words in my head to make sure I would say them correctly.

Arigatou gozaimasu. A-ri-ga-toe go-za-i-ma-su.

When it was my turn, I placed the basket on the counter. The young man took each item out, scanned it, and announced the price as he did so, then he placed it in a bag. He totaled the items, then called out the number to me. I removed my wallet and remembered to put the cash on the money plate. He took it, then made my change, and placed it on the plate. He pushed the plastic bag to me.

"San-kyu," he said, and bowed a little. I took a few seconds to realize he was speaking English. Thank you, he had said.

"*A-ri-ga-toe go-zeye-ma-su*," I said slowly, trying to make sure each pronunciation was right.

****

When I woke up in the morning, my head was congested and my throat felt itchy. I must have picked up some bug from being around so many people.

Whether or not I was sick, I had to meet Haruyo at the bank. I got ready, made sure that I had my hanko, and went to find the place. When I got off at the station, I had to look around for longer than I wanted, trying to find the bank, and then worrying that I'd gone to the wrong place or come at the wrong time. After going back and forth, going back to the station, and looking at the local map, I realized I had taken the wrong exit. I put myself in the right place and found the bank just outside the south exit and Haruyo waiting outside. I walked up, apologizing as soon as I was close enough for her to hear me.

"I got out at the wrong exit," I said.

"It's okay. Shall we go in?"

The bank was exceedingly white, like the waiting room at a hospital. I took a number and we sat and then were soon called to a cubicle. The entire thing went by in a flurry of Japanese and stamps on documents. I had to give some money to deposit at one point, then stamp more documents.

After a few minutes, I was handed a moneybook and then asked to choose a cash card design from a placard. Having no preference, I chose the first. Since I had no permanent address yet, Haruyo gave the school's address that my card would be sent to.

Another twenty minutes, and the entire thing was done. I offered to get coffee with Haruyo, but she shook her head. "I am too busy," she said. I said that I understood, but I worried that the "I'm too busy" meant something else. I had kept her waiting. And though it was unintentional lateness, she could have been upset and not want to spend time with me. I didn't want to blurt out my worry, so we said our goodbyes and I was free. Now that I had a bank, I had a place for my money, and I could finally get my apartment.

****

A day or two later, I met with Mr. Findle at the address he sent to me. He was a man who I would describe as "interesting". He was well dressed in a sky-blue suit with matching color shoes and a tie. He had a trimmed black beard and dapper hair. In his arm, he held a small white bichon frise who sat comfortably in the crook of his arm. The dog was well-behaved as it barely twitched from that spot in his arm the entire time I was with him. The apartment was in a small block of apartments near a train station.

The place was small, being just one large room with a separate small section for a kitchenette and a shower. Small, but it was all I needed. I didn't have much with me and I didn't intend to buy very much in the way of furnishings. Being near a train station would make my work commute easier, even if it meant I didn't have a full bath to submerge in or a large kitchen to cook in. I liked the window, a large sliding door window that led to a narrow balcony. Having sunlight was on my mind. I wanted to make sure I could soak in enough of it.

I recalled too many dark days during winter when working in my classroom which had windows facing away from the sunlight, so what little there was could barely be seen. I had ended up investing in a light therapy lamp for my desk so that I got enough daylight, even if it was artificial.

Having a window that let in light was perfect. I could put my bed just in front of it so that the sunlight could wake me up in the morning.

"I like it," I told him.

"Wonderful," he said. "There *are* other non-Japanese living in this apartment building."

I wasn't sure why that was relevant.

"Actually, this apartment is not so expensive because it is *jiko bukken.* Unfortunately, two years ago the occupant died here. That's what this is for," He pointed at a thin piece of paper with *kanji* on it tacked on the wall above the entrance. "To keep the ghost at peace."

I exhaled sharply. "Having an apartment that someone happened to die in doesn't bother me."

Mr. Findle raised his eyebrow slightly. He glanced away, stroked his dog's head, and then said, "Well, then, in that case, the owner will not charge for the first month until after your first paycheck and he will include some furnishings. I will prepare the paperwork and I think you could move in by the end of the week."

"Great!"

Having my own place would make it real. I would be finally settling into the experience. It would mean that I was here, that my new life was starting.

Back at the hotel, I went over my finances. I would be making close to 190,000 *yen* per month, a little over fifteen hundred dollars. The one room with a small kitchen apartment I found in Ogamicho in Akishima was

54,000 per month. Then there was the cost of my cell phone. I was glad I'd opted for an inexpensive *keitai*, a simple flip-phone that could send SMS messages and make phone calls. I needed internet access, and then some money for food and travel. I should have enough left over for some savings.

Rather than moving in by the end of the week, Mr. Findle called me back later that day to tell me the paperwork was ready. By the end of the week, I was out of the hotel and in my own place. The apartment had been furnished, as Mr. Findle had said it would, with a futon for a bed and a small white table. The futon was in the middle of the room so I moved it closer to the window to give some more space.

It took me days to finally sleep without waking up. The busy streets and the sound of the passing train was more sound than I was used to at night. Every night at nine o'clock, an announcement would bellow that it was late hours. I could never catch what the rest of the announcement was.

Chapter 4

My first day of teaching. I was nervous but excited. I got to the school and went to the teacher's room and waited there until I saw Haruyo. She greeted me briefly, picked up a stack of folders, and said, "Shall we go?"

I helped her carry some of the folders and generally followed her lead. The morning went by quickly as I helped Haruyo pronounce words and explain certain parts of grammar. Except for the younger children, all the students all kept their eyes focused downwards. When I asked Haruyo about it, she said that "We Japanese don't always make eye contact. So, that's why I have it in some lesson plans for the older students. We have to practice eye contact."

It must have been a social norm. I always considered that a person looking downwards, avoiding eye contact, was usually a signal that someone was either shy or dishonest.

In one of the elementary school classes as we were getting ready, one of the boys touched my hair.

"*Orenji*," he said.

It took a little bit for me to figure out what he said. Orange. I wouldn't consider my hair orange or even red. It was a kind of strawberry-blonde. But, to them, my hair must have looked strange. In every class it was almost the same. I introduced myself and as soon as I did, one or two would start to laugh or to make faces. One would puff out their cheeks or flap their hands by their faces. By the third class I decided that there must be a reason for it that I didn't know about.

"They keep saying my name and making faces," I said. "Is it my hair?"

"Oh," Haruyo said, and lowered her voice. "I think because 'Tara' is like a fish, see," She opened her electronic dictionary, tapped the keys, and then showed me the screen. On it was a picture of a fish with the Japanese writing and under it the English, "Cod". I chortled. No wonder the younger students laughed whenever they had to say my name.

Tara-sensei: Teacher Cod Fish.

I laughed.

"It's not very flattering," I said. I thought about the nicknames some students in my hometown gave me. "Bitch" and "Cum-muffin" came to mind. Compared to those, being called a fish was quaint, "but I've been called worse."

As I went through the day, I was more in awe of Haruyo than any other teacher I'd met before. At first, Haruyo reminded me very much of a rabbit standing on its hind legs as she often took to resting her arms so that they bent at the elbow and then she held her hands hand-over-palm in front of her chest. She was patient with the students, more than I might have been if I were in her class. She stood and waited for the students to quiet, and they did. I'd tried that before and the kids kept talking for ten minutes. With Haruyo, there was an implicit respect. She was stern with them, but also understanding and kind. She was the kind of teacher who I wanted to become.

The next evening, Ami sent a message that she

would be off work that evening and could meet me for dinner at MoriTown, a mall in Akishima that I hadn't been to yet.

I stopped back at my apartment to change out of my work suit and into more comfortable wear. Haruyo had given me the lesson plans for the month that I needed to review. I put on some music, opened my window, and sat on my futon to go over the lessons. I corrected some grammatical mistakes. One lesson that was rife with errors was on the subject of prepositions.

Some of the uses were uncommon, like "Going to a walk" instead of "Going for a walk." It was understandable. There were some grammatical choices that made logical sense but weren't used in English. It could be hard to understand the reasoning behind most of the rules of English. Some rules just existed from centuries' old conventions that remained stuck in modern English for whatever arbitrary reason.

By the time I got through half the lessons, it was nearing five thirty and I got up to leave.

****

Moritown was on the other side of the train station. I hadn't figured out how to use a public bus yet, so I opted to walk. It took about twenty-five minutes to get from my apartment to the Moritown entrance.

The mall was gigantic. It was two or three times the size of the local mall in Minot and the design was modern and chic. The exterior was painted in a tan color with white accents and there was a high tower which had the name of the mall and a white geometric design inside a green circle. The surrounding areas had all sorts of plants and trees and there were little islands on the main pathways that had seasonal flowers planted in large pots.

I walked down the main pathway. Not long after, a small crowd of people came from behind me. A train must have recently arrived. Students who had just finished their after-school activities were scattering into the mall, along with other workers who were lining up outside restaurants or rushing to get inside. I was still early. Ami wouldn't be finished with work for another hour, which left me with enough time to look around.

As I neared the entrance, I passed an Indian restaurant and the smell of the food wafted out, stopping me for a moment so I could stand and savor the aroma. I'd only had Indian food a few times in my life but I always enjoyed it. I saw that next to the main entrance to the restaurant was a small window that had a "Take Out" sign posted and a short menu on the inside of the window.

I went up to it. A short lady came to the window to help me. She was younger, with her hair tied back in a bun, and she wore a plain white t-shirt with a green apron over it. She spoke English with a slight Indian accent. I was thankful to hear it. I was becoming so used to hearing Japanese all the time that for someone to use English meant that neither of us had to struggle to understand one another.

I ordered something small, since I would be eating with Ami, and decided on a bowl of curry and a serving of naan bread. In less than ten minutes, it was ready, and a line had already formed by the time I received it. I walked over to one of the outside benches and ate my snack. Everything about it was delicious, from the soft, slightly buttered bread that dissolved on my tongue to the mildly spicy curry that warmed my stomach. I sat there for a few minutes after I'd finished eating to savor the taste that settled on my tongue as I listened to the sounds of people walking past, catching bits of conversations.

Finally, I stood up and deposited my trash in one of the nearby bins. I walked inside the building, passing a fancy-looking tea shop as I did. Inside, I was struck by the size of the place. I knew it was big, but being inside made me realize just how big it was. There was a floor map on a column that I went to. There were at least two floors and, by my estimate, about thirty or forty stores. There were also other buildings on the other side of the mall, including a Toys R Us and a movie theatre.

I decided to start where I was and walk around. I went from one end to another, mostly window shopping. One such shop I went inside was a small store where everything in it was five hundred *yen* or under. I couldn't resist buying a squishy pillow formed in the shape of a sleeping cat.

After, I went upstairs and my phone buzzed. Ami. She said she would meet me at the food court. I went in search of floor map. The food court was on the second floor, so I went there and waited out in front. I didn't think it would be hard for her to spot me.

About fifteen minutes later, I had a tap on the shoulder and saw Ami. I gave her a hug and she let out a long exhale. She smelled of cigarette smoke and floral perfume.

"Long day?" I asked.

"I'm happy it's over." She pulled away and looked down at my bag. "What did you get?"

I showed her. She smiled.

"Cute. Be careful, though. If you keep buying those, you'll end up with half your room full of plush animals."

I thought of half of my apartment stacked with

fluffy, soft plushies and coming home to lounge on them. That seemed like a wonderful way to fall asleep.

"Is that a bad thing?" I asked.

"Not if you like it. Ready to eat? I'm so hungry. I haven't eaten since breakfast."

We went into the food court and Ami set her purse down on a vacant table and started walking away.

"Wait," I said.

She stopped. "What?"

"Are you going to leave your purse there?"

"Yeah, so no one takes our seats."

"But someone will take it."

She smiled and shook her head. "Not here."

I was confused. I never let my belongings leave my sight, even when I was working—*especially* when I was working. Some students had sticky fingers and I had no doubt that they would take something if given the chance.

"Let me hold it," I offered.

"Just leave it," she said. "Trust me, it'll be there."

Ami went to one of the food places that made noodles. "Udon," she said. "Have you had it yet?"

"At the airport, I think."

"Oh, this will be better."

We waited in line but I couldn't take my eyes off of her purse, just in case a passerby thought to swipe it. When it was my turn to order, I chose my item quickly so I could keep looking back at the purse. Although I kept watch, Ami had been right. No one took a second glance at it.

We sat down with our food. I still couldn't believe that nobody touched her bag. Ami stood up and went to one of the center columns. I looked over and saw that she was washing her hands at a small sink affixed to the column. That was certainly convenient. I considered following her to do the same thing, but I didn't want to seem like I was copying her or that I needed her to show me how to do everything. I was becoming mindful that I often leaned on her to answer questions about the area or about understanding a situation and I wanted to stop relying on her so much.

Ami wasn't exaggerating when she said she was hungry. No sooner had we sat down than she had her chopsticks in her hand and was blowing on and eating her noodles.

"No finders-keepers here?"

Ami slurped some noodles and swallowed. "Finders-keepers?" she asked. "I don't think I know about that."

"It means that if you find something, you can keep it."

"Is that an American thing?"

"I think so."

"Oh. My mom never told me about that." Ami knitted her eyebrows. "That sounds like it's stealing."

Ami ate some more.

"Not really. If it's something that nobody pays attention to or something that's lost, then anyone can take it."

"Just because it's lost doesn't mean it belongs to you."

"No," I agreed. I didn't have a good answer for her. It was just something that was done, that was normal. Normal to me, but maybe it wasn't so normal. "It's just what happens."

"Is that something *you* do?"

I thought back to a few times in my teenage years when I found some misplaced ring or trinket in the school hallway and decided to pocket them.

"Once or twice," I said.

She pressed her lips together in thought but then continued eating. I took my chopsticks and gathered some noodles to eat. Like Ami told me, these were much better than the ones I had at the airport. It was like everything I was eating was tasting better and better. The noodles were thick and warm, the broth was savory and strong, and the boiled egg that was on top of it was soft and seemed to melt in my mouth. After eating bite after bite, I stopped to give my stomach a rest.

"The food here is so good," I said.

"At Moritown?"

"In Japan."

Ami smiled. "I think so."

I looked around the food court and thought about the options that I had for food in my hometown. They were all slight variations of the same food items: hamburgers, pizza, pasta, maybe a Mexican restaurant or two, family buffets or homestyle diners. There was the odd Thai or Chinese place, the one restaurant that masqueraded as serving Japanese food. And there were always a few cafés besides the bigger coffee chains. From where I sat, there was more variety in this Japanese mall than in my entire town of Minot.

I shook my head.

"You know, it almost isn't fair," I said. "Where I'm from, there are so few options for food. It's mostly fast food chains or just the same variation of it."

"Is that what's popular?"

"It must be." I thought. "Everyday after I left work

I'd drive home and there would be a line of cars at McDonald's or a line at Starbucks. On Sundays, the parking lots at food places were always full. It's like a meat and potatoes kind of town."

Ami chuckled.

"A meat and potatoes town?"

"Sure. Mostly meat for meals and a side of some kind of potato."

"No vegetables?"

"Sometimes."

"Only sometimes?"

"Depends on the person. Like, I don't think I've ever seen my dad eat any greens except for a green bean casserole and I don't think that really counts."

"That can't be healthy."

"Not really, but it's also a little expensive to buy fresh produce."

"Too bad," she said. "I thought there were many farms around there."

"There are, but they grow wheat and corn, and maybe some other crops."

"I see."

Ami finished her food and leaned back, sighing, and holding her hands over her belly. I was drawn to her fingers and how she held them one over the other, relaxing her fingers so they spread out, touching the top of her pants, with one pinky resting on the top button. I felt myself staring and looked back at my food.

"How was your work day?" she asked.

I looked at her. "Not so bad." I shrugged. "I'm getting used to the routine. I like it. It's definitely less intense than my last job, but I wish I could converse with the students more. So, after I'm done with work, I try to study Japanese for an hour each night."

"That's good," she said. "I was kind of lucky with English since my mom always spoke it at home. I didn't need to study too much."

"Could she speak Japanese?"

"Perfectly!" she answered. "She told me that it took her years. She even passed the N1 test," she said. "It's the highest level of the Japanese language proficiency exam."

"She sounds amazing."

"She was."

Ami looked away at some far-off point or to nowhere in particular, lost in thought. I shouldn't have asked about her mother.

"I'm sorry," I said.

She turned back to me. "Why?"

"I shouldn't have asked about your mom. It makes you sad."

She nodded. "Of course it does. Still, I can't go around my whole life without talking about her, or thinking about her. I get sad, but it also makes me happy to remember her. So, don't worry about it. *Shinpaishinai*."

Her attitude about living through a major death was insightful. I didn't know if I could deal with my mother's death with such acceptance. "Wow, that's really mature."

Ami tilted her head to the left as if in thought and then gradually straightened. "Hm. I don't know if it's mature; it's reality."

"I don't know how I'd deal with that."

"I didn't do very well in the beginning. It's been a long time, so it's not so bad now." she smiled. "And I work with sick or dying animals everyday. I'm used to death." She said cynically but with an upbeat tone that made me unsure if she was joking or not.

I wasn't sure how to move on to a new topic or if I should talk at all. Thankfully, Ami broke the conversation by getting up to return her tray. I finished eating and did the same.

"So, what kind of sightseeing do you want to do while you're living here?" Ami asked.

I had ideas in mind before I left America but I also didn't want to be too strict in my plans. I liked seeing where the day would take me.

"Just being in a big city is fun," I said. "There's always something happening."

Ami nodded. "That's true."

"I think I'd like to see the major touristy things and probably try to climb Mt. Fuji."

"Oh," Ami pursed her lips. "That's such a difficult climb."

"So I've heard."

"I did it with my dad and brother maybe ten years ago. I practiced before, hiking shorter mountains and doing some running after work, and it was still the most challenging climb ever."

I was now reconsidering. I thought I could do it, but being from the Midwest I was definitely not used to hiking. "I think I should practice, too. There aren't any mountains where I'm from, well," I stopped to think. "There are the Turtle Mountains. They're more like big hills and tall cliffs."

"Turtle Mountain? Like, *Kame-yama*?" she asked. "We have a place called that here."

"Really?"

"I think it was also the name of one of the emperors." She smiled. "That's interesting. A half a world away there is someplace that is the same."

"Maybe I'll take you there someday."

"Yes, that would be nice." She turned and smiled at me.

We walked around the mall and were on the third floor by a noisy arcade. It had loud pop music playing, flashing lights, and the interior was lined with crane game machines and the label at the top of each machine said, "UFO Catcher". Ami stepped over to one which displayed a gray cat-like plush animal that held a leaf.

"Oh, Totoro," she said.

The name sounded familiar. Then I remembered that I had seen the character before at a display in a Barnes and Noble, but that was where my knowledge of it ended.

"Who is that?" I asked, as Ami rummaged through her purse for some coins.

"You don't know Totoro?" She asked wide-eyed.

I shook my head.

"He's a character from a movie: *Tonari no Totoro*."

She put her coins in and moved the joystick to where she thought it would pick up the plushie. She then pushed the bright pink button and the crane lowered. It picked the plushie up by the ear, moving it closer to the hole, but then rose back to its original spot. Ami let out a disappointed noise. She tried again, each time getting the plush closer to the edge of the hole.

"I used to be good at these," she said.

"Is it actually possible to win?" I asked, remembering the few crane games I'd played before.

Ami groaned at another failed attempt as she searched for more coins. "It is."

She put more coins in the slots. After she lined up the crane and pushed the button, she said, "I'll have to show you my place sometime. I have so many little things I've won from these."

The crane barely moved the plushie. Ami clicked her tongue. "I'm out of change," she said.

I removed my wallet and took out the coins I had been accumulating since I'd arrived. She put up her hand to refuse.

"Then I'll try," I said.

I stood in front of the machine and attempted to win the prize. Ami took a spot beside the machine and told me where I should aim the crane. I kept slipping coins through the slot after each failed attempt, but all the time the plushie moved closer.

I wanted to win it. I was too invested to step away. One thousand *yen* later, I had gotten the plushie close to the edge. One more try and I was confident I would have it.

Ami stood by.

I tried again and on the press of the button, I stared at the crane, willing it to grab the prize. One of the crane arms grasped the underside of the leaf and caught it, forcing the plushie to be dragged up and positioned directly over the hole. I held my breath. The crane released; the plushie fell through the hole.

I jumped in excitement as the crane machine lit up and played a sprightly tune. I grabbed the Totoro from underneath.

"*Jyouzu!*" Ami said.

I handed the Totoro to her. She shook her head. "No, no. You won it."

"It's for you," I insisted.

She shook her head again and waved her hands in a dismissive gesture.

"Take it," I said again. "Besides, I already have a companion," I said, jiggling the bag at my side.

Ami considered that and reached out to take the plushie. She smiled and held it in the crook of her arm. "Thank you," she said.

We walked back through the mall and to the train station.

"So, did you teach in your hometown?" Ami asked.

"I did. I wasn't very popular with the English department," I said, "because of my 'radical' views about Shakespeare."

Ami scoffed. "What does that mean?"

"I once shared that I didn't think Shakespeare's plays should be taught in English class at all; they should be in Drama. Shakespeare wasn't meant to be read sitting down, it was meant to be heard and seen. I still taught some of the plays in class since it was required, but the teachers never forgot what I said. All those other teachers were older and had this weird loyalty to Shakespeare. I preferred Milton."

"I didn't read Shakespeare until college. What are a bunch of middle schoolers doing reading that?"

"It's in the curriculum."

"Seems a waste of time," she said.

"Most of the kids thought so."

"What's school like in the States?"

"That's a long story," I said. "I can only talk about my own classes, but I liked to have an open-type of room, use incentives, collaborate, and I never gave homework."

"You what? No homework?" Ami leaned back and

raised her eyebrows as if questioning my teaching. "Wow."

"Is that a problem?" I asked, a little more indignant than I intended.

She put her finger to the center of her lips. "I think the kids must like it," she said. "I know I would've loved not to have any homework in school."

"But?"

"But…don't kids need discipline? The real world is hard and they need to learn that early. Hard work is the way to be successful."

"They do work hard. I just have them do it all in class so they don't have to bring work home. There have been studies that show that homework doesn't improve academic achievement."

"What studies?" she questioned.

"I remember researching one from Duke University and I did my own research project on it when I was interning," I said, more defensively than I wanted to sound.

Ami looked off into the distance.

"*Saa*, maybe it's like that in America. I don't know how kids can be successful in life if they don't know how to work hard."

I didn't like arguing about it.

The other English department teachers had told me I was being too soft on the students. I had too many memories of the teachers meetings where one of them would inevitably mention my teaching methods and how they disagreed. I used new methods that were seen as easy; I thought they used old methods that were outdated.

Thinking now about how I had observed the teachers at Tachikawa, and especially how Haruyo taught, I had to admit that Ami may have had a point. Maybe there were times when I'd been too easy on a student when they needed a firm hand. It was difficult to toe the line between efficacy and effectiveness. I had wanted to be effective, to have students learn as fully as possible and to enjoy the subject as I did. While efficacy was important, I wasn't as concerned about it as I was that the students were learning. Had that been the right thing to do?

"You could be right," I admitted slowly.

"I had lots of different teachers," she said. "You learn something from each of them. It's like fate."

"You think so?"

She turned back to me. "Everyone we meet in our lives, we meet for a reason. Like how we met," she said.

She then lifted her hand in a fist and kept her pink straight. "It's '*Unmei no Akai Ito*.' The red string that connects our hearts by fate."

She took my hand and grabbed my pinky with hers. "The vein from the heart flows directly into this finger. Now our hearts are touching."

That was an encouraging thought. I didn't hesitate; I kissed her.

Chapter 5

March 2011

The first time I felt an earthquake I was left feeling incredibly dizzy. The floored rolled underneath me; the lights shifted above me. To me, it didn't seem too bad, just weird.

The students and the teachers, however, had different reactions. Their panic, their fear, told me that it was more serious. Everything after that went by so quickly that I didn't have time to think. I followed Haruyo as she led the class outside, then the parents came to pick up their children, and we waited until all of them were accounted for, late into the evening. Afterwards, I was told to go home and wait for a decision.

The trains, buses, and taxis were either full or had lines. Taking the train was quicker on a normal day, but I could walk. It would take over an hour, but I would rather be halfway home than standing and waiting for a ride. I wanted to be home, safe. I wanted to call my parents and tell them I was alright.

"I'll walk," I said.

"Are you sure?" said Haruyo

"Yes. My place is in Akishima."

I started walking, following the direction of the train tracks. I was not the only one.

My phone buzzed. It hadn't been working all afternoon so I eagerly withdrew it from my pocket. It was a message from Ami:

Ami—*Can't get a train home. Can I stay with you?*—

I stopped and stared at the message for a long time. Long enough that several people passed me. I didn't care if it was convenience or sentimentality that made her send the message. I wanted to be with her.

I replied immediately, giving her a time when I should be at my place, along with my address. I rushed home, running when I got to Akishima station. All the streetlights were out.

When I got inside, everything in the apartment was off. I looked through the few cupboards for a flashlight or some candles and found a large camping flashlight. Since my apartment was so small, I could place it in the bedroom and have a soft glow illuminate the interior. I checked the faucet to see if the water was running. It sputtered and then flowed in a soft stream. I took a quick shower while the water was available and then changed. I didn't think Ami would care that I was in my lounge clothes. I made sure to tidy up my small space and to open the window to get some fresh air.

The lights suddenly came on.

I turned out the flashlight and started my computer. I was worried about my mom and sent her a message that I was alright.

A knock came at the door.

My heart beat rapidly. I took a breath and opened the door. There was Ami, dressed in her work clothes, skin moist with sweat, her hair was pulled back into a ponytail and she smelled a little musky. She held her purse in one hand, which bulged at the sides since it contained her high heels. She was barefoot.

When she saw me, she gave me a hug. I was too startled to reciprocate at first, but then put my arms around her. She smelled like the train, fresh air, and sweat, and I didn't care. She was holding me and I didn't want her to let go.

"*Arigatou*," she said and let out a long exhale that smelled of cigarettes and coffee. "I tried hotels, but they're all booked, and all the *friends* I called gave me the run-around. I was worried you would think I was being weird, asking something like that when we haven't known each other too long."

"It's no problem," I said.

She backed off and though I wanted to keep her there in my arms, I relaxed.

"Think I could shower?" she asked.

"Yeah," I said and pointed at the room, "It's there."

"Thanks."

"Do you need a change of clothes?"

"No. I stopped at the Seven Eleven and picked up some stuff on my way here. There wasn't much by the time I got there."

She took a shower while I went on my computer again. When she was done, she had changed into a simple white t-shirt and shorts outfit. She looked clean and fresh and her eyes were a little drowsy. She looked like she could fall asleep standing up. I knew that we hadn't been seeing each other for long, but offering some comfort seemed the polite thing to do and it would be nice to have someone I cared about be with me.

"You can sit down by me," I offered.

She gave a little smile and did not hesitate to walk

softly over to my futon and sit down. When she did, I nudged her on her shoulder playfully.

"Uhm," she mumbled as her fingers tapped on the phone. "I'm just messaging my dad to check how he is."

"And?"

"He's fine. His house is outside the city so there wasn't any damage. He's worried about me. My apartment is in a more populated area and it's on the ninth floor. I told him I was with you, so he's a little calmer."

"You told him you were here?"

She nodded. "Mhm. He's less worried now."

"Does he know we're dating?"

She looked at me. "Yes."

I felt like there was more she should have said or more that I should have asked. I was used to my sexuality being criticized, used to the opposing arguments that inevitably came when my orientation was obvious, used to being lectured or at the very least, silently judged, and at the best, moderately tolerated with the rare occurrence of being openly accepted—that was usually by very few. The open admission that I was dating a woman would have been met by apprehension and mild acceptance by my family and prejudice by most of my co-workers and general people. That Ami's father was so open and accepted without question made me feel an immense appreciation for the man and I had yet to meet him.

"Your dad sounds great," I said.

She sighed. "He is." Then she rested her head on my shoulder and glanced over at my computer screen. "What are you working on?"

"Mostly checking my email. Letting everyone know I'm safe."

Ami reclined and settled her head on my pillow. I flicked my attention from my messages to her face, getting glimpses of her fidgeting to find a comfortable position. I finished and logged off, placing my laptop next to my bed.

"This is a nice little place," she said. "You were lucky to get something close to the station."

"*Chotto*," she said. I looked at her and she was pointing to the slip of paper tacked above the entrance. "Did you know that was here?" she asked.

"Yeah. Why?"

"Did they tell you someone died here?"

"Yeah. Is that what that thing says?"

"It's to purify the space from spirits," she explained hastily, "But, *ano*, you didn't feel worried about sleeping where someone died?"

I crossed my arms and leaned back to consider what she asked. "Not really. I mean, people die on the street and in hospitals, but I don't stop going to those places."

I know I must have made some sort of confused expression because she looked at me as if I were missing some obvious point.

"Yes, but, it's different to *live* where someone died, especially if you didn't know them."

We stared at each other for longer than I wanted. I didn't want an argument but I also thought she was overly concerned with the idea that someone died in my apartment. It seemed silly to be superstitious about it.

"You believe in ghosts," I said as I uncrossed my arms and rested my hands at my sides.

She tilted her head to one side. "A little. You don't?"

"No."

Ami's eyes widened. "Eh?"

"Is that weird?"

"I think I've never met a person who didn't."

I didn't know what I should say but I thought I should give more of an explanation. "The stories are interesting to hear about but I think they're just stories. Most of what people see that they think are ghosts can be explained."

Ami scowled. I braced for an impassioned explanation from her, which was what usually happened whenever I had a view that contradicted some else's. Instead, she relaxed her face and shook her head.

"At least it's good that you have the blessing. I won't have to worry about anything creepy touching me."

"Like this?" I asked playfully and tickled the back of her knee.

"Ah!" She twitched her leg away and when she did, she inadvertently pulled the blanket with it, making me lose my balance and shifting closer to her. She turned over and faced me. Her eyes were half closed as she nestled into my arms and thread her arm under mine. She stared down at my leg and stroked my tattoo on my left thigh. It was inspired by one of Georgia O'Keefe's paintings and was another way of being able to express myself without being overly direct.

"You feel so good," she murmured as she kissed my neck. "Do you want to?" she asked.

I melted into her touch. I had wanted to be with her since she came to my door. "Yes," I answered.

****

I woke up the next morning feeling groggy. Instead of getting up right away, I lazed around on my bed looking out the window. There was some condensation fogging the glass, making the view outside look like an impressionistic painting.

Looking closer, there were four small stars that had been drawn into the condensation. I smiled. Ami must have done that. When I turned, Ami was not there.

I sat up, worried that she left. Then, I heard a plastic bag rustling from the kitchen. She must have gone out to get food. I got up and went to her, giving her a hug from behind. She leaned her head back and put her hands on mine. Then, she let go and withdrew the contents of the bag. A squatty can with red markings, a bag of sliced bread, a container of margarine.

"There wasn't much there," she said. "So, I found what I could."

I picked up the can. On closer inspection, the red markers were pictures of beans and there was black *kanji* on it.

"What's this?"

"*Anko*," she said. "I will make *ogura* toast."

She took the bread out and toasted it in the small counter range that I had, then spread a healthy amount of margarine along with a spoonful to the red bean paste. It didn't look very appetizing but I was hungry enough to try it.

I took a bite. The sweetness of the beans combined with the savory, melting margarine made me keep eating and I didn't stop until the entire piece was gone. I ate another.

"Almost better than peanut butter and jelly," I said.

Ami made a gagging sound. "That is the grossest sandwich," she said.

"It's a staple."

"Yeah, my mom made it for me once. She said all

the children in the States ate it. I could never get used to it."

"Why not?"

"It's everything: the soft bread, the weird peanut texture, the smooth jelly. It's like eating a dead jellyfish."

I laughed. "Maybe you need to try it again," I suggested.

Ami eyed me mischievously. "I'll make a deal: I'll eat a peanut butter and jelly sandwich, if you eat *natto*."

"What's *natto*?"

"Fermented soybeans."

That didn't sound too bad. Weird, but I had already eaten octopus so my openness to other kinds of food was increasing.

"Fine," I said. "Deal."

Since I didn't have a television, I had my laptop open to stream some videos while I cleaned my small apartment. One of the positives about living in such a small space was that it was easy and quick to clean. With Ami's help, it took less than an hour.

I searched the news and immediately saw footage of a building with smoke coming from the top. The news I was looking at was in English and explained that the tsunami and earthquake had caused major damage, and the nuclear reactor faced issues. The power plant was having radiation leaks. They were evacuating anyone who wasn't already gone.

I closed out of the page. I couldn't think. When I checked my email I found dozens of messages from family members, all of them asking if I was okay. I answered every single one and then I shut down my laptop.

It couldn't be happening. Something that terrible

couldn't be happening. Not right now. Not to me. I distracted myself by folding my laundry or hanging it up in my closet. But my thoughts kept returning to the tsunami, the earthquake, the melting reactor. Was there radiation in the air we were breathing?

When I was finished, I sat next to Ami and rested my head on her shoulder. She was still on her phone, but had it plugged in and charging. I kept thinking about how everything was suddenly changing. I had a plan and now it was all unravelling. I wondered if I should leave. No. I had barely been in Tokyo for a month. I didn't want to have to leave. I had to trust that the problem would be fixed.

At the same time, I was afraid of the possibility of a melting nuclear reactor. What kind of effect would that have on the water or the air? There was no way to protect myself from that. It was insane that a six-minute earthquake could change so much. It made me feel small; it made me feel powerless.

"What do you think is going to happen?" I asked.

Ami took a deep breath. "Who can know? *Shouganai.*"

Ami got up and went on my narrow balcony to smoke.

I didn't know what else I could do, so I opened my laptop again and zoned out by playing *Chrono Trigger*. Ami gave me updates every now and then. Some of it was reassuring. The workers shut down the reactors and they were supplying coolant. Ami watched a Japanese news report, telling me what little she learnt. The workers were trying to fix it.

Finally, I took a break and fell asleep. When I woke up, it was evening. It was quieter than I was used to. An eerie sort of quiet. There was no hum from the electronics or the sound of the refrigerator cooler. I checked the nearest light switch. The power was out. Again.

I was a little drowsy. I could hear the shower running. Looking out the window, all I saw was the black street. The shower stopped and Ami came out with her hair wrapped in a towel and wearing the clothes she bought at the *conbini*.

She jumped when she saw me. "Ah, I thought you were still asleep."

"The power's out."

Ami rubbed her hair with the towel. "I know. They're trying to give more electricity to the reactor."

"Is it bad?"

"It's the same. The news was covering the earthquake damage around Tokyo and showing more about the tsunami before the power shut down. I don't think I can watch any more news. It's just giving me tension."

Ami removed the towel and took it back to the bathroom to hang it up. She came back and sat on my futon. "My work already called me to say they would be closed on Monday," she said. "I think most schools will be, too."

"That's a silver-lining," I said with a smile. "We get a three-day weekend."

I thought about the air and the radiation that could be coming from a failing nuclear power plant. "Do you think it's safe to go outside?"

Ami stretched her legs out in front of her. "I don't know. If anything is in the air, it'll get in here through the aircon or under the gaps. The news said they were testing the air. Maybe we can never know for sure." Ami tilted her head to look out the window. "I think many people will be scared."

"That's because it *is* scary."

"Yes. There's a history of fear about anything nuclear."

"Why?" I asked at first, but then stopped. I shook my head, remembering the two nuclear bombs the Americans had dropped on Japan at the end of the seond world war. "Never mind," I mumbled, scratching my head.

"I remember my grandmother talking about it," Ami whispered into the dark. "how scared she was when she learned about the atomic bomb. What it did. I must be feeling the same as she did."

Guilt panged me. Though it wasn't me who was directly responsible for what happened to her family, it was *my* country. In school, when I learned about the bombing of Hiroshima and Nagasaki, it was presented as a kind of victory over the Japanese. We had defeated them and secured our safety. Now? I was ashamed that I had rarely considered the human impact of it. How many had died? It was my countrymen who had made Ami's grandmother feel fear.

"I'm sorry," I said.

"Yes." Ami looked at me. "It is a sorry situation."

"Maybe we should talk about something else?" I offered.

Ami smiled. "That's a good idea."

"Do you have any siblings?" I asked.

"Two," she answered. "A brother and a sister. My brother is a salaryman—"

"—A what?" I asked, unsure of the term.

66

"Like someone who works for a company for a salary. He works all day from seven to maybe nine at night, then has to do *nomikai*—drinking with co-workers—and then goes home. It's depressing. But, he's married, and lives in Nagoya now. My sister is a dentist in Yokohama. No children yet, though my dad hopes for one soon. You?"

"Oh, yes. My parents are Catholic."

"How many?"

"Six, including me."

"Six!?"

I nodded. "Six. We had a small house, too, so I shared a room with my sisters. And we had one bathroom. I don't know how we all managed it."

"What are they doing now?"

"Most of them are still in Minot. My eldest brother moved to Nevada after college, he works as an electrician, and two of my sisters moved to Canada. Everyone is married, except for me, and I have," I had to stop and think. "Seven nieces and nephews."

"Big family."

"Like I said, they're Catholic."

"And that means they have to have many children?"

"They don't *have* to." I tried to remember all the intricacies of the religion but long ago I had stopped thinging about it. It wasn't my religion anymore. "I don't really know all the reasons why."

Ami sat for a long while looking out the window, not saying anything.

"Do you miss them?" She asked, finally, and turned to me.

I had to think about that question. There was a time in my life when I did, but as I grew older and more independent I grew apart from them. Partly religion, but mostly that I wanted to be on my own, especially after so many years being in a crowded house with many eyes on me. When I'd started college, even though it was in the same town, I got my own dorm room across from the university to have a place for myself. Over time, I was too busy studying or working to be homesick. It was only during holidays or on frigid cold days when I felt their absence more than usual.

"I used to," I said. "And then I went on my own. I was busy with my own life and what I wanted to do. I guess that's just what happens when you get older."

Ami tilted her head. "Here, you never leave your family, no matter how far away you are. At least that's what I've been told."

"My family is like that. *I'm* not. When I told them I was coming to teach in Japan, they begged me not to go. They wanted me to stay there, to find another job, but I couldn't. I couldn't stay there anymore. Not after everything. It's a small town, so word travels. Even if I tried to get into another school, I don't think they would have accepted me. I tried to make a life there but I just don't think it's for me after all. I was trying to fit into a place that wasn't right for me, I think, or maybe *I* wasn't right for *it*."

"That's why I don't like small towns," she said. "It's the same here, too. Your public face is always on show."

I thought about how much trouble I had in my town. How different I was to everyone else and how I was often judged for it. When I still went to my parent's church, I sometimes went to a Sunday School class.

When I was about eight, on a hot July day I took off my stockings. Once I got one stocking off my left foot, the teacher tapped me on my naked toe and told me that, "God loved modesty and didn't I want to make God happy?" I shouted at her and took them off anyway. I was promptly removed from the class and taken to my parents in the sanctuary where I listened to a reading from The Bible while I daydreamed about unicorns.

When I was older, I held hands with a girl at school. Her name was Lucy. We played every day, sat next to each other when we could, played with Barbie dolls on weekend playdates. Then, one day during recess, impulsively, I told her I loved her and I kissed her on the lips. I thought it was the most natural thing to do. She even kissed me back. The following Monday, my desk was moved far away from hers and I wasn't allowed to play at her house anymore. Two weeks later, Lucy was put in a different classroom. "I guess they didn't like mine."

Ami shook her head. "They sound like assholes."

I was reminded of the teachers who came to me to tell me privately how they agreed with me or how they were also frustrated with the administration. There was quiet support, quiet tolerance, but that was often where it ended. Quietly.

"Not all of them, just not enough to make a difference."

"Yeah," she said. "It's easier for people to follow what's normal. It's like that here. Some things change, but so much stays the same. I mean, offices still use fax machines."

"They do? The last time I saw one of those I was in first grade."

She nodded. "I guess people like to keep doing what makes them comfortable."

"That's true."

My stomach grumbled.

Ami laughed. "Maybe we should figure out what's for dinner."

"Do you think anything will be open?"

"We could try to see." Ami rubbed her eyes. "Could I borrow something to wear? I don't want to put on my work clothes."

"Sure."

I liked the idea of Ami wearing something that was mine. It made me feel closer to her. She went to my closet and picked out a pair of blue jeans and the Minot State University t-shirt that I'd brought with me. While the shirt always fit a little short on me, it went to Ami's hips and the jeans were a little long on her so she rolled them up at the bottom.

She looked down and smiled. "Is this where you went to school?"

"For college. I always thought it was funny that the mascot was a beaver."

Ami gave me a look of puzzlement.

"I mean, because beaver is slang for vagina."

Ami laughed. "Do they know that?"

"Some do. It's like an inside joke for students who know about it."

"Maybe I should get one, too. We can be beaver twins."

I smiled.

As we were getting ready to leave, I thought that it might be good to wear a face mask, just in case. I went through my backpack and pulled out two masks for us.

"You're already getting accustomed to things here," Ami said as she took it.

"They're good for the train," I said.

Ami nodded and put on the mask. So did I. We went outside to a dark street. There was an elderly man walking a small brown poodle on the opposite side of the street. When we passed, the poodle looked at us and sniffed the air.

"I always wanted a dog," Ami said. "We always had a cat but never a dog."

"What kind of cat?"

"He is a persian. My brother was little when we got him and kept calling him '*fuwa fuwa*'. It means, like, kind of fluffy? So, that's the cat's name."

"That's cute. My parents have a dog. She's about six now. She's a big husky."

"Oh, a husky! That's a big dog."

"She is. Her name is Baby."

Ami laughed. "That's funny to call a big dog that name."

"Oh, it's funnym because she acts like a baby. She always cuddles and whenever anyone leaves the house, she cries."

"Aw. I will have to see her sometime."

"I'll show you a picture later. Well, I guess whenever the power comes back."

At first, we tried the *conbini*. They were closed. I should have gone earlier instead of hurrying back after Ami told me about the power plant.

We then walked to a nearby grocery store, which was open and operating with flashlights positioned around the store. There were a few others in the store as well who were trying their best to see and get what they needed. One woman had a small baby in a front carrier and was looking around the boxed and bagged cereals.

The refrigerator sections had tape on them to stop anyone opening them. We were able to find bread, noodles, cereal, some filled buns, and some fruit, but not much else. I was happy to have something.

Reminded of my deal with Ami, I went looking for peanut butter and jelly. While the jelly was easy to find, I could only spot a kind of peanut cream that came in a small container, but not actual peanut butter. I guessed it would have to do. Ami made sure to take a package of *natto*.

The man at the register was older, and also wearing a face mask and had a pad and pen to mark the sales. He had a large flashlight set up at the till. Once we went through the *genkan*, I said, "So, are you ready to try it?" I asked, holding up the grocery bag.

"Are you?" She asked, taking the *natto* from the bag.

On the walk back to my apartment, a black and white cat crossed our path, jumped up to sit on the dividing wall, looked at us, and gave a loud, "Nyaow". I stopped, startled by the odd sound.

Ami stopped as well. "What?"

"That cat," I said, nodding to it. "It made a weird sound."

"Did it? I think it's normal."

We kept walking until we reached my apartment door.

"Oh," Ami said. "because in America cats say 'meow'."

"Yeah?"

"Here they say '*nyah*'."

I unlocked the door. "I didn't know animal's sounds were location specific."

Shaking my head, I focused on preparing her

sandwich, while she had a cup ready for me with *natto*. We stood next to each other in the kitchen, ready to follow through with our dare.

"You first," she said.

I took a deep breath, which was a mistake, since I inhaled the rotten bean smell. I gagged. Ami giggled. I took a pair of chopsticks and picked up one bean from the sticky, putrid mass of beans. I held my breath and put it in my mouth. My initial reaction was to spit it out, like I was a toddler who ate a piece of undercooked broccoli. The taste reminded me of a time when I accidentally ate a soggy carrot but the *natto* was much worse than that. After swallowing that one bean, I washed my mouth with water.

"I think I can only do one."

"Not bad. So, I'll take one bite."

Ami brought the sandwich to her mouth and took a small taste. She made a frown and then let out a disgusted groan. She shook her head and handed the sandwich to me, which I gladly took and ate.

"*Muri*," she said.

My phone buzzed. I didn't recognize the number but I swallowed the piece of sandwich and answered.

"Will you continue to teach?" Haruyo asked.

"I plan to," I said.

She let out an audible sigh. "Oh, good. I will tell the principal. Today the school is closed, but class will start again the next day."

"Ok. Thanks."

"See you at school."

She hung up. I explained what happened to Ami who nodded.

"I think I need to take a rest," she said and went to

my futon to lie down.

I showered and brushed my teeth. Ami was asleep, so I had a snack and started my computer. Inevitably, I would shift from video gaming to looking at news updates. NHK had an English language site with updates and even a live feed of what was happening at the reactor. I managed to finish half of a level and then stopped so I could study some Japanese. I practiced writing the *kana* and after that tried writing some vocabulary words. I was starting to practice some grammar points when Ami woke up. She stared at me for a little with half-opened eyes.

"Is it all normal?" she asked.

"Not exactly," I answered.

"*Kuso*. I hoped it was a dream." She sat up and scratched her head. "I'll have to check on my place today," she said. "See if there's anything broken. I'm a little worried about some of my things." She rubbed her eyes. "Do you want to come with me?"

"Yes!" I said, more excitedly than even I had expected. I wanted to see her apartment, how she lived. Plus, it would be a break in the constant news coverage.

"Oh, good. I didn't really want to go by myself." She looked over at me and smiled. "Studying?"

"Yes. I thought I was prepared, at least a little bit, but I need to learn more."

"You will. You'll hear it everyday and it'll stick."

I hoped so. I stood up to stretch my legs from sitting for so long. Ami got up, too, and before doing anything else, she went to the balcony to smoke. I didn't like that she smoked, but I couldn't tell her what to do, either. She had told me that she didn't like it. In time, maybe she could quit.

I got ready. After Ami came in, she changed back into her clothes from the day before.

The trains were running, but there weren't as many as usual. We waited half an hour for one. Once we got on the train and started to the destination, the screen that showed the destination changed to a news feed covering the Fukushima power plant. All the smoke, the rubble, and the flashing *kanji* on the screen wasn't very reassuring.

Chapter 6

Her apartment building was elegant. It had an office with an attendant and security cameras. The attendant told Ami something and I heard the word "elevator". Ami thanked the attendant and then told me, "The elevator isn't working so we have to take the stairs." She led me to the staircase.

"What a nuisance."

We started walking. After the third flight, I asked. "What floor did you say you lived on?"

"The ninth."

I sighed.

"Sorry," she said.

"*Shouganai*," I answered.

Ami laughed.

We kept walking up the stairs. Finally, a long time later, she stopped and we were on the ninth floor. We walked down the corridor and Ami rustled through her purse for her keys. She stopped at number 67 and unlocked the door. I followed her inside and removed my shoes at the entryway, the *genkan*. She turned the lights on to light the short hallway.

Immediately, I noticed that her apartment was bigger. That wasn't a surprise. What was surprising was how many little mushroom decorations were tacked around the place. In fact, the entire apartment was like stepping into a small forest. There was a tipped over large vase that contained overly-large flowers. Her floor was wood but she had forest-themed carpet over several sections. The hallway had a green carpet which resembled grass. When I stepped on it, it was soft and silky. Her walls were decorated with framed pictures of various plants, some of the frames contained pressed leaf drawings and pinned mushrooms with their names written below in English. I focused on one, a framed watercolor of a tiny chartreuse mushroom with the title penciled in as "hydrocybe psittacina".

"I painted that in my tenth year," Ami said when she noticed me staring at it. "It's one of my favorite mushrooms: the *Parrot Waxcap Mushroom*. I've tried looking for it here but…no luck. I read that they are in, um, Denmark, so I want to travel there one day. Also, this one," she said excitedly, pointing to another framed watercolor of a cluster of deep violet mushrooms, "The *Amethyst Deceiver, Laccaria Amethystina*. This one you can eat but it looks similar to the *Lilac Fibrecap*, which is poison. This one is also in Northern Europe. I wonder how many people ate it by mistake."

She paused and I waited for her to talk some more. I liked listening to her talk about a thing she loved, even, or especially, because I knew so little about it. She didn't say anything right away, so I asked about another framed picture, this one was a print of a lavender purple mushroom with a thick stalk and a wide cap.

"This one is *Murasaki Shimeji*. I drew that on a trip to Yamagata when I went mushroom hunting."

"Is purple your favorite color?" I asked, noticing the trend.

She made a gesture of putting her hand vertically in front of her face and waving it as if she were waving away a bad smell.

"No. It was when I did these. Now I like indigo. What about you?"

"Green," I answered. I looked at another picture that had circular pictures with lines in the center. "What's this one?"

"These ones are mushroom prints," she pointed at each one and named the mushrooms, "*Saketsubatake, chichitake*, and *fukurotake*."

"It's amazing," she said. "Mushrooms reconstruct dead life and make something new. Even if the mushroom dies off, the mycelium spreads out underground, and stays there for hundreds, thousands of years. Then, they can grow again!"

"I've never thought about mushrooms that much."

She looked at me after a short pause. "What do you think ?" Ami asked.

At first glance, her place seemed comfortable, cozy; a refuge from the city.

"It's great," I answered honestly.

Ami smiled. A string of fairy lights hung over the door frame that led into the main room. There was a table in the room that remained stable, but it was at an odd angle and everything that had been on it had either fallen to the floor or had tipped over. She had a small television that had fallen off of the small cabinet it sat on and was on the floor.

There was a computer desk that had shifted, and the desk items were spread out on the floor. The laptop remained on the desk, along with the mouse and a risqué looking mousepad that had a picture of an anime style character and whose padded wrist rest was formed into plump breasts. In front of the desk was a large toadstool that must have been used as a chair. There was a fluffy, low set lounge chair that was level to the television. On the ground in front of the chair were cushions that were made to look like tree stumps.

Ami went over to the set of black curtains and pulled them open, letting the sunlight into the room. On the glass, she had window decals of trees and forest creatures.

By her computer was a shelf with six small plastic pots which had white mushrooms poking out of precut holes. She opened her balcony door and shouted, "*Kuso.*" She crouched over a cut log on the ground that had some sprouting mushrooms.

"What's wrong?" I asked as I walked over.

She lifted the log gently to reveal several damaged mushrooms, and a few which had fallen. Ami picked up the log and set it against three others that had been set in a square with all three growing mushrooms.

"Ah, I'm growing *Nemeko* here," she said, tapping a finger on the log she replaced. She bent over and picked up the ones that had fallen. She showed them to me. "Feel the top. It's *tsuru tsuru*. Slippery."

I touched the top of the slippery mushroom.

"My father likes them. Next time I see him, I'll give him a bag." Ami rubbed her hands together and said, "I'll go wash."

I followed her back inside. Along one side of the wall which separated the living room from the kitchen was a squatty white bookcase filled generously with both English and Japanese books, some of which had fallen in a pile on the floor.

Her kitchen was a decent size and she had a thin refrigerator with magnetic mushrooms arranged in no particular order. Some of them were used to keep photos stuck to the surface. Most of which were of Ami at work, Ami with some friends just in front of a lake, Ami with those who I assumed were her family, and another of her in a colorful *kimono* in front of a shrine.

"This is a nice picture," I said.

Ami glanced over.

"Oh, that was for my *Seijin no Hi*, my coming-of-age day. My dad made sure that I dressed up and did all the traditional things."

"What's a coming-of-age day?"

"It's when we turn twenty. It's to show that we're adults. So, there's a ceremony and everyone dresses up. I guess I never cared about all that. I was still in college, studying, and didn't want to take a day off when I could have focused on doing something productive."

I could understand that. I had done the same thing before, focusing on work that needed to be done and ignoring celebrations and time for relaxation. I now knew that it was important to take the time to celebrate. "What's all that hard work for if you can't take a break?"

"That sounds like what my dad said."

"Well, sometimes parents are right."

Ami smiled. "Sometimes."

She passed by me. "Think you could check if anything is broken in the bedroom? I'll start cleaning up here."

"Sure," I said.

"It's there," she said, pointing to a closed door framed with a string of ivy next to her desk.

Ami picked up the television from the floor and replaced it on the shelf. I was a little anxious, though it was silly for me to be. We had slept together more than once. I shouldn't have been nervous to see her bedroom. I opened the door and found the switch on the inside wall.

She had a brown wooden bed frame. Her sheets and bedspread had a forest design. The background was white and along the bottom were trees and wildflowers. Folded neatly over the pillows was a minky pink blanket and on that blanket was the Totoro plushie that I had won for her. I walked over to it and touched it on the nose.

The bed looked like I could sink into it. I wanted to fall on it and snuggle under the covers. As I looked down, I startled at the pairs of eyes that I saw under the bed. I laughed at my surprise. Lined up along the bottom were all kinds of plush animals, mostly rabbits and dogs, and one chubby hamster.

The bedroom had a large closet and on it were tree decals. In each corner of the room were fabric houseplants, one which was a large tree whose branches stretched out halfway into the room, making a canopy over the bed. The tree trunk and branches had white lights strung around them.

I went to find Ami in the living room tidying up her books. The television was on and playing the news. I stooped down to help her.

"Thank you," she said. "It's not as bad as I thought. The mess, I mean."

I put the books back on the shelves. Most of them were about mushrooms, given the pictures on the front, others were manga, and some didn't have pictures, but I supposed that they were academic or nonfiction. There were books with English titles which were on subjects of animal research, laboratory research, and medical ethics, one of which was titled *The Mouse in Biomedical*

Research.

"Interesting reading?" I asked.

She peeked at the book I was holding, which had a Japanese title. She scoffed. "Not that one. It's about processes in biomedical research. It's one of those boring-but-necessary books."

Ami stopped, still holding a book in her hand, and turned to the television. She watched for a few minutes while I finished putting the books back. I got up and shifted the computer desk back against the wall.

"Will you go back?" she asked quietly.

Was she asking if I was going back to my apartment? "What do you mean?"

"Will you go back to the States?"

"Oh." I sat on the mushroom chair, looking at my fingers.

I didn't expect to have this conversation with Ami yet, but it was reasonable for her to ask. Other people were already leaving Japan. I knew what my mom wanted, what my friends wanted. They wanted me to be safe; I was somewhere that might be *un*safe. I wanted to stay with Ami. I wanted to keep my job.

I wasn't sure what I would do. Both choices had a risk. I could stay with Ami, where I wanted to be, and face the uncertainty of all that came with a failing Nuclear reactor in a small country. Was there radiation in the air I was breathing, in the water I was drinking? I didn't know. I could go home and be safe from it, safe from uncertainty. Yet...I wanted to be with Ami, even if it was during a disaster.

"You know how I was in a relationship before?" I asked. Ami nodded. "Well, it didn't work out because she left. She finished her degree and went to a hospital in Mexico City. We tried to figure it out in the beginning, the long distance, but…well, she worked weird long shifts and so did I." I exhaled. "I'm worried that if I leave now, the same thing will happen to us."

Ami slunk next to me and hugged me gently.

"I like you," Ami said. "And I don't want you to go." Ami took my hand in hers. "But I think it's important for you to be safe," she said.

"I don't know. It's a lot to think about. My parents want me to come home. They said they'd pay for the flight, which, I don't think they can afford."

Ami chewed the inside of her lip.

"I don't want to," I said suddenly.

She didn't speak for a long time. We sat together. The murmurings from the live feed were the only sounds in the room. Eventually, I couldn't stand the silence.

"This is all so messed up," I said. "It wasn't supposed to be like this." I shook my head. I thought about the news footage of the tsunami and the stories of the ones who were stuck in their homes when the water had come. "Why should I complain? There are people who are dead."

Ami kissed my hand. "It is messed up. But, *shouganai*. I learned that so much is out of our control, no matter how much we try. We just make choices to make sure we're in control. You have the choice to go home."

This is my home now, I thought. For better or worse, I had to see it through. *I came to teach, to try a new way of living. What would I learn if I left now?*

I didn't really want to go back to America. It might have been safer. I didn't want to go, whether it was safe or not. I didn't want to quit. There was so much I still wanted to do. And, I thought that I could help. I would be more useful where I was than back in North Dakota with nothing to do and little prospects. No. It might be safer to fly away, but it wouldn't be *better*.

"I think I should stay." I took a breath. "My family will be worried. Maybe it's a stupid thing to do, but I'll stay."

Ami smiled. She placed her hand on my cheek and kissed me. When she pulled back, she rested her forehead on mine.

"So that's your vice," she said. "Stubbornness."

I shrugged. As much as I would have argued about that when I was younger, insisting that I was not and proving that I was, Ami was right. I hoped that my stubbornness was leading me in the right direction.

I kissed her again.

She took my hand and led me to her bedroom where she turned off the lights. I started taking off my clothes and leaving them on the floor. Ami did the same.

Soon, our bodies were together, warm, laying on the soft sheets on her bed. The dark room and forms of the plants and trees made it feel as if I were in a summer forest. It was comforting, relaxing. In those moments together, I didn't think about anything except of her, of us, and our shared pleasure.

Chapter 7

The next few days were anxiety-ridden.

It was difficult to find certain food at the grocery stores. What wasn't there was limited per person. A bag of rice, a staple in most homes, was limited to two bags per person.

I noticed fewer people out on the streets, but the crowded commute was the same. Even more, in some places, since certain lines were shut down to save power.

What was happening at the power plant changed daily. One moment, everything was under control, or was reported as under control, and the next there would be doubts.

Watching American news didn't help. They focused on everything that could go wrong. My dad called me asking when I would fly back and telling me outlandish stories he read online or saw on the news about the death toll being three million people. Where he got his sensational stories, I didn't know. I had long since tuned it out. After two days of streaming American news, I couldn't take it anymore and stopped looking altogether.

After a few days of watching Japanese news and them playing the song *"Hana wa Suku"* in what felt like every half an hour, I also turned that off. Instead, I played Christmas music and pirated old 90s sitcoms.

There was still school. Every other day or so, one of the teachers would ask, "Are you staying?" or "I thought all the foreigners were leaving?" Hearing it so many times made me want to remain even more. The question almost seemed like an accusation, like they expected me to leave when things got difficult, like I was someone who was weak or couldn't take the challenge. I would always answer, "I'm staying here," and they would nod and walk away, placated for a time until they saw me again.

This was the third day back. Three days since the earthquake happened. When I came to work on that day, Haruyo said, "I am glad you decided to stay." Why she was saying this to me now and not the first day I saw her, I didn't know. Delayed reaction, I supposed.

"So am I," I answered on our walk to the first class.

"I saw many other ALTs that were leaving, so now there are schools without a teacher. I was worried you were going to be a *flyjin*."

"A what?"

"*Flyjin*. Some people were calling the foreigners who are leaving that name. You know the word *gaijin*?"

I knew of it. I had been called that and knew that it could be an insult depending on how it was used. It was the word for a foreigner, a non-Japanese person. "Yes."

"So, they use the English 'fly" and then "*jin*" for person. "

"That's too bad."

"Hm. Yes. It's sorry for the students. They have no chance to speak English with a native teacher."

"I guess I can understand it. The people leaving are scared."

"Hm. Yes. It is scary, but *shouganai*. This is not the first time such a disaster happened."

"It's not?" I said, then I thought that was stupid to

say out loud. Of course disasters like that had happened before. Japan was located on fault line.

"I think about eighty years ago there was the Kanto earthquake and also a tsunami that destroyed many buildings and many people died."

"History repeats," I said.

"*So desu ne.*"

We got to the first classroom and prepared for the lesson. The students were talkative, as usual, until the bell toned and they began to quiet. We did as usual. I greeted every student, and once that was finished, we taught the lesson.

The lessons for the day followed teaching some adjectives using the simple subject, "to be" or "to have" verb, adjective method. It was simple for me, but there were some students who were having some problems. Kaide kept confusing how to say the verb and would say, "She has tall." Haruyo would explain the reason why to use a certain verb.

Explaining the intricacies of English helped keep my mind off of everything else.

****

I went through that week of work and the ones that followed in much the same way as always. Having a routine helped to keep my mind off the disaster for a little, though it would creep up at certain points of the day or when a student would ask about it.

I was a little thankful for my ignorance of the Japanese language because I could tune out the news and the conversations that were focused on the disaster. I wouldn't call it blissful ignorance. It was more comforting ignorance. I knew they were talking about it when I would hear "Fukushima" or "*Jishin*", but I could ignore it.

It was the details that I couldn't deal with for a few days. It was easier for me to focus on work, on English, and to know that I would be able to do something concrete to help rather than sitting and worrying.

Chapter 8

April 2011

The disaster passed and cherry blossoms began to bloom. The bright beauty they gave made it seem like the terrible things that happened with the earthquake could be forgotten, if for a little while.

Ami and I planned to go on what she called an "*o hanami*" to look at the cherry blossoms and have a picnic. We met at the Akishima station and took the train to Showa Park in Tachikawa. The parks I was accustomed to were small affairs, but this one was gigantic. I felt that I could have walked for hours and still have more to see. There were flower fields, trees, smaller gardens, even a small lake where a few paddle boats floated around. We found a spot amongst others who were also picnicking under the blooming branches.

"How is the teaching?" Ami asked when we sat down.

I shrugged. "It's fine." It was a non-answer. "Actually," I said, "It's a little hard some days. I don't like the way they teach English,"

"How do you mean?"

"Well, it's all 'listen and repeat'. I mean, I guess that's great to learn basic English but then when I try to actually talk to the students or even the teachers, they have no idea what I'm saying. Honestly, it's like I'm teaching a classroom full of parrots." Then I remembered that Ami had said she grew up in Japan. "Was it like that when you were in school?"

"I guess so. I already knew English, so that class was always easy. Most of the time I goofed off if I could get away with it. But, Japanese schools are strict like that in every class."

I remembered passing by the math class and how the teacher rapped at the board, and how the Japanese teacher would swiftly, and hopefully gently, strike the back of a student's head when she found them sleeping.

"It's shocking," I admitted. "When I was finishing my degree I had to do a teaching internship. I cared about making sure the students understood—*really* understood—what they were learning."

I remembered then about how difficult it had been to track student achievement, to make sure that all of my nearly one hundred and sixty students were doing well. The sleepless nights I spent grading papers, finishing administrative paperwork, writing my action research paper, my nearly twenty-page paper on my teaching philosophy and how I could apply it in the classroom.

I knew that there had been places where I failed. I was not as strict in some places, mostly in classroom management. I was better with smaller classes. Once the number of students went beyond about fifteen, the ability to control them became difficult, if not impossible. The students must have known this. Even as I told Ami that I made sure that the students understood what they were learning, I wondered how true that had been.

"At least, I tried my best," I added.

"That's school," Ami answered. "It's sink or swim; the kids either shape up and study or they fail. There aren't as many chances here as in the States. In the States, I could get paper extensions, excused absences, I could bullshit my work and still pass, and this was at a university. If I did that at a school here, I don't know. Everything is competitive. To get a good job, a good place in society, you have to work hard and succeed. If you fail in the States, there are more options. If you fail here, you're stuck." She shrugged. "That's why the teachers are strict; to prepare them for the world."

What she said was insightful and I appreciated her for it. "I'll have to think about that," I said. "How'd you figure that out?"

"Perspective, and lots of therapy," She said and flashed me a smile.

"Really?" I asked. "You seem so put-together."

I wanted to ask a little more about it, but decided not to. Therapy wasn't outside of the norm, at least not back home. I knew plenty of teachers who had gone and some students, too. Actually, I was impressed that she so freely admitted to it.

"Now, maybe. If you'd seen me six years ago, I was a mess. Still am, in some ways." She reached inside her purse. "This is one of them." She pulled out a packet of cigarettes along with a slim yellow container.

"Your smoking?" I asked and grimaced. I never dated a smoker before and didn't understand how a person could do that to their body.

"Judging by your face, you have never tried," she said.

I relaxed my expression. "Sorry," I offered.

She shook her head. "Nothing to be sorry about. You made the right decision. I didn't." She tapped some ash into the container. "I go through waves. I don't touch them for months and then I get the itch." She placed a cigarette in her mouth, took out a lighter, and lit the end. She inhaled and exhaled out of my direction. "And before you say anything; I know it's bad. Like I said, I'm still kind of a mess."

I thought about my own faults. "I guess all of us are, in one way or another."

"So, what's your vice?" she asked.

"Mine?"

"Everyone has one."

I shrugged, not wanting to be so honest right away.

When the cigarette began to burn, she would slide open the top of the container she was holding and tap the ash into the top.

"That's ingenious," I said, pointing to the object.

Ami glanced at it. "An ash container. Most people who smoke here use one, well, the people who aren't assholes. Smoking makes enough of a mess without leaving ash and butts on the ground." Ami finished her cigarette and put the spent end in the container, and then placed the container back in her purse.

It was quiet for a while, so I felt compelled to say something. "What do you get up to outside of work?" I asked.

"Hobbies?" She asked.

"Sure."

She crossed her arms. One of her purse straps fell from her shoulder and she adjusted it. "I was into puzzles for awhile. Oh, that makes me sound like a grandma, but it's true. Every Saturday I'd go to some craft store or hobby shop and find a puzzle to do over the weekend." She shook her head and smiled. "That doesn't make me sound very interesting, does it?"

I imagined myself sitting with Ami on a quiet Saturday, drinking coffee, listening to music, and doing a puzzle. It didn't seem boring. It seemed to me like it would be the most interesting and lovely way to spend a weekend. "Actually, that sounds nice."

"Ah, you're just being polite." Her eyes brightened and her mouth twitched into a half-smile. I smiled, too. It was thrilling to see her happy.

I tilted my head back to admire the trees and the warm air.

"I think Tokyo is good for you," Ami said.

I grinned. "Why do you say that?"

"You have more pink in your cheeks."

"I don't think it's the city that's making me pink," I said and stroked her shoulder with my finger.

Ami chuckled.

We stayed like that for as long as we could. I had even fallen asleep at one point. The day was getting late and Ami said, "I know what you'd like." She turned to me with a smile on her face. "Have you been to Donkihote?"

I didn't know what she was talking about. I knew the story about *Don Quixote*, but judging by her excited face, that probably wasn't what she meant. "It isn't the story, right?" I asked.

"Story?"

"*Don Quixote*, about the old guy who fights the windmills."

She furrowed her eyebrows and then her eyes lit up. "Oh, no, nothing like that. It's a store just a few minutes from here."

She started walking towards the train station. The ride was a few minutes and then she led me to a tall building with a blue penguin statue in front. From inside came loud music, bright lights, and excitement. The shop sign took me a few seconds to read, and I mumbled to sound out the *katakana*, "*Do-n-ki-ho-te*" or Donkihote. A blue penguin mascot was on the other end, waving as if to summon me inside.

There were so many things everywhere that I could barely focus on just one item.

"It's a *gacha-pon*," she said. "I'll show you,"

She looked around at each one and then chose the machine which had pictures of mushrooms, some of which were glow-in-the-dark. She removed her wallet from her purse, and unzipped it to wriggle her finger around and pulled out three one-hundred *yen* coins. She put these into the machine and turned the circular crank. Out popped a clear ball. Inside was a translucent mushroom. She hopped a little.

"Oh, I love these kind," she said.

She opened the ball, took out the small toy inside and deposited the ball into the plastic bin above the machine.

I wanted something, too.

"Let me see," I said. I looked around at all the different machines. There were about twenty of them, each with a different toy. I decided on one which had tiny cat toys, each one in a funny pose. I put in my coins and out came a ball and inside it was an orange cat with its mouth open in a wide yawn.

When I found Ami, she was still at the mushroom machine and five of the small mushrooms in one hand. She did one more and then saw me.

"I like mushrooms," she explained.

She lit another cigarette as we walked towards the

station.

"You didn't smoke the first night we went out," I said.

She exhaled. "No, well, I wasn't nervous that day."

"You're nervous?" I asked.

She looked at me, smiled, and then looked away. I didn't like her smoking but I couldn't tell her what to do. She found the packet and yelled a word in Japanese that I didn't know but suspected was a swear given how she said it.

"You don't have to make that face," she said.

I didn't know that I was making one, but I changed my expression just in case.

"I know you don't like it," she said and lifted her cigarette to show me. "I don't like it much, either."

"Have you tried to quit?"

She scoffed "Of course I have. I quit for a while and then I start again. It's been a habit for so long. That was my mistake, starting so young."

"How old were you?"

"Fifteen. All the cool girls were smoking and I wanted to do it, too. Someone should've smacked me in the head." She inhaled the cigarette. "Mom would've done it, if she was there. My therapist said that it was a coping mechanism."

"Sounds like it," I said. I thought that I might have sounded rude, so I said, "I mean that I think it's normal to do whatever you can to keep yourself together after something like that."

She smiled and kept smoking.

"When my grandpa died, my mom became obsessed with fishing. It's funny because she always complained about how much grandpa went fishing and how she hated going with him. After he died, she did the same thing. She'd collect all these lures, rods, whatever."

Ami finished the cigarette and took some mints from her purse. "It's becoming late," she said. "The trains will stop soon."

I took out my phone to look at the time, which was nearing eleven o'clock. "We can hurry," I said.

Ami shook her head. "I don't think there's enough time, but," she started and tapped her finger against her bottom lip. "I think I know what we can do."

Ami hailed a taxi. In another few minutes we were in front of a beige tower complex. I would have guessed it was her apartment building until I saw the neon sign on top which said, "Hotel Festal". Ami paid the driver and we both got out.

"*Ano*," Ami said with a nervous looking smile as the taxi drove away. "This is a different kind of hotel."

"What do you mean?"

"It's called like a 'Love Hotel'. Uhm. Maybe, you'll see?"

Intrigued, I followed her inside. The lobby was empty except for touch screen panels that displayed the different kinds of rooms. I let Ami figure out the details since everything was in Japanese. I followed her to an elevator and I passed a man and a woman who were leaving. The woman wore a large black hoodie with the hood pulled over her head as she lowered her mask-covered face. We rode the elevator to the sixth floor and exited. The room was down the hall and had what looked like an ATM next to the door.

"So, we have to pay before we go in," she said.

"Oh, you need some cash?" I asked.

"No," she said.

I took out my money anyways and gave her 5,000 *yen.* "You paid for the taxi," I explained.

She reluctantly accepted. Once the bills went through the slot, the door unlocked. As soon as I got inside, I understood what she meant by "Love Hotel." A large bed sat in the center of the room in front of a flatscreen television which played gratuitous pornography. I had the unfortunate luck of looking at the screen when it showed a close-up of a man's crotch as he received a blowjob. When I looked away, I saw clearly on the table a red package of condoms.

"Ah!" Ami shouted when she noticed and rushed to turn off the television. In the silence she said, "Sorry about that."

"So, it's a sex room?" I asked.

"Eh, well, yes," she said. "It's less expensive to stay at a Love Hotel for a few hours until the trains start again." There was a short pause as she glanced around the room and back at me. "Is it weird?"

My idea of what was weird and what was normal had long since changed, now that I lived in Tokyo. It would be out of place in my hometown, that was for sure, but here in a busy city, it didn't seem so strange. "I don't know if I like the idea of sleeping where I know other people have had sex."

"Not everyone at a hotel has sex."

"And everyone who stays here does? What about us? Are we going to sleep here or..." I trailed off and turned to look at her with my eyebrows raised.

Then I laughed.

I sat on the bed beside her and ran my fingers through her hair. She closed her eyes, moaned lightly, before we kissed.

Chapter 9

It was the end of March. The end of the school year.

I attended the graduation ceremony. Rather than a raucous celebration, as my high school graduations had been, this one was serious. It was more like a Sunday sermon than a graduation.

We sat when the Principal spoke, then stood when the student graduates walked down the center aisle. The Japanese National Anthem was sung first, then the school song was sung by the students. As each student's name was called to the stage, they walked up, received their certificate with both hands, bowed, and walked off stage and back to their seats.

As the graduates received their certificates, many of the teachers and parents began to cry. It almost felt like a funeral, that they were mourning the end of their youth. I couldn't tell if the tears were happy or sad. They could have been both.

Haruyo pointed out the new students to me that I would be teaching after the spring holiday. After the ceremony, she had me greet each student and each told me their name. I tried to remember each one but at some point I couldn't remember their names anymore. Once I was able to write them down and memorize a seating chart, I would try to match the names with the faces I had seen today.

Before I left, Haruyo gave me my schedule for the

next month. I had a few days off and then would be expected to come in to help with the lesson plans.

****

I stayed up late that night to play games and fell asleep sometime after two in the morning. I slept in and when I woke up I saw a message from Ami. She wanted to meet for coffee.

I replied eagerly. I was hungry for breakfast and coffee sounded great. On the walk to the station, I grabbed a bottle of warm tea from the street vending machine. The trains were a little crowded, but not so much that I was vying for personal space. I met with Ami at the Mister Donut in Tachikawa. All the seats there were full so we took our food and drinks outside the shop. The weather was clear and warm and the sun was shining. I couldn't help but think about how the April weather must be back home in Minot. Even in April, there could be snow.

"How was your Friday?" I asked Ami.

She shook her head. "Hard. We were testing on mice this week. It was a cancer drug trial. There was this one little mouse that was really cute and sweet. Every time I held him, he would lick my finger and squeak." She drank her coffee. "He died yesterday."

My heart sank. Death was never easy. To watch it happen to a small animal must have been difficult. "I'm sorry," I offered.

"*Shouganai*." She said and sipped again, then took a bite of her bear shaped doughnut. When she swallowed, she said, "I went into lab research so I could do something important, *deshyou*. Mom died from cancer. If I could help to get better medicine to people so they don't get sick, then I think there would be a point to her

99

death. So, every animal that dies is for a bigger reason. Does that make sense?"

"Yes. Helping people is always a good thing to do."

Ami stared at the street, deep in thought. "When I first started studying in an actual lab, it was hard for me to do the tests on the animals. We have to give them the sickness, sometimes, and then test the medicine. We do it on mice first, then guinea pigs, pigs, and monkeys. I've only done it on pigs and monkeys a few times. My job focuses on the small animals. When I started, I didn't like to inject them. I would cry. My *sensei* told me that it was to help people. The more we could understand sickness, the more we could stop it. So, I have to think about it like that." She took a deep breath.

"Do you like working there?"

"Most days. I learn a lot. Actually, one of the medicines we tested a few years ago is used in hospitals now to treat *ninshishou*, uhm," she stopped to think. "Dementia."

I couldn't hide my astonishment. "That's amazing."

She bit her doughnut. Her nonchalance was interesting. I would have thought that such an achievement would have made her feel accomplished. "It was my job. I was happy to do it."

"Make sure to put that on a resume."

She laughed. "It is."

I ate my sandwich as I watched people pass by. I liked to see the different fashions that people wore. It was nice to see so many put thought into their appearance and how different styles were worn. There were young teenagers dressed in their school uniforms. Some older ladies wore high collared blouses, usually with a scarf. There were other younger adults who were in casual wear or else in suits. I noticed a few non-Japanese people, maybe Americans, passing by.

I caught them speaking in English as they passed and tried to listen to what they were saying. I wondered where they were going and would have liked to have asked them. At home, it was always easy to start a conversation with someone, for better or worse. I remembered there were times I went grocery shopping and got stuck in a conversation with a stranger that would last for fifteen minutes or more. At those times, I would be a little annoyed at the random strangers wanting to talk, but I missed it a little.

"Do you have plans for Golden Week?" Ami asked as she folded her wrapper and held it in her opposite hand.

"What's that?"

"It's a week vacation in April. I usually have it off."

"Oh, so like Spring Break?"

Ami tilted her head. "Yes, I think so."

I shook my head. "No. I'll probably wander around the city. There's a lot I want to see while I'm here."

Ami took out her carton of Lark cigarettes and held them in her hand. "I thought about visiting my father."

"Oh?"

"It's been a few months since I've gone by." She turned to me. "Do you want to go with me?"

I perked up. I wanted to spend more time with Ami. "Really?"

"It'll probably be boring," she said.

"It'll be great!"

Ami smiled. "I thought about staying for a few days. The house is in Ome, so not too far. We could still do other things."

"I don't think it matters what we do. I'll be happy to just be with you." I thought the last admission might have been too much, but it was the truth and I wanted to share it.

Ami smiled and kissed me gently on my cheek. "Are you sure?"

"I don't have any other plans. Oh," I said, having a thought. She always took me somewhere and I wanted to show her something. "Maybe we can go hiking."

"Hiking?" she asked.

"Sure."

"I don't usually go."

"You don't like hiking?"

"It's okay. Oh! I can collect mushrooms while I'm there. Where were you thinking about?"

"Takao," I said.

"Oh, Takao-*san*. I don't think that's so bad…"

"That'll be perfect." I thought a little more. "I don't have hiking clothes. Want to go shopping?"

"Now?"

"Yeah."

"Sure. Oh, we should go to Hard Off."

I thought that might be a joke. "What's Hard Off? It sounds like an innuendo."

Ami furrowed her brows and then relaxed when she realized what I was saying. "Oh, no. It's like a second-hand store. I'll see if there's one nearby. But, I'm going to smoke. I'll be right back." She got up and walked over to a smoking area and took out her phone as she was smoking. By the time I finished my food, she came back to sit down.

"There's one in Sakaecho. We can take the train and walk."

"Let's go."

We brought our drinks with us. Since they had tops on them, I figured they would be alright to take on the train. I had seen people bring their to-go cups on the train before.

****

The train stopped and we got off. Ami had her phone out to follow the map to the store. We walked out and down the street until I saw the large building with giant lettering saying "HARD OFF." There were bicycles parked outside and I noticed the parking lot was nearly full. I could hear music coming from inside.

Once stepping inside, I was in awe. I was used to small thrift stores that had the same basic items: old toys, dated clothes, damaged furniture, and all the leftover items from after an older relative died. Here everything was neatly lined and many new clothes, even brand names, were on the shelves. I was able to find nice second-hand fleece lined hiking clothes but no luck on any shoes in my size. I'd have to make do with the sneakers I brought from home.

Once home from the shopping, Ami having returned to her own apartment, I pulled up my laptop and looked up things to do since I had the next few days off. I settled on spending the next day in Akihabara. I hadn't been there yet and was eager to go. Whenever I saw a video about Tokyo, it would eventually show clips of Akihabara, the Electric Town. A place full of people, electronics, and anime fanatics. Although I did like to play Japanese RPGs and had watched some anime on Saturday mornings when I was a kid, I never considered myself obsessed, just mildly interested. Still, it would be fun to see if I could find any merchandise from *Chrono*

Trigger.

I woke up early, in part to avoid the usual commuter traffic. I was a little more confident in finding my way around the stations as I looked up train routes before heading out. I checked the train tables, charged my pass, and once I was inside I stopped at the *conbini* in the station to pick up breakfast before heading to the platform. There were some people already waiting, but not so many that I would have to scramble for a seat if there was one.

While I waited, I ate the packaged maple and margarine pancakes that I bought and washed them down with a dark coffee. By the time I was done an announcement called that the train was arriving. As I watched it arrive, I was disappointed to see the majority of the cars filled with people. They must have had the same idea as I did.

There was nothing else I could do, so when it was time to get on after the few passengers got off, I tried to find a decent spot. All the seats were taken. I didn't want to have to stand holding a rail. The only other open spot was in a corner next to the door. I took it. At least it had a barrier between the door and the seats so I could lean against it if I needed.

When I arrived at the station, I followed the signs to the exit. I stood where I was for some time, dumbfounded by the sight of all the towers and the sounds. It was still amazing to me that such a place could exist. Being in the middle of Akihabara was like falling into the wormhole from *2001 A Space Odyssey*. It was a blur of color and sound. I stopped at all the small electronic shops and some of the bigger ones, as well as being lulled to a game center where I played some of the

UFO catchers and, after spending about two thousand *yen*, ended up winning a small pink teddy bear with long bloody claws.

Ami sent me a message asking me where I was. When I answered, I got a message from her telling me she would meet me outside the station in a little over an hour.

I weaved my way through the crowds back to the station, though I got lost a few times and ended up in some alleys. By the time I got to the station, I was hungry and needed a quiet break from the city noise, so I stopped at a pub just outside called the "Rose and Crown". I sat there, delightfully alone while I drank a cup of warm green tea and practiced reading Japanese in the manga I bought. Ami sent a message that she arrived. I told her where I was and in a few minutes, she was in the pub and sitting across from me, still in her work clothes and smelling faintly of cigarette smoke.

"Thank you for letting me join," she said.

"No problem. How was work?"

Ami smiled. "Oh, very good," she said in relief. "We finished the trial on mice. Now I have some reports to write before the next trial."

"That's great. I know you were stressed about it."

She smiled and reached out to squeeze my hand. She glanced at the manga on the table. "*Sangatsu no Raion,*" she said, reading the title out loud. "You're practicing Japanese?"

"Yeah. It's going slowly."

"Better than nothing. At least you're trying, which is more than some people do." She drank her wine. "*Sa, renshyuu shimashyou ka*? Do you want to practice?"

"Now?"

"*Hai. Shinpaishinai you.*"

I straightened my back a little and placed my hands on the table. "Ok."

For the next hour, I tried speaking basic Japanese with Ami. She was patient with me and would repeat what she said more than once while I tried to understand her. After a few more drinks, we decided to take a break, and a needed one, since I was getting a slight headache after trying to understand the difference between using "*ni*" and "*de*" as a preposition for going somewhere. If I were going to ride a train, I would say, "*Denshya de ikimasu,*" but if I were going to work, I would use, "*Oshigoto ni ikimasu.*" It was all a little confusing.

"Why don't we walk around?" she asked. "I want to go see if I can find some things at Mandarake. It's a kind of hobby store."

"Looking for mushrooms?"

She smiled coyly. "Now you know me."

We left the pub and walked down the streets to a tall triangular faced black building with multiple floors. Inside, there were all kinds of collectable figurines that were similar to the boxed figures that I had seen at GameStop. There were model figures of anime characters, stuffed animals, and some expensive dolls. I was slightly uncomfortable by the plastic figurines of scantily clad young pre-teen girls, or girls in a school uniform who were in such a position that their panties were showing. I was disturbed by the fact that there were school aged children around me who were also looking at the figures and responding to them without more than a glance.

Ami looked around on racks where there were hundreds of bagged toys. She rifled through them and I decided to look as well. All sorts of tiny toys, dolls, insects, animals, anime characters, and everything in between were in those plastic bags. Then I stopped. In one of them was a small figure of the Frog character from *Chrono Trigger*. He was in a fighting stance with his sword drawn and his shield raised.

"Ami," I said and held up what I'd found. "From *Chrono Trigger*."

"*Yatta!*" She held up three bags of her own, all filled with tiny mushrooms. "Me too."

We paid and then left to return to the station. By then it was dark and all the neon lights lit up the sidewalk. All of a sudden, a young woman in a maid costume said something in fast Japanese.

"*Ano*," Ami said and looked at me with her eyebrows raised, "Do you want to go to a maid café?"

I looked at the young woman who wore a performative smile.

"I'm not sure what I'm agreeing to."

Ami chuckled.

"Let's find out."

So, we both followed the overly cheerful maid to a narrow elevator inside a building. The elevator door opened to loud pop music and the strong smell of cigarette smoke. The tiny room was filled with older men sitting at tables and young girls dressed in pink maid costumes. There was a small front desk with a cash register where one of the maids stood.

"*Irrashaimase*," she said.

Ami and I looked at each other and she visibly cringed.

"I didn't think it was like this," she said.

I looked behind me and the other maid was still in

the elevator, waiting for us to walk forward. "Too late now," I said.

The maid led us past the tables, mostly occupied by older men, and to the bar. Three of the maids were singing and dancing on a small stage. Because of the noise, it was barely possible to speak without either yelling or talking straight into each others' ears. One of the maids handed us menus and then bowed before she left.

"Let's just order drinks and get out of here," I shouted.

Ami nodded.

Once they were finished, we asked to leave. I stood up, and a group of maids called my name. A spotlight was turned to me and I froze. I looked at Ami helplessly.

"They want you to go up there."

I tried to refuse, but that made the maids and the drunken men clap enthusiastically.

"I'll come with you," Ami said. She took my hand and we walked to the stage together, passing all the older men, most of them drunk, and standing on the tiny spot lit stage with six young women. The bright lights hid the rest of the room in a shadow. I looked over at Ami, who was smiling, but said to me, "Make sure you smile." She put her hand around my waist and I returned the gesture.

That was when I saw the camera in front of us and heard the count down, "*San, ni, ichi*." I smiled. There was a round of applause from the girls and one of them led us back to our seats.

"I'm still ready to go," I said.

We got up again. This time, one of the girls came over and offered music CDs, cigarettes, lighters, and other souvenirs with the maid cafe logo on it. We declined.

At the register, the lady gave us the receipt on the money tray. The amount couldn't have been right. It was over one hundred thousand *yen*, one hundred dollars. I couldn't leave without paying. The elevator was the only way out. I put my money down but then Ami took some and gave it back to me, replacing half with her own *yen* notes.

Before I could refuse, the maître d' took the money. She returned the money tray with change and a tiny polaroid of the picture with some hearts drawn on it with pink and blue markers. Ami picked it up. The girls gave us an overly-enthusiastic farewell and we were back in the quiet elevator.

We didn't say anything to each other until the doors opened up to the hallway and we were in the street.

"I don't know what I was expecting," Ami said. "but it wasn't that."

"And," I said. "We have a souvenir to always remember it."

Ami chuckled and looked at the photo of me smiling awkwardly and her looking perfect.

"Why don't you keep it?" she asked and handed it to me.

"Are you sure?"

She answered by slipping the picture in my pocket and kissing my cheek. I went home with Ami that night.

Chapter 10

After the intensity of my first time in Akihabara, the rest of my off days were spent away from the city. I preferred instead to spend one day being alone and lazy at my apartment and gaming for several hours. I had placed my Frog figurine next to my laptop and stuck the picture of Ami and I together at the maid café between his shield and arm. The day after, I met Ami for dinner at an *izakaya*, a Japanese pub.

I'd made a habit of video calling my parents every week. Because of the time difference, I talked to them on weekend mornings. The conversations always amounted to the same talk about what our days had been like. I would show them the weather outside and they would comment on it and then they would show me the weather at their house. Seeing the snow dusting the ground and the wind shaking the oak tree in the backyard made me thankful that I was somewhere else. I hadn't realized how lonely I had felt when I was living in Minot in my year of teaching. My girlfriend and I had broken up and my first year of teaching at a public school was harder and less rewarding than I'd thought. Everything there was lonely.

Soon enough, it was time for me to work. On the first day, there was a meeting with other ALTs like me but who were teaching at different schools in the area. After introductions, I noted that other than myself and another older man, none were formally trained in education. Most of their qualifications began and ended with having English as a first language. It frustrated me that they would teach English and knew little about the rules that governed the language. Just because a person could *speak* English, didn't mean they could teach it. I thought it best to keep that thought to myself.

It was on that occasion that I met Hannah, an Australian woman who had married a Japanese man and had lived in the area for over five years. She was a svelte, middle-aged woman, with long wavy brown hair that she kept in a fishtail braid. She was one of those women who didn't take much stock in make-up or appearances. I saw her with a red mark or two on her hand and face. Another woman might cover it with foundation, but she didn't. When I asked her about it, she explained, "I keep bees for honey."

"Really?" I asked excitedly, "One of my teachers, Mr. Fjeldahl, in elementary school had a small farm and kept honeybees as a hobby, going as far as selling homemade honey at the farmer's market during summer weekends. At the end of the school year, he'd always give each of us a small jar of chokecherry honey."

Hannah furrowed her eyebrows.

"Chokecherry sounds like a sinister fruit. It sounds poisonous."

I smiled. "I guess I've never thought too much about it, but it's fine to eat. What kind of bees do you keep?"

Her eyes widened when I asked the question, as if she's been waiting for someone to ask it to her for a long time. "First, I started with the European honeybee, and I have a hive at the house, but two years ago I went to Tsushima to learn the traditional beekeeping and I'm trying to use Japanese honeybees now."

So, it was our shared knowledge of bees that made us friends from then on.

The remaining work week was boring. Despite being scheduled to work on lesson plans, I came to understand that what was expected of me was to sit at my plain desk and review the English lesson plans for grammar and accuracy. It took me one day to do it, so the rest of the time I spent at my desk memorizing the seating charts for the classes, studying more Japanese, and trying to look busy so no one would notice that I had nothing else to do.

On one of my breaks I went to the restroom and in the corner I noticed a scale. I decided to step onto it. It was in kilograms, so I had to remember how to convert that to pounds. Even with all the walking I had been doing, I guessed that I managed to gain five pounds. I would either have to stop eating so many snacks, cut back on eating out, or accept that I would have a muffin top. I looked at my belly and the roundness that had softened there. I knew I'd hate myself forever if I didn't sample everything the country had to offer. What was a few pounds compared to lifelong memories?

On the first day of school being back in session, I followed Haruyo to each classroom and we went through the lessons. Each one was the same and amounted to me greeting each student one-by-one and then standing at the front of the classroom with Haruyo and repeating the English words that she wanted them to learn, then the students would repeat after me. After that, I would go to each student as a group or individually to either check their pronunciation or we would practice a simple conversation.

And that was how most days went, with the exception of the lunch hour which I would spend with the students from the ninth-grade class. I was surprised by Haruyo's answer when I first asked about where I needed to pay for the meal.

"The school provides lunch," she explained, "So, if you want, you can eat with the homeroom class or take lunch in the teacher's room."

"The school gives lunch?" I asked. "The students don't have to pay?"

"No."

"Who pays for it?"

"I think it is from the consumption tax or the city tax." She paused. "Do the students in your country have to pay?"

"Yes, but there's a special program for students who can't pay so they can get something."

There'd been students I had in my classes who were on reduced-priced lunches and the backpack program. One boy named Thomas who wore worn clothes and had one winter jacket that he had grown out of was so often without a lunch that I bought granola bars to keep in my desk. The school offered breakfast but because of his family schedule, he could never arrive to get it. He would get the reduced lunch and the food backpacks, but it never seemed like enough.

"It must be hard for the students."

I thought about Thomas who came into class early one day so he could eat one of the snacks I had in my desk and afterwards he sat at his desk, laid his head down, and cried. I'd wanted to help him, but there were limits to what I could do. I talked with the school counselor, to the principal, to other teachers, and the solutions they gave me were to encourage him to be in time for breakfast. The principal told me to stop giving him food in class. All of it seemed wrong. Children needed nutrition. Learning couldn't happen if a student was hungry.

"It is," I answered.

When lunchtime came, the kitchen staff brought a bus tray of food, which the students helped to pass out. I was surprised at the plate of food I was given. It was a complete meal of rice, vegetables, cooked fish, bread, soup, and milk. I stared at the meal and thought about the paltry school lunches back home where it was common to have a slice of pizza or a hamburger for lunch and that was all.

I was hungry and ate the entire meal. I wasn't used to eating fish regularly but was enjoying it. The last time I ate a fish was when my mother was in her fishing obsession and would bring home four or five trout to cook. As I ate, the students talked amongst themselves.

One student, Natsumi, a short, stocky girl who wore her hair in a short bob, liked to practice her English with me once she finished her meal. She had a good understanding of basic grammar and could express simple thoughts.

"What do you like to eat?" she asked in punctuated diction.

I answered in kind, with clear English. "I like to eat candy."

"Ohhh," she answered and smiled. "Me, too. I like to eat choco and fruits candy."

"Good."

"Do you like animals?"

"Yes."

"What animal do you like?"

"I like cats," I said.

"Oh, I like...*ano*...*hebi*...snakes."

"Eh? *Hebu suki desu ka*?" another girl across from her asked. "*Henna no.*"

"Snakes?" I asked.

Natsumi nodded. She took out her keitai and showed me a picture of an orange and white snake in a glass cage.

"This is Rio-*chan*. She is my pet. She is a *ko-nu* snake."

I tried to look up "*ko-nu*" in my phone dictionary and then realized that she was saying "corn."

"*Mise-te*," the girl asked.

Natsumi turned her phone to the other girl.

"Eyah, *kimochi wauri.*"

Natsumi put her *keitai* away. What the other girl said, the way she said it, didn't sound like a compliment.

"I like snakes," I told Natsumi.

Natumi smiled.

The tone rang to signal lunch ending. We all worked together to help put the trays back. The food kept me full for the rest of the day.

****

When I walked to the station at the end of the day, I noticed how when people ate outside they stood in one place until they were finished and then continued on their way. I did not see anyone walking and eating, though drinking from a bottle or can seemed acceptable. Maybe that helped to keep the streets cleaner. What struck me was how clean everything was. Rarely did I see any trash on the streets or sidewalks. It was nice to see that so many people cared about the environment in which they lived.

Seeing the way that another country dealt with community issues made me question how I had seen the response in the States. I had accepted things as being the way they were and would always be that way. I saw how it didn't need to be like that, how what I accepted as a concrete way of life was changeable.

I had been in Japan only a few months but it felt like I had been there longer and I didn't want to ever leave. I didn't know quite what it was that made me like it so much, maybe it was being in the city, maybe it was that I felt useful, or it could be that I felt like I had a purpose, and that there were people who cared about me. After my upsetting experience being a first-year teacher, I was happy to be somewhere where I was appreciated and where they seemed to care about the students.

Whenever I had lunch, Natsumi always made sure to sit beside me. Each day, she showed me some drawings she made in her school notebook. When I told her I liked them, she spent the rest of the lunch hour drawing a picture of a snake that she gave to me when lunch was over. I thanked her and taped it to the wall behind my laptop when I got home.

Soon enough, Natsumi gave me so many drawings that my wall was full of them. Most of them were anime characters, animals, and one was a picture she drew of me.

Chapter 11

May 2011

It was Golden Week. A week off from working. I thought about the conversation Ami and I had about hiking and about Mt. Takao. It was close enough to the city and there were other sightseeing places nearby. There was even a monkey park on the mountain. I read about the temple that was near the summit, the Yakuoin Temple, which was built in the year 744 and was rebuilt in the 14th century. It was amazing that something so ancient still existed.

I packed my usual backpack with my hiking clothes, enough clothes to last me a few days, and toiletries. I debated bringing my laptop with me but decided against it. I didn't want to be distracted by technology while on vacation.

Ami and I agreed that we would meet in Ome at nine. As I waited at the station, it started sprinkling so when the train lurched to a stop, the droplets from the overhang had soaked my sneakers. There were no seats or a corner spot available so I stood and held one of the handrails. At one of the stops, I lost my footing and my book tumbled out of my hand. As I was reaching for it, a young boy, probably in middle school, picked it up and handed it to me. I thanked him and then noticed that he had an English study book.

"Do you want help?" I asked, then adding, "*Watashi eigo sensei.*"

"Oh, *jibun ga eigo-no sensei de suka?*

I caught "*eigo*" and "*sensei*" for English teacher and answered, "*Hai*".

He smiled.

"Ah, *tasukette kudasai,*" he said. "Eh, helu-pu."

Helu-pu: Help.

"Okay." I put my book in the bag and stepped so that I was near him. I looked at the textbook, a thin, colorful book titled, "Let's Go 3." The page he held open to show the uses of "at the" in a phrase. It looked like it was being used with locations, like "at the bakery" or "at the bus stop." The next page showed pictures of people in situations and places and prompted the reader to ask and answer questions, such as "where are they now?" "They are at the…"

The young boy pointed at the question section and said, "This, you teachyar."

I pointed to the first number and asked the question "Where were they yesterday?"

"Zey ah in za eyar-ru-poh-tu."

"Where *were* they yesterday?"

"Wa-ur. Ah. Zay wa-ur in za eyar-ru-poh-tu."

"Good. Not 'in', *'at'*."

"A-tsu. I-nu *ga tsukawanai.*"

The young boy took a highlighter out of his pencil case and highlighted the preposition "at." He repeated the phrase, using the correct word in the sentence. We practiced a few of the sentences and then I tried to help him pronounce the "the" sound. I opened my mouth to show him how to place the tongue to make the sound, which may have been a poor choice because the old woman sitting next to him made a twisted face of disapproval. The young boy moved his tongue into the same position and then pushed air through to make a deliberate "the" sound.

"Good!" I said, louder than I intended, startling the old woman again. She shifted in her seat so that she faced away, showing her back to us. I stifled a laugh.

"What's your name?" I asked the boy.

"Oh, my nay-mu izu Kaito. Wha-tsu yo-ah nay-mu?"

"My name is Tara."

"Tara?' he said, crossing his eyebrows. I thought he might use the same fish gesture that the other students used with me before, but he didn't.

"Whe-ah ah yo-ah fu-ro-mu?"

I suspected that he had memorized these phrases, like most of my students did, but he was doing well.

"I'm from America," I answered.

"*Kakui*. Ai lai-ku wa-chi Su-tar Wa-zu."

It took me a few seconds to figure out that he was saying that he liked Star Wars. I smiled. Most young kids did. I had been one of them when I was younger. I recalled a scene with Princess Leia in a skimpy outfit. My fascination with it then should have made me realize I was a lesbian sooner than I did.

"*Demo*. Ba-tsu, Ai don-tu lai-ku Pokemon."

"No? Why not?"

He stared at me. I don't think he was ready for a follow-up question.

"Wha-tu do you lai-ku?" he asked me.

Now I was sure he was using memorized lines. Natsumi asked me the same question before, almost in the same way.

"I like reading and listening to music," I said. It was a generic answer, but it was true.

I would have liked to have continued the conversation. Unfortunately, the train was slowing to a stop at Tachikawa. Kaito said, "Ekskyuzu mi," packed up his textbook in his black leather backpack, stood up, and went to the automatic doors.

Before I could move, another passenger slithered beside me and took the open seat. It was as fast as that. A conversation, an exchange, and then gone.

I couldn't help but wonder how Kaito would do in his English lessons, where he was going, and how he did at school. One thing about a small town, for better or worse, was that I could easily run into my students to see how they were doing. It gave us a familiarity that I noticed was lost in a bigger city.

Maybe that was why Haruyo and others that I'd met made time to connect with students while in school. I saw Haruyo once in the office on her lunch break on a phone call that she later told me was with a student who was refusing to come to school. She had then gone to the student's house on the weekend to meet with the family. I can't say that I would have done that as a teacher. A telephone call would have sufficed or a parent-teacher meeting. I wouldn't have gone to the house, as a matter of safety. But that kind of in-person, intimate, meeting helped.

With Kaito, I had to change my thinking from missing a connection to being thankful for it. I had long pined for my girlfriend who had moved in search of better opportunities. Maybe that was wrong. I supposed that some people came into my life for the time that they were meant to, and I needed to appreciate the time I did have with them.

I was lost in the what-could-have-been that I hadn't considered what I had gained during our time together. How we had loved each other. It wasn't lack of love that separated us. We had different paths to follow, my ex-girlfirend and I. Now, I wonder if I could ever look back on her and think of our relationship fondly instead feel the sting of her absence.

****

At Ome station, I exited and waited in front of the bench under an overhang. I was struck by how quiet it was. There were some small noises of cars passing or people walking, but otherwise it was still. It reminded me of home. The station had an old wooden waiting room. I peeked inside where there were framed retro posters. I sent Ami a message and then settled in to wait, watching the sprinkling rain on the broad leafed trees.

A tap on my shoulder startled me. There was Ami, her hair misted by the rain, holding a rolling luggage bag in one hand and a plastic bag in the other, filled with the *Nameko* mushrooms inside. She had said her father liked them so she must have been taking them to him.

"Sorry, I'm late," she said and gave me a quick hug. "I was feeling a little dizzy this morning."

"Are you feeling okay now?"

"Yes, *daijyoubu*."

We walked down and out to the street. Ami waved to a silver car parked just outside. The man sitting behind the wheel opened the door and stood up. I was struck by how tall and lean he was. I couldn't see much of his face as it was shadowed by the blue ball cap he was wearing.

"That's your dad?" I asked

"Yes."

Ami walked over and I followed. She hugged her father and he walked up to me.

"Nice to meet you!" he said with a smile that showed his white teeth which were somewhat crooked, especially his left canine, which jutted out slightly. "I'm Junsei,"

"Tara," I said.

"I'll take your bag," he said in a deep but caring voice that spoke perfect English.

"It's okay," I said, trying to be polite.

"I'll open the trunk," he said, smiling in a way that was so charming that I could not refuse.

Ami handed him the bag.

"*Sugoi!*" he said.

He went to the driver's side and opened the trunk. I walked behind the car to stow my bag and Ami did the same.

"*Kita-nai*, papa!" Ami exclaimed.

Her father looked back and waved a hand dismissively.

When I looked at the trunk, there were all sorts of things stowed away. Three bottles of water, extra tennis shoes that were significantly worn, an umbrella, a box filled with old radio parts, and a plastic bag filled with packaged snacks. Ami shoved the things out of the way and put her bag in. She also picked through the plastic bag to remove a packet of tiny sugar cookies.

"You want something?" she asked.

"Sure," I said, putting my own bag in.

Ami took out another snack and handed it to me.

"I think you'll like this one," she said.

I took the colorful packet that had pictures of jellybeans and the writing "Poifull." I opened the packet and ate a few. A burst of fruity flavor tickled my tongue.

"Wow," I said.

"Good, right?"

I finished them before we got into the car.

When getting in, I noticed the car was decently clean. It seemed that all the mess was located in the back. Ami sat in the back seat with me and her father began to drive.

"So, Tara," he said.

"Yes?"

"You have been here for how many months?"

"Since February."

"Ah, very nice. Ami told me you were from North Dakota?"

"Yes."

"So far. I went to South Dakota, oh, when I was twenty, to visit Yellowstone."

"You did?" I asked, happy that there was something in common we shared.

"Very beautiful place. That was the first time I saw a bison. First time and almost last time."

"Aw, here comes the story," Ami whispered.

"I could not believe there was an animal like that. I got out my camera to take a picture. 'No one at home will believe me', I thought, so I went to take a picture. Well, I did, but I didn't think it was close enough. So, I walked closer, closer, until I could really see its face,"

I cringed. It was dangerous to get so close to a wild animal, even more so with a buffalo. I couldn't imagine that his story ended well.

"I took the picture and then the bison kind of got closer to me, stomped the ground, everything. I started running away and the bison followed me. I heard it

123

making noises," her dad stopped to make some gruffing noises to imitate the animal, "And I didn't stop running until I was maybe a kilometer away. Once I was calmed down, I looked down and my shirt was torn in the back."

I exhaled sharply. "You were lucky," I said.

"I was stupid," he answered with a laugh.

I had been worried about how her dad would act around me, but he was easy to be around, and I felt calmer as we went on.

"Did you ever eat bison?"

"Did *you*?" Ami asked me.

"Sure, you can pick it up in most grocery stores." I shrugged.

Ami raised her eyebrows, then turned her attention to opening her cookie bag and eating the contents.

"I don't think I did," her father answered, "I kept eating hamburgers and fried chicken. I think I gained ten pounds by the time I left."

He turned onto a road to park at a house that was much like the other Japanese homes I'd seen. The difference was that there was a oversized wisteria tree in the front yard that obstructed the door.

"Let's change and then we can go hiking," I suggested.

"Sounds good," Junsei said.

He turned off the car and went to the door to unlock it, then helped to unload the bags from the trunk. I helped as well. As soon as everything was inside, Ami said, "I'll show you where we'll sleep."

Where *we* would sleep. I smiled, happy to have been so welcomed. If it were reversed and I had brought Ami to my parent's house, I wasn't confident that they would reciprocate.

The room was up a narrow set of wood steps and wood paneled walls.

"Actually, it's my parent's old room," she said and went down the short hallway to open a sliding door and when she did I smelled what I guessed was dry reeds. "Dad doesn't sleep here anymore. He says his knees hurt too much when he uses the stairs."

Inside the room was a large futon in the middle of the *tatami* mat floor. I set my backpack down.

"Oh, *suteki*," Ami said. She crouched and spread out on the blue satin comforter.

I started changing. Since Ami said her father didn't use the stairs, I didn't bother closing the door so I didn't notice when her Persian cat walked in until I heard a loud, "*nyah,*" and turned to see it nuzzling under Ami's chin.

"That must be, um," I tried to remember the cat's name. "Puff?"

Ami chuckled. "*Fuwa-Fuwa.*"

"Oh, right." I pet it on its head.

"*Chotto, yasumitai,*" Ami mumbled.

As I changed, I looked around the plain room which remained undecorated except for a dried flower wreath hung below the windowsill.

"Are you going to get dressed?" I asked Ami gently.

"Mm," she mumbled and sat up. "I think I'll need some coffee."

I went downstairs carefully as my socks slipped easily on the polished wood. My intention was to go to the kitchen to make coffee while Ami got ready but I found a wedding photo of Ami's father and mother hanging on the wall. I stared for longer than I should have. They were an attractive couple. Ami's father was lean, handsome, and had a charming smile. Ami's mother was glamorous in her white *kimono*, with her chestnut hair swept into a bun, surrounding a heart-shaped face, full lips, and a pair of bright blue eyes.

"It's a nice picture," Junsei said.

"Yes." I chuckled nervously at being caught staring. "Is there coffee?" I asked to shift the topic, "For Ami."

"Oh, *hai*, in the refrigerator." He pointed towards the kitchen.

The kitchen was large enough for a few people to fit into, with a full stove, sink, and a countertop. I took out a can of coffee from the fridge and returned to Ami. She was dressed and had tied her hair up halfway. She looked so tired; I handed her the coffee without comment.

"*Arigatou.* Of course it's black."

With everyone ready, we got back into the car, parked at the station, stopped at the *conbini* for food and snacks and got on the train to Takao. I knew it was a bit unseemly to eat while on the train, but since it was *onigiri*, a type of rice ball, I didn't think anyone would mind. The worst I got was a disappointed glance from an older gentleman. Although that could have easily been attributed to his possible prejudice against non-Japanese people. I ignored him.

We changed trains and in a little over half an hour I saw the mountains and the trees. There were others on the train similarly dressed, more carried trekking poles, and I noticed that most of the hikers were wearing brand named clothing from head to toe.

When the train stopped, we got off onto the platform and went into the main area. A small store with more snacks, drinks, some hiking items, and souvenirs was just next to the platform exit. Ami's father stopped to buy another cup of coffee. I wondered how much he drank in a day.

When I exited the store, there was a stand just next to it selling roasted fish. The way it was being cooked was interesting and I'd never seen it done that way before. There was a circular stove and around it was a circle of tightly wound straw. There were fish poked onto long skewers and those skewers were stuck into the straw. I bought one and the older woman who stood there took my money, plucked one of the fish and held it over the heat for some time before handing it back to me.

I stood a few steps away and started eating. It was salty, savory, and delicious. No sooner had I started eating it, I was finished. That was when Ami found me.

"I thought I'd find you around here," she said. "Those look good. I haven't eaten one yet."

Ami bought two and stood next to me to eat them. Her father found us and once he saw the stand, bought a fish as well. We tossed the skewers into the trash bin next to the stand. The old woman thanked us.

Finally, we started walking.

"How long will you be in Japan?" her father asked.

"A year, at least."

"Good. You can see all the seasons."

"That'll be nice. Spring and fall are so short where I'm from that it's hard to notice them. I came here just before the *sakura* started to bloom."

"So, you got to see *sakura* for the first time?"

"Yes," I said, beginning to breathe a little heavier as we started walking up a concrete slope.

The ground leveled out and there were some storefronts that were shuttered. To the right was a red torii and a path up the mountain, enveloped by all kinds of trees and bushes and calling birds. To the left was a line to the lifts.

There was a sign and Ami mumbled something. When I looked at her, she spoke up. "I can't take any mushrooms," she said.

"Why?"

"Because of radiation."

"But we're so far away from Fukushima."

"They're being cautious." She sighed. "Maybe I can take pictures instead."

"Sorry," I offered.

Ami nodded. I looked up towards the trail entrance.

"*Keiburu kar tsuakimasuka*?" Ami asked her father.

I knew that *tsukaimasu* meant "to use" and it sounded like she was saying "Cable car".

"Ah! I don't need it!" her father said. "I'm still young."

Ami didn't say anything as her father led the way to the walking path. He bowed before the torii and started walking.

"Just wait, you'll hear him complain about his knee in a few hours. Don't say I didn't warn you."

"He might not be the only one. I've hardly hiked before."

"Well, *ganbatte*."

I looked up at the mountain, at the lush body of green. I had never seen so many different shades of green. The mountain stood in beautiful majesty, compelling me to enter its embrace.

"It's so…" I started, trying to find the accurate word to define it. "Glorious."

Ami gave me a nudge on my shoulder and smirked. Initially, the walk was a mild slope and then as we continued on, the concrete path became a dirt pathway with some roots growing up through the soil.

There was a sudden, steep incline.

A three person group before us took the slope slowly, with one of the ladies using a trekking pole to gain her footing. I hardly had the breath to talk at all.

When we passed the steep slope, there was a level area where her father was waiting. He took out a bottle of water from his pack and drank. I did the same, sharing my bottle with Ami. I looked up to see the overhanging branches that seemed like a canopy over my head. Behind me was a wall of dirt where at some point the mountain had been dug away to make the path and along that wall were thick root systems, mossy plants, and verdant vines. Moisture trickled down some of the leaves from the morning mist. I touched one of the moss fibers to feel the wetness between my fingers. It seemed to me that every part of it was brimming with life. It reminded me of the early days of summer when the threat of winter was finally over and the plants rushed to grow, eager to feel the sun and the rain.

"Ready?" Ami asked me.

I nodded. Her father started walking and I followed. As I did, I stopped when I passed a stone statue of what looked like a small child. On the statue was a red bib.

"What's this?" I asked.

Ami looked.

"It's a *jizo*. It's like a shrine." Ami paused. "Actually, I don't remember exactly what they're for." She turned to where her father was resting beside a knotted tree. "Papa. *Jizo ga imi wakaranai.*"

"Ah," Her father leaned forward to stretch his back and spoke too swiftly for me to catch much.

"Oh." Ami glanced at me and then at the statue. "They are to protect the earth and to protect children. My father said that they are like spirits for the forest."

"I see. It's like the statues of patron saints for Catholics."

"Maybe."

"Why do they have red bibs?"

"Oh, red is for protection."

We kept walking up the dirt path. Ami stopped towards the side of the path under some scraggly trees and crouched. "*Mi-te*," she said. She took out her phone as I stooped next to her to see a small tea-green mushroom poking out from some underbrush. "I'm not sure what this one is."

She pushed some of the fallen leaves and twigs from the base of the mushroom and then stood up. She swayed a little and I reached out to steady her.

"*Gomen. Memagurushi.*" She drank some water. "*Iko?*"

Ami's father was already some distance ahead of us. We didn't talk much. I didn't feel the need to and I was using my breath to keep oxygen in my lungs. My heart was beating strongly and I wondered if I could make it all the way to the top. Maybe I should have taken the cable car. Ami stopped at a gigantic tree that protruded out into the path and showed its exposed, thick, roots. Other hikers in front of us stopped there and touched the large knot.

"This is the Octopus Tree," Ami said as she took a deep breath. She touched the bulbous knot. Her father did as well, and took the chance to wipe the sweat from his forehead.

We kept going, taking short breaks, until we got to

a point where there were two split paths.

"There are two ways to go," he said, "the man's path and the woman's path."

On the left was a steep stone staircase with what looked like hundreds of steps and to the right was a level, curved, pathway. I didn't care for gender norms. Ami went silently to the left and I followed. I thought her father would join us but he was going to the right. Ami looked over and laughed.

"*Doko ni iku*?"

"*Hiza ga itai dakara*!"

Ami chortled. I had to think about what he said. I caught the words "*hiza*": knee and "*itai*": hurt. I chuckled. Ami had been right about her father complaining about his ailment.

The trek up the stairs was one that required multiple stops. Fortunately, we were not the only ones who were pausing. Muscles that I didn't know I had were tightening.

When we finally reached the top, we caught our breath and drank more water. We kept walking on the trail. Lining the sides were tall stone pillars engraved with *kanji*. Red lanterns lined the left side and wooden plaques with *kanji* hanging from a wooden frame lined the right, leading far ahead without end. We eventually reached a more flattened area with a restaurant, shops, and an observation deck.

"Let's take a break here," I said.

I badly needed one. My muscles burned and I was getting a tinge of a headache.

Ami nodded.

A vending machine stood next to the small noodle restaurant. Though the price was more expensive than what I paid at the *conbini*, I bought three water bottles anyway. I found Ami leaning against a wooden fence made from quartered logs. As I walked towards her, I saw that behind her was an unobstructed view of Tokyo. The gray of the city buildings was sprawled out beneath.

"I can't believe we hiked so high," I said, handing Ami a bottle of water.

She placed the bottle on the back of her neck.

"*Ne*. I can believe it. Oh, my feet hurt a little," she said. "I'm out of practice."

I sat down on a bench next to her, beside us another hiker who was also resting. It felt good to sit and let my body rest. I took off my backpack and took out the bag of snacks. Some of the bread had been smushed during the hike. I offered a snack to Ami but she refused. She took the water off her neck, twisted the cap, and began to drink until half of it was empty. Even after eating something and drinking water, my headache was worsening. After a few minutes, Ami started smoking. Either because of my tiredness, my headache, or both, I wasn't in the mood to smell cigarette smoke.

"Can you do that somewhere else?" I snapped. I didn't mean to be so harsh.

Ami removed the cigarette from her mouth and turned to me slowly. She gave me a look that I couldn't really decipher; something that was a mix of amusement and offense.

"Are you okay?" she asked.

"Fine," I said. I took a deep inhale and exhaled sharply out my nose. "I just don't know why you have to do that *now* or at all."

"*Saa*, it's my body. So, if it bothers you, I'll stop."

She put out her cigarette.

"Just give me a minute," I said, closing my eyes. "I want to be by myself."

Ami took a deep breath and stood up. "Okay. I will go mushroom hunting around here."

I leaned my head back on the wooden fence and closed my eyes. The fresh air and cool breeze lulled me into a light sleep. The air smelled like warm cedar and moist leaves. When I smelled the aroma of smoke, I opened my eyes. I lifted my head, which now had a dull, subsiding ache, signaling that I was recovering. Across from me was a stall that was roasting what looked like round marshmallows. My stomach groaned. I walked over to buy one. Reading the *hiragana* on the sign noted that they were called "*dongo*" and rather than marshmallows, as I guessed they were, they were rounded balls of sweet *mochi* rice.

That was where Ami found me, holding a stick with my mouthful.

"Feeling better?" She asked.

I nodded. "Sorry," I offered.

She waved a hand in front of her nose. "*Totemo nashi*. If you need to be alone, I understand." She pulled out her phone, "Look at these." She flipped through her pictures to show me the mushrooms she had found. Most of them were white or brown and looked similar.

"I wish I could take some," she said.

I looked around for her father. "Where's your dad?" I asked.

"He went ahead. Are you ready?"

I finished the rest of my food and gave the skewer back. I adjusted the straps on my backpack that were loose. "Sure."

I stopped at one of the drink vending machines that

was next to a noodle restaurant. Of course there would be a vending machine on the mountain. They were everywhere else, why not here? The price for a bottle of water was high, but I paid it.

"How are you doing?" Ami asked.

"I think I'm fine now. Tomorrow, I'll be sore."

"Oh, yes. When I climbed Fuji-*san* the first time, the next day I could barely walk on my own."

"Fuji-*san*? Mt. Fuji?"

I didn't have to read far in my initial research of Japan to have come across Mt. Fuji, the tallest mountain in Japan.

"Yes." She stopped to rest and then a smile spread across her face. "We should climb it next."

I stopped. "Oh, I don't know about that."

"Why not? Oh, we could do it on *Oshougatsu*. We climb up at night on December 31st and we can see the first sunrise of the new year." She looked at me, no doubt puzzled by my reaction. "It's romantic, *deshyou*?"

"Breaking my back climbing an insanely high mountain isn't what I would consider romantic."

Ami walked to me and thread her arm through mine. "Think about it," she said.

****

After much more walking that seemed endless, we finally reached the bottom of a set of stairs. Just above there was a red gate and on either side were giant stone statues of figures with bodies of men but one had an elongated nose and the other had a beak instead of a mouth and bird wings. I stood between the two winged statues, which were inside a cordoned area, protected on all sides by mesh wire in a wooden frame. I passed through and on the other side was another of these statues.

I watched as the hikers performed a certain ritual by a covered water basin. There was a large stone basin about half my height and over it was a long length of bamboo with short bamboo spouts sticking out of it. From the spouts flowed water. One by one, each hiker took one of the bamboo ladles and held it under one of the spouts until it filled with water, then they would pour the water on one hand, then the other, and then on the other again before sipping some and then holding the ladle vertically to let the remaining water spill down the handle and then placing it along the bamboo in between the spouts with the end of the ladle resting on the stone basin and the cup facing downward.

It reminded me very much of dipping my fingers in the holy water and making the sign of the cross before going into church. I considered whether I should also take part but I felt out of place, so I kept walking, past a marble circle standing by itself and on the other side a metal pole and at the top of the pole were two bars holding metal rings. A person walked through the circle, then took a long pole in hand and tapped the top against the rings, making them jingle.

Beyond this was a small shrine. Next to it was a metal frame with horizontal bars. Tied with red string on each bar were countless bright five *yen* coins. When a breeze happened by, the coins clinked against each other. Farther down were stalls selling goods. I wandered towards one which had charms and other items for sale. The man behind the stand wore a white robe and a long strand of dark beads. A few other hikers were also perusing the stand, one of them having picked out a red fabric charm with *kanji*.

I looked at each piece and all of them were interesting. I recalled my parents and their saint medallions and I guessed that the charms I was looking at were similar. I didn't want to buy something that I didn't know what it was for. I played it safe by buying a black bead bracelet. In one of the stones was a small piece of glass. I picked it up to give to the man. He said, "*Mi te*" and picked up the bracelet to put one of the center beads to his eye. He gave it back to me. When I looked through it, it magnified a picture of one of the statues. I smiled at the ingenuity. I gave it back to the man so he could put it in the white paper bag and I paid him. I stepped aside, took it out, and put it on my left wrist.

The temple was intricate and beautiful. I stood before a building whose founding was far older than the country that I was from. I had to stand there for some time as I watched tired hikers approach the large incense burner. One or two of them stopped before the burner and deposited coins into a wooden box, then took small batches of incense wrapped in colorful paper. They lit the tips of the incense until they began smoking and then placed the blunt end into the ash.

I noticed that Ami held one of the white envelopes.

"What did you get?" I asked.

She opened the bag and briefly pulled out the fabric charm and then put it back.

"An *omamori*. It's just for good luck. What about you?"

I showed her the beaded bracelet on my wrist.

"Very nice."

"So, all those little charms are for luck?"

"Not all of them. Each one has a different purpose. So, when I was a student I would get the ones for helping to pass an exam or to help with studying."

"Ah. I thought they were something like the Catholic saint medallions that my mom had. Each saint would help with different problems."

"Kind of. There are other gods or goddesses, uhm, I think they're called bodhisattva, who can help also. It's all really complicated, but if it helps, then it helps."

We stood off to the side to let others through.

"My dad swears by them. There was one year that he kept getting into car trouble: a flat tire, engine problems, or another car would bump into his and leave a dent. Finally, he made us all go with him to hike some mountain that would help protect travelers. So, we all went, and he bought the special *omamori* there that he hung from the rear-view mirror. Since then, he's never had car trouble."

"How much of that is divine intervention and how much is a placebo effect?"

"Hopefully, a little of both."

We walked along the outside of the temple where there was another stand selling charms. Ami looked there as well. The charms were similar but they had some other things that I hadn't seen. Ami bought a wooden board.

"It's an *ema*. You write your wish. Maybe it'll be fun."

Ami went to a place where a small table sat before a section where there were wooden frames and horizontal bars where other written wooden boards had been tied. A cursory look showed short or long pieces of writing, a few of which were in English. One I saw, written in slanted handwriting, read "I want to find love!"

I thought that must be everyone's wish. I hoped the person would find it. Ami called my name. She had already written a line in *kanji* with a marker that was attached to the table with a red piece of string.

"Your turn," she said.

I picked up the marker, not knowing what to write. I stood there for longer than I intended, thinking about what I should write or what my wish would actually be. There were many things that I wanted. If I were to write them all, the small block of wood could hardly hold all the letters. I looked at the short line that Ami wrote, wishing that I knew what it said. That would be my wish. I took the cap off the pen and wrote "I want to understand."

"Good wish," Ami said.

I put the cap back on.

"What did you write?"

"Eh," she started and looked down. "I wrote about love." She pointed to one of the *kanji* that looked like 恋 . "This one means 'love'. The rest, uhm, maybe it's embarrassing." She tilted her head to the side in thought. "I think I will tell you about it." She pointed to some *kanji* that looked like 恋の予感.

"I wrote. It's called '*koi no yokan*'. It's like—*Eigo janai*—uhm, feeling about falling in love with a new person."

Why would she be embarrassed? We had been dating for long enough that feeling love wasn't unordinary.

"*Koi no yokan*," I repeated. "I think that's true."

She didn't say anything. Instead, she kissed me on my cheek. I had to smile at her sweetness. She took the *ema* and tied it to a spot on the bar.

Chapter 12

I slept in late the next morning. Once I woke up, I felt how strained my muscles were and how it ached to move. Ami was still asleep beside me. She didn't look well at all. She was pale and even though she was under the blanket, she was shivering. I felt her forehead. It was burning. I found her father in the kitchen washing the dishes.

"Is there a thermometer?" I asked.

"I think there's one in the cabinet under the sink. Why?"

"Ami's sick."

He put the dish down, wiped his hands on his pants, and followed me. I found the thermometer and went to her room. Her father was there with his hand on her forehead. I passed him the thermometer. We both waited until it beeped.

"*Kuso*," he said. "I'll start the car. We have to go to the hospital." He passed the thermometer to me and I saw where it showed forty degrees Celsius, or one hundred and four degrees Fahrenheit.

"Ami?" I asked.

"Mm?"

"We're going to the hospital."

She nodded weakly. "*Tsukareta*," she said.

I helped her up off the bed. She could walk a little bit but was wobbly. I put a sweater on her, along with her socks, and held her so that she wouldn't fall down the stairs. I heard footsteps and her father came in.

"*Hayaku*," he said, and motioned to the door.

I slipped on my shoes and helped Ami with hers. She was breathing hard and kept trying to keep her eyes open. We got in the car and her father pulled out quickly, speeding along the road. I worried that he would hit another car, but he was a good driver. Ami fell asleep on my lap. None of us said anything while in the car.

"Don't you have to pay?" I asked, remembering that whenever I had gone to the emergency room or care clinic, that my parents had to pay first.

"Pay?" her father asked. He looked puzzled for a little and then explained, "Oh, no, Japan has national health."

He took out his wallet and showed me a card filled with *kanji* I couldn't read.

"It's the health card. We all pay taxes so we all get healthcare."

I remembered my time in college, worried about getting injured and going to the hospital and putting medical debt on top of my student debt. "That sounds nice." I said.

We sat in the waiting room for an hour, and then her father helped her into a wheelchair, aided by a nurse.

"*Gomen*," he said. "Only family."

I nodded. "I'll wait here."

He smiled and then rummaged in his pockets to hand me a one thousand *yen* note.

"For *tabemono*. Food."

I took the money and almost cried at his generosity. He left to go with Ami.

I couldn't keep from worrying, despite thinking she

would most likely be fine. There was still the worry that the fever would get worse. She did work with lab animals. What if something had bit her and she got some disease? I'd once watched a movie called *Outbreak* where a diseased monkey had caused a virus to spread. What if that was happening to Ami?

That's stupid. It's only a fever, I kept thinking. *You've had fevers before and it's been fine.*

But what if it's something else?

I walked around the hospital waiting room where there were others, mostly elderly people, similarly waiting, watching the television that was tuned to one of the many Japanese talk shows.

There was a vending machine where I bought a warm bottle of lemon tea. I thought Ami would like something, too, when she came out, so I bought her a milk tea. In the rush, I had forgot my backpack. I occupied myself by trying to read the Japanese that I knew in the magazines on the stand, and for what I didn't, I would try looking it up in my phone's dictionary. Focusing on a problem to solve kept my mind too busy to think about anything else. Eventually, I was tired of looking through Japanese *kana* and got up to walk around. I kept checking the doors so that I wouldn't miss Ami and her father when they appeared.

About an hour later, the doors clicked open. I saw Ami first, still in a wheelchair but alert and resting her head on the back of the chair. When she saw me, she smiled, making her tired, puffy eyes more obvious.

"Everything's okay?" I asked. I remembered the milk tea I got for her and gave it to her. Her expression relaxed and she smiled a little.

"Oh, *arigatou*. Just what I need." She twisted the top

and then took a drink.

"What was it?"

"Influenza Type A," she said.

There were types? I'd have to ask about it later.

"How did you get that?"

She shrugged.

"She didn't get her vaccine this year," Her father explained.

"*Papa*," Ami said with a tone of annoyance.

The rest of their conversation was in rapid Japanese, punctuated by Ami coughing periodically.

"At least," I offered, to stop what seemed to be a beginning argument, "it's nothing too bad."

"It's spoiling our holiday," Ami said. "I'll be sick the rest of the week. All the plans we had are ruined now."

"We can always find something else to do," I said.

"Very good," her father said. "We will get to the car and go back."

"Okay," I said. "Oh," I remembered the money he had given me and took the change from my pocket to give to him but he put up a hand.

"No. I gave it to you."

I returned it to my pocket. We walked out together and back to the car. Her father drove slower this time, more in line with the posted speed limit. A few minutes after driving, Ami rested her head against my shoulder and fell asleep. She smelled like dried sweat and alcohol sanitizer.

"That was exciting," her father said.

"Just a little. I was surprised that the hospital was so nice."

"Yes, it's good. Ami doesn't get sick often, so I was

worried."

"Me, too."

I noticed that his eyes flicked to the rearview mirror to better see my face, then he glanced back at the road.

"Ah, I wish she would relax more." He laughed. "I wish *I* could relax more."

Thoughts came back of late weekend nights grading papers and early mornings to be at school to plan for the day and to be in the class in case students arrived early.

"I know the feeling."

There was silence for a while and he had the radio playing some low volume pop music. I looked at the older man for longer than I intended to. He was lean, fit but not overly muscular. He had wrinkles, and all the normal signs of age of a man of his maturity, and most of his hair had grayed. I could imagine that, thirty or forty years before that he would have been very attractive. I wanted very much to ask him about his late wife, how they met, how they fell in love. I knew she was important to Ami and I knew so little about her mom. I knew better than to ask, though. It was a delicate subject and now was not the time. When we drove off the highway and into the city, he turned off at a restaurant. I recognized the *kana* for "ramen" but not much else. Ami was still asleep. Her father unbuckled.

"I will get take-out for us. Do you like *tonkotsu*?"

I didn't know if I did or not, but I wasn't about to refuse food. "Yes."

"Okay. You can stay here with Ami." He opened the door and stood up. I tilted my head back and closed my eyes for a little until I heard the car door opened again and the rustling of plastic bags. The smell of the ramen wafted through the car. Ami must have smelled it. She lifted her head up suddenly and looked around, bewildered.

"*E-ni-o-i*," she said. I knew that expression. My students said that every time the lunch cart came in the room.

"We are almost home," her father said as he pulled out of the restaurant.

Ami, more alert, drank from her milk tea bottle.

When we returned home, I helped hold the food while her father opened the door and held it open for us. Ami refused any help and walked on her own through the door.

"I need *ofuro*," she mumbled.

We went inside and I put the food on the table.

"I'll start a bath," her father said.

He walked down the hallway and into the bathroom.

"Should we eat?" I offered, unpacking the delicious smelling ramen.

"No," Ami started, but then took a deep inhale. Her stomach made an audible grumble. We both chuckled. "Or, maybe I should."

She sat on the other side of me.

"I don't know whose is whose," I said.

"It doesn't matter. Papa isn't picky." She slid one of the bowls to her and opened the top. When she did, the steam rose to her nose. "Mm," she moaned. She took a pair of chopsticks and a soup spoon. With the spoon, she dipped it down and drew up a spoonful of the ingredients: noodles, pork, and bean sprouts. She used her chopsticks to take the contents out of the spoon and into her mouth, slurping the noodles. She closed her eyes and let out a satisfied groan.

I opened the lid to my bowl. I could see why her

reaction was the way it had been. Everything about it was delectable.

"You and Papa would get along in that way," she said. "You both like all kinds of food."

"Coming from where I'm from, there wasn't much variety. Here, there's so much. I don't want to miss out on something good."

She smiled. "Like when you ate *natto*?"

I cringed at the memory of eating the slimy, rotten, fermented beans. "At least I tried it."

"Good," she said. "I'll have him make you *Sunagimo Yakitori*."

"Should I ask what it is or be surprised?"

"Isn't a surprise better?"

Her skin looked a little pinker now and her mood was improved. The food must have helped her. I started eating my own bowl. It was fantastic. The broth, the noodles, the pork, everything about it warmed my stomach and filled my belly.

Her father came into the room.

"Bath is nearly ready," he said. "How is the food?"

I had my mouth full so I gave a thumbs-up. He smiled and sat down to eat his own bowl. None of us said much as we ate, focusing instead on enjoying the food. Her father ate quickly and then held the rim of the bowl to his lips to drink the broth. When done, he put the trash into the garbage and went to the bathroom.

Ami drank some of the broth and stopped, leaving a bowl still half-full.

"Oh, I think I'm done," she said.

"I'll eat it," I offered, then thought again. Ami was sick. If I shared food with her, I might get the flu, too. On the other hand, we had already slept in the same room and spent time together so I was exposed anyway. She slid the bowl to me and I happily ate from two bowls until I was full. That might have been a mistake as I soon became bloated. "Maybe I'll skip breakfast in the morning," I said.

Ami laughed.

Her father came back. "Ready," he announced.

Ami stood up.

"Do you need help?" I asked.

She shook her head and went down the hall to the bathroom.

****

On Saturday morning, I woke up earlier than usual and dressed. Ami was still asleep, but her father was awake and typing on his computer in the living room. He was also dressed in his hiking gear. Every item of clothing had the brand label "Patagonia" on it. He also had a small Fjalraven backpack by his feet. "I'm just going to get snacks before we leave," I said. "Do you want anything?"

Her father stopped and looked over at me.

"Black Boss Coffee," he said. "Two."

I went to the *genkan* and put on my shoes. The *conbini* was a few blocks away. It was a Lawson. I stopped in and filled my orange basket with all different kinds of snacks. I found the coffee in one of the coolers. The can had the image of an older man's portrait with a pipe in his mouth. I made sure to also get two large bottles of water. While perusing the few aisles, I made sure to get some sweets. One looked interesting. It was a soft cookie with cream and raisins. The *katakana* read "Raisin Sando."

I paid at the register, thanked the cashier, and

walked back to the house. The sky was somewhat overcast and the sun poked through the clouds at points, making me squint against the bright light. I picked the Raisin Sando and ate the soft, creamy cookie, on my way back. It was sweet but there was a taste that I couldn't quite figure out.

I got back to the house, stopping to look at the wisteria blossoms. Some bees buzzed back and forth, skittering inside the blossoms to gather the pollen. I went inside, removing my shoes, and first went to give the bottles of coffee to her father. He thanked me and opened one. Her father offered me a drink from his can. I shook my head. I wasn't one for the taste of straight black coffee.

Instead, I went to the room Ami and I were sharing. She was still asleep. I put a hand on her forehead to check her temperature. She felt normal. I began packing my backpack with the snacks. I felt a little drowsy. I thought my drowsiness might be because I was hungry, so I ate one of the *onigiri* and drank some water. Ami rustled awake. She turned to look at me through half opened eyelids.

"How are you feeling?" I asked.

She stretched her arms over her head and scratched her scalp.

"Much better," she said.

"Are you sure?" I asked. "We don't have to go if you want to stay here."

"No. I'm tired of being inside."

She sat up and smiled at me. She got up and came to where I was and hugged me from behind as I packed. I stopped to rest my head against her shoulder.

"Thank you," she said. She kissed my forehead. I

took a moment to bask in the feeling of her warm, sleep-laden skin against mine.

"You got snacks?" She asked.

"Yup."

"Any *onigiri*?"

I took one from the backpack and handed it to her.

"Oh, *arigatou*." She released me from the embrace and unwrapped the *onigiri*. She took the empty plastic bag that I had left on the floor and put the *onigiri* wrapper inside.

"Raisin Sand?" Ami asked, no doubt seeing the empty wrapper I left inside. "That has alcohol."

"No it didn't. They wouldn't sell a cookie with alcohol."

"Yes. It's like, uhm," she paused and shouted something down the hallway at her father. Her father responded.

"Rum Raisin," she answered. "I think there isn't much alcohol."

"Well, I was wondering why I was feeling sleepy..."

"I'll get dressed," Ami said after she finished eating. She went out the door and to the bathroom. I was ready, so I went to the living room to wait. I took out my Japanese study book. Ami's father glanced over at me from his typing.

"Can you help me with some English?" he asked.

"Sure."

I stood up and went to him. Glancing at the screen, it looked like he was working on writing a narrative. I skimmed the document and read a few sentences about what I assumed was his memoir. He highlighted a sentence on the screen.

"I'm not sure about which is the best word to use to

make these two be put together."

I read the sentence: "I never liked swimming and chess."

"So, it's best to use 'or' in this sentence instead of 'and.'"

"Why?"

I had to think about that. I'd never had someone ask me about that. There was no clear reason. Using "and" technically made sense. If I were to make it a positive sentence "I liked swimming and chess", that would make sense. The only reason really was that it was a negative sentence. I told him so.

Ami laughed. She said something to her father and he groaned.

"I was wondering when he was going to show you his book," she said.

I looked back at where she was, dressed in her hiking clothes and with pastel blue knitted hat on her head.

"That's great," I said.

"Yes, I am writing about my life."

"And he won't let me read it," she said. "He was so excited for you to come so he could show you what he had."

"*Ami*," he said. "*Yamette. Hazukashii daiyou.*"

I smiled a little, for a grown man to admit that he was shy about his work. It was cute. "I'd like to read it," I said.

He smiled nervously. "Thank you," he said as he gave a little nod.

"Why did you decide to write in English?" I asked.

"Huh?" he said. "Oh, I did write it in Japanese first. Now, I want to put it in English so that my wife's family can read it."

I noted that he used the present tense to talk about her. That seemed very sweet to me.

"Are they your memoirs?"

He nodded. "Mostly. There are things I don't write about."

"He started writing after mom died," Ami whispered.

"I was writing before that," her father said. "that's why Jenny said I should write more."

"He's been working on it for…" Ami trailed off and then turned to her father, "*Dono gurai?*"

"Sixteen years," he answered in English.

That evening, after the hike and dinner, Ami went outside to smoke. She came back in and said that she would take another bath.

"Can you help me?" she asked me. "I'm worried I'm going to pass out and drown if I go by myself."

"Of course," I said.

She moved slowly to the room and took out a pair of her soft yellow and pink pajamas.

"Can you start the bath?" she asked. "Just push the middle button on the wall there." She pointed at the wall outside the bathroom. I found the button and pushed it. I heard the bathwater begin to fill the basin.

"I should get one of those," I said to myself.

Ami was soon next to me and opened the bathroom door. She hung her change of clothes on the hook outside the frosted glass. I went in the bathroom with her. Like most Japanese baths, the area to wash was separate from the actual tub. Ami undressed and tossed her dirty clothes on the floor outside. She turned on the shower and washed her body and her hair, then rinsed. The bath water stopped and there was a little chime that rang from the button pad outside. The bath water had a warm, milky, color to it and smelled of flower blossoms. Her father must have put some salts in it. Ami stepped in the tub and inhaled sharply.

"Ah, he always has the water too hot," she said. She then relaxed a little more, dipping farther down so her shoulders were below the milky surface. "Feels good."

She shook her head.

"I'm sorry, Tara. Everything is ruined."

"What? It's not your fault you got sick."

She didn't answer me. She leaned her head back and closed her eyes. The steam from the bath was making my head tired and I rested against her shoulder. She let out a tired moan. She lifted her head and kissed the top of my forehead.

After the bath, we both went to sleep, one of those deep sleeps where only the sound of a lightning crack would wake. I always loved that kind of sleep. It felt like the world and all its stresses vanished into a beautiful dark.

Chapter 13

June 2011

After the vacation where Ami recovered from her flu in a matter of days, I was back at work teaching. The issues with the aftermath of the earthquake and nuclear disaster continued. This meant that trains and most shopping areas were not using air conditioning or sparing as much electricity as possible. As such, to combat the heat, most people were using hand fans. It was on one of these commutes one morning, that my phone rang. I generally did not like to talk on the phone on account of the phone manner sign on the train, but in my tired morning stupor, I did.

"Hello?" I asked softly to try not to arouse attention.

"Tara." It was mom. The background noise was fuzzy and I heard noises of shuffling items.

"What is it?"

"There's a flood. We have to leave the house."

What she was saying didn't make any sense. "Mom, what are you talking about?"

"The river is flooding. There was too much rain or, I don't know…but we have to leave in case it comes to the house. They put up levees, but the water's coming over them."

Their dog, Baby, barked in the background. "Are you going to be okay?"

"All the hotels are full," she said quickly, her voice panged with anxiety, "we have to stay with John and Lori."

John and Lori Tollefson, family friends that went to the same church. Friends of my parents, and to me for a time until I stopped going to mass, and then their friendliness towards me turned into ministry. However they acted towards me, I knew they were kind, and had been friends with my parents for decades. I knew they would help. Still, I felt powerless from where I was.

"Do you need money or anything?"

She scoffed. "You should have come back," she said spitefully.

From the other end, my dad yelled at her from the door. There was the scuffled sound of movement, the sound of her dropping the phone, and then picking it up again.

"I'm sorry," I offered.

"I have to go," she said.

"Call me when you get to your friend's house," I said.

"Sure."

"I love you," I said.

"I love you, too."

The phone turned off. I held it in my hand for some time. How could so much go so wrong in the span of a few months? A disaster in Japan and, now, one in North Dakota.

It was selfish of me to have stayed. Had I left in March, I would be there with them. I had decided to stay in Japan those months ago. If I had gone back home, would I be more helpful or less? I would be there, but I would also be an extra body that needed an extra room.

Without me, at least my family could focus on their own needs. I didn't know what I could do, if there was anything I *could* do. I would just have to hope they would be alright.

The river they were talking about was the Souris River, a body of water that divided the town. It was where my mother went fishing, where I drove and walked over before and after school every day. It was the river where the geese would gather each spring. My parent's house was not far from the river. They lived in a pre-war house by Roosevelt Park where the river was a few minutes away.

If the river grew high enough and the flood was severe, my childhood home would be damaged. All the precious items that my parents had collected over the years would be gone. If I had been there for them, I could have helped. I dwelled on that for a long while. Even if I bought a plane ticket and left in the morning, it would be too late to do anything. I would be there to help them pick up the pieces, but not much else.

After work, when I had a moment, I checked the news on my laptop. Sure enough, there was coverage about the on-coming flood. I couldn't look at the information for long. It all reminded me of what happened two months before. The panic, the desperation, the inevitability of disaster and even death. I couldn't sit still. My heart was beating quickly. My apartment felt stifling. I needed to get my mind off of thinking about what may or may not happen to my family. What would they do if their house was destroyed? Where would they live?

The response to the earthquake and tsunami in Japan had been swift and supportive, from what I had seen.

Almost immediately afterward, temporary houses were erected, food and water was provided, even relocation services. Where my parents were, I wasn't sure how much help they would get. Their church should help, but I had my doubts. There was too much that was unknown. I snuggled into my futon, pulling the blanket over my head. I tried to sleep but couldn't.

Our house was as good as gone, sunk under water, and only the roof could be seen. I thought then about my grandmother's pine trunk, the one she brought when she immigrated all that way from Sweden, the one that I used to hide in when playing hide-and-seek with my brothers, under the folded quilts that smelled like lavender fabric softener and dusty wood. If they spent too long looking, I would fall asleep under those quilts, like a kitten curled up in warm laundry.

Was that trunk sunk under dirty river water? I needed to know. I called my mother, not caring about the time. She must not have either, since she picked up the call. "Tara?"

"Did you get grandma's trunk?"

She sniffed. There was a long silence that told me everything.

"I can't believe it," she said. "I forgot."

I wanted to swear. I wanted to scream.

I planted my face into my pillow and did both. I didn't notice my mother's voice on the other side until I was done screaming. She kept saying "Tara? Hello? Are you there?"

I took a deep breath. I remembered what Ami had told me about when bad things happen that no one could control.

"Yeah, I'm here."

"I'm sorry."

"*Shouganai*," I said.

"What?"

"Nothing. Are you okay?"

"We're settling in. The house is up on the hill. They've been nice to let us stay here."

I took a deep breath. "I'm happy you're safe," I said. "Are you sure there's nothing you need?"

"I just wish you were here," she said.

"Mom," I said, "I wish I were there, too."

"It's fine. I'm sorry for what I said before. It wouldn't matter if you came back or not. It wouldn't stop the flood."

"I—"

"It's that I miss you."

"I know. I miss you, too."

"Oh, it must be late there."

"It's alright."

"I'll let you go to sleep. Your dad and I are going back to the house to grab some more things. It hasn't flooded yet. I think we have time."

"Well, be careful."

"Of course. I'd," she hesitated. "I'd really love it if you prayed for us."

When I heard her ask it, I opened my mouth to give her a sharp reply. I halted. She was stressed, and arguing with her about religion and faith would make her more stressed out and leave me angry. I didn't care to be angry. If it gave her some peace of mind, it was a small concession to make.

"I'll pray for all of you," I said.

"Thank you."

"Love you."

"Bye."

I hung up the phone. I could hope for her, for all of them, but I could not pray as she wanted me to. My hope and well-wishes would have to be enough for now. I took a deep breath.

The next morning I went to work. It helped me to keep my mind off of what was happening. The lessons were the same as usual and when I got back to my apartment I read and watched updates on the flood, the good and the bad. And I read and watched the updates on the aftermath of the tsunami, the good and the bad. I thought about donating money, but my money was in a Japanese bank and I couldn't use my card online. I could send cash through the mail, but I didn't trust that it would arrive there unstolen. If my parents let me transfer money to their account, they could donate it, but they refused when I offered to give them money in the first place. I couldn't help with the issues with the tsunami either. My limited knowledge of Japanese made looking for information difficult.

At a certain point, I couldn't look anymore.

What I could do was send a package to my family. I looked up the Tollefson's address online where I could send the care package. I went out that evening and bought snacks, toiletries, and little gifts. I asked Ami how to send a package and she told me to go to the Seven Eleven. There, I found a section with flattened post office boxes. I ended up having to ask for help from the staff. The young man who helped me knew some English and after about fifteen minutes, I was able to pack everything, fill out the address form, and pay for the postage. All I had to do next was take it to the post office, which I did on my way to work.

It wasn't much, but it was something.

I called Ami after getting home from the post office and told her what happened. She insisted I go to spend the night at her place. It was closer to the school and I wouldn't be alone. I brought a change of clothes and my laptop and was at her place in less than an hour.

What I didn't expect was that as soon as I was inside and sitting on a chair in her living room, I would start crying. She sat next to me and held my hand, saying nothing while I let the tears flow.

I stayed at her place for a few days. Even though she was usually at work and didn't come home until late in the evening, it was nice to know that someone else would be there, that *Ami* would be there, and I wouldn't be alone.

Chapter 14

July 2011

Rain came to Tokyo one day. And didn't stop for three days. I hadn't thought to need rain boots, but after thoughtlessly walking to work and returning with soaked-through shoes, I went out to buy a pair. With the moisture and the heat, my apartment became musty, so I took to keeping the balcony window open to have some fresh air.

Homes in Minot were being recovered. My parents emailed me as often as they could, but there were no more phone calls or video chats. It was too expensive for them.

During classes one day, Haruyo stayed to keep talking to the student and I went to the next class. The students were in the hallway, some taking their break time to go to the bathroom or just to be away from their desks.

As I approached the classroom, I noticed that there were two or three girls in a corner with their backs to me yelling at someone. I delayed entering the classroom and walked over to them. As I did, one of the girls saw me coming and said, "*Eigo-no-Sensei kita.*"

It was Miu, the same one who teased Natsumi about her snake pet. The two other girls were Jyumi and Fuuka. And in the corner, looking down with her shoulders hunched forward was Natsumi.

I was not supposed to speak anything other than English in the classroom but I wanted the girls to listen to me. I asked in stern Japanese *"Nani shiteru no,"* even though I knew exactly what they were doing. It wasn't the first time I had seen a student getting bullied and I had no tolerance for it. The girls looked at me wide eyed.

"Nihongo shabette."

"Majide."

I stood before them. *"Ijime dame,"* I said. Stop bullying.

"Ijime jyanai yo," Fuuka said with a smile. I'm not bullying.

Bullshit, I wanted to say. They knew what they were doing, cornering Natsumi, making a wall with their bodies so no one could see what they were doing. The class bell rang and the girls dispersed, leaving Natsumi by herself, still staring at the floor. I knelt down so I was face-to-face with her. She didn't seem to be crying, but had a blank expression that looked like she was in shock or disassociating from the situation.

"Natsumi," I asked, and I touched her on the shoulder. *"Daijoubu desu ka?"* They were empty sort of words. "Are you okay?" Of course she wasn't okay. How could she be? It was the only thing I could think of to say. I wished I had a bigger vocabulary, knew more Japanese so I could tell her that what was happening wasn't her fault and that the other girls were wrong.

She remained quiet for some time. I noticed Haruyo coming down the hallway.

"Ma-ma," Natsumi said. So-so. She played with the charm on her cell phone and walked away from me without looking up.

"Is everything alright?" Haruyo asked as she stopped. Then she approached the classroom door and looked over at me.

I watched as Natsumi walked away and into the girl's bathroom. I wanted to go with her, to tell her that I could help her, or to say nothing at all and for her to know that there was someone who cared. Was that what she needed? Whenever I was less than tolerated, I didn't need platitudes, I needed to be alone. Maybe that's what Natsumi needed, too. I'd leave her alone for now and talk to her later in the best Japanese I'd be able to muster.

I turned to Haruyo. "Some girls were bullying Natsumi," I said plainly.

Haruyo took a deep inhale. "Which girls?"

"Miu, Fuuka, and Jyumi," I said.

"*Saa*. It is always them. I will talk with them. Shall we go?"

I would have to set my emotions aside for the next hour. The three girls were in the class, except for Natsumi who hid in the bathroom. If there had been bullying in my class, I would have sent the students to the principal or to the office. I did not tolerate that kind of aggression. But here, I was limited in what I could do. I would have to trust that Haruyo would do what was needed.

We went into the classroom and immediately Haruyo went to the telephone on the wall and made a call. Haruyo waited for the classroom to settle before she began. We started the lesson, with me announcing the month and day, as usual and then greeting each student. The classroom door opened and it was a person from the front office who called the three girls to come. They obliged, but as Jyumi left, she passed me and said,

"*Nechi, nechi, sensei.*"

Haruyo then made a long, stern speech to the classroom. I noticed only a few words from what she said, but the gist of it was that she was lecturing them about bullying.

I ignored her and continued with the lesson, passing Natsumi's empty desk and not expecting her to return from hiding.

By the time the class was over, it was lunch and so I had time before I would sit with the other students. I went to the bathroom to check on Natsumi and brought my keitai to use the dictionary.

"Natsumi?" I called out. "*Daijyoubu?*"

I checked under the stall doors but didn't find anything. She could have her feet on the seat, to better hide from others. She could also have left.

"Natsumi," I started. "*Ijime, gomen-nasai.*" I took out my dictionary and looked up the word "fault". "Natsumi *no shogai jyanai.*"

I heard a stifled giggle. Someone was there.

"Tara-*sensei?*" she asked. "*Shogai ga chigai yo.*"

I knew the word *chigai*, or *machigai*, "mistake". Had I said the wrong word? It didn't matter. At least she was talking.

"It's not your fault," I said in English.

The door at the far end clicked open. Natsumi came out of the stall, gripping her phone in her hand. She turned it around to show me the display screen. She had written a sentence in English that said: "Hate the 3 girls. Thanks to helping me."

I smiled. I hoped she would be alright. I knew first-hand how insidious bullying could be. It didn't happen just in school. There were the "mean girls" who would take their bullying online or do it just outside school property so that teachers like me were limited in what we could do. There were the "brutal boys" who would take the aggressive route and fight both in and outside of the classroom. If I could stop even one instance of bullying, that might be enough to stem the cycle.

That night I received a phone call from Haruyo while I was gaming on my laptop.

"Tara-*sensei*, sorry for calling so late. Are you available tomorrow afternoon?"

"I think so."

"The three girls who were bullying have to come to school and apologize to Okabe-*san*, Natsumi. They will be with their parents and it was requested that you be there, too."

It was a delightful surprise to know that there would be some meeting. That their parents would be there was a great feat. So often it was difficult for me to get parents involved.

"It will be after the club activities tomorrow at two o'clock. Please meet in the teacher's room."

"I will," I almost hung up and then thought about my clothing. Somehow I thought that it wouldn't be appropriate to show up in jeans and a t-shirt. "Should I wear something nice?"

"Yes, your regular school suit is good."

"Ok. I'll be there."

"Thank you."

The phone call cut off. I was planning on doing my laundry in the morning. If I needed my suit tomorrow, I'd need to do my laundry tonight. I took my full laundry bag, my backpack, and went out to the nearest coin laundry.

****

I arrived at the school ten minutes before the meeting and went to the teacher's room. Haruyo was there and dressed in an extremely formal suit, making mine seem dull in comparison. She greeted me.

"We can go in the room, here," she said.

She guided me to a room I had never been into before. It was a conference room. There were already a few people there. Miu, Jyumi, Natsumi, and adults who I assumed were their parents or guardians. With Miu there were two parents, a mother and father, while Jyumi had a grandfather with her, and Natsumi had her mother. On the table before everyone were single ceramic cups of green tea. The principal was at one end. He rose when I entered and gestured to an empty seat for me to sit in. I complied.

At two o'clock, a man rushed in, and stood a moment to catch his breath. He bowed and apologized, then took a seat. Fuuka was still missing and I wondered if she would show.

Haruyo sat next to me. The principal spoke and as he did, Haruyo whispered the summarized translation in my ear. We were all there to hear the girls apologize to Natsumi for their bullying. Fuuka was absent so her father was there to apologize for her.

The principal lectured in a calm manner, but I could note where he was stressing the seriousness of the issue, and no doubt shaming them for their actions. Haruyo said that he was telling them how embarrassed he was that the English teacher had to see them misbehave and how badly they represented their school.

Miu apologized and bowed deeply to Natsumi and then to me. Jyumi refused to bow and her grandfather exclaimed, put his hand to the back of her head, and pushed it down firmly to force her to do so. Then, Natsumi and her mother bowed and thanked them for their apology. It was all very formal and very quick. Once finished, the principal told them that that was to be the end of their bullying.

I wondered how successful that strategy would have been in America. Most Americans I noticed didn't care about being told what to do and even fewer might care about being shamed. I found it intriguing that the parents and the guardians were made such an integral part of the apology, as if they were culpable as well. I had heard the phrase before, "Meet the parents, meet the problem," a phrase I found to be true in most cases but at the same time, older children were also influenced by peers. At least here, the parents seemed to take the issue seriously, and took ownership of what their child was doing.

Chapter 15

A chittering hum that came from the trees, I noticed on the way home from work at the end of the week. It sounded like insects. On my way to the station, I stopped briefly to examine one of the trees and saw a brown, oval-shaped bug clinging to it. Curious as to what it was, I decided I would have to ask Ami. I texted her and she replied that they were cicadas.

The heat and humidity made it impossible for me to keep from sweating. Since the issues with the nuclear reactor, little electricity was being used, so the trains and stores were without air conditioning. As a result, myself and other commuters used paper fans to try to cool down. The fan I had was a simple black and blue, that I bought on a whim from a Seven Eleven when I couldn't take the heat anymore.

I flapped it incessantly, trying to cool my body down and getting brief relief. When the train doors opened at a stop, a rush of cool air would relieve the humidity for a few minutes until the doors shut again. The inside was muggy and smelled of body sweat. It was then that I decided I would start wearing face masks on the train to have some filter from the intense smells that came from being so close to other sweating, hot bodies. There were a few people around me who would periodically remove a decorative hand towel and wipe the sweat from their foreheads.

My hair stuck to my neck and I fluffed it to keep it off my skin. In a strange realization, I found that I missed the prairie winds that would cool down the air in the summer. In the winter, those same winds were harsh and unforgiving, causing skin to burn or my eyes to dry, but in the summer those winds cooled the air and my sun-soaked skin. I had a vision of spending Fourth of July weekend camping on Lake Metigoshe, when the summer temperatures could rise over ninety degrees Fahrenheit and feeling the breeze against my cheeks as I swam in the lake surrounded by rushes and trees.

I had barely started the day and I was already sweating and tired. I had a few minutes to stop at the *conbini* for a cool drink. There, I bought a pack of pink face masks, two cold bottles of water, a can of coffee, and what I guessed was perfume.

I sprayed the perfume under my shirt so that I wouldn't smell all day. I drank one bottle of water immediately and with the other, I held it on the back of my neck to cool me down. As I walked, I noticed how other commuters dealt with the sun. There were some women who carried umbrellas and covered their arms with thin sleeves. Others had a towel rolled around their necks.

When I put on the pink face mask, I was pleasantly surprised that it was scented with a light floral aroma. It made the ride home infinitely better. Still, I was sweaty so by the time I got home I took a shower.

That night had been hot as well and I'd slept in my underwear without any covers. I felt something tickling my thigh and looked down. I screamed and jumped up. Sitting on my thigh, as if wishing me a good morning, was a cockroach.

I jumped up, grabbed one of my shoes from the *genkan* and looked round to find it and squash it. After scouring my apartment and becoming sweaty in the process, I couldn't find the creature.

It made going back to sleep almost impossible, knowing that the cockroach was still there somewhere.

The summer heat became insufferable. I didn't want to go out but Ami was coming over so that we could go to what she called the *Tanabata Matsuri* in Asagaya. I had to look up what that was.

The festival was to celebrate that a god and goddess were meeting after being separated all year. The story went that Orihime, the weaver, and Hikoboshi, the herder, fell in love. But after being so in love that they ignored their work, Orihime's father became angry and made them separate. Orihime begged her father to let them be together so once a year the two lovers were allowed to meet. It was one of those stories that explained the movements of the stars Vega and Altair. It sounded like it would make for a romantic night, if it weren't for my complexion.

With the humidity and the heat, my face was breaking out in acne spots. I washed my face every morning and night, but it did nothing to heal the spots. I sweated too much in the heat. My skin couldn't stand it. I thought I'd try some foundation to cover it. It worked fine when I was indoors but tended to weep once I spent a few minutes outside. I didn't want Ami to see my face so splotchy, but I couldn't do anything to remedy it either.

When she arrived, she had a sanitary mask over her face.

"Oh, the heat's gotten to you, too," she said. When

she pulled off the mask, I saw that she had a few pimples on her nose and chin. She sighed. "*Shouganai*. It happens to me every year."

I sighed in relief and then laughed. "My co-worker said it was called '*mushi-atsui*'." I said, recalling a day when Haruyo complained about the weather. "But I thought '*mushi*' was 'bug', like an insect."

"Oh, *hai*. Different *kanji*."

She took out her smart phone and went to a drawing screen. "This is bug." She showed me the *kanji* 虫. "This is steamy." She showed me another *kanji* 蒸し.

"I don't think I'm ever going to figure out *kanji*."

She nodded. "It takes a long time. There are still some that I don't know."

She came in and took off her shoes. She wore a pair of socks that had little toadstool mushrooms. She had a plastic *conbini* bag with her that she set on the kitchenette counter and two hangars with black garment covers. She took out a bottle of water, dripping with condensation and began to drink until a quarter of it was gone. She put it down on the counter and inhaled deeply, wiping the sweat from the back of her neck, and glanced at me.

I kissed her. Her skin smelled like warm leaves and musty silt.

I took the items out of the bag and set them on the counter. She unzipped the garment bags to uncover two matching cotton *kimonos* with patterns of pink hibiscus on a deep blue background.

"I thought these would be nice. They're *yukata*. The flowers were a little like your tattoo."

I stared at the pattern and then at Ami.

"*Nani*? Is it okay?"

169

"It's great. I just don't know how to put it on."

She smiled in relief. "I'll help you."

We both showered. After that, Ami put on some makeup and helped me do mine.

"I don't usually wear makeup," she said as she brushed the dusky pink eyeshadow over my lid. "I'm not allowed to at work because I am in a lab and it's too *mendokusai*."

"I've heard students say that word before."

She laughed.

"It means trouble, right?" I asked.

"In a way."

She finished my makeup and then moved on to styling my hair. With the heat and humidity, my hair had gone from being normally straight to wavy which made it difficult to get it to behave. She took a decorative comb with small blue fabric bobs from her makeup bag and swept up my hair on the left side.

"*Owari*," she said. "Now we can get dressed."

I removed the *yukata* from the bag and put it on. I took the sash and tried to tie the *kimono* closed. Ami came over after drying her hair and giggled.

"Are you going to a funeral?" she asked.

"What?"

She came closer to me and drew a line with her finger on my collar.

"We only fold it this way at funerals."

She untied the sash, opened the front of the *yukata* and folded the front the opposite way so that the cloth was tight against my body. She had me hold the front and then gathered some of the material around the waist and folded it up so that the hem was at my ankle. She wrapped the sash tightly and then tied it at my back.

"My turn," she said.

She put the *yukata* on and I helped to wrap the sash around her waist and did my best to make a decent bow knot. I was going to grab my backpack to bring but Ami stopped me and showed me a red fish-shaped bag.

"That's what this is for." So, I put my wallet, keys, and train pass in the bag.

We left and walked to the train station. I did my best not to trip as I got used to walking in the sandals. It was still hot even in the evening sun. We exited the station and into the main street where I was bombarded with color and sound. Streamers hung from the tops of bent bamboo and the ends reached the street surface. Food stalls lined the sidewalk and in between those were crowds of people either in street clothes or in colorful *yukata*.

"I didn't think there'd be so many people," I said.

"*Hontou*? It's a summer festival! You have children who can play the games and eat sweets, the couples who come out to drink, then you have the girls who are looking for hook-ups."

I wondered about that last part.

"Did you ever hook-up with anyone here?"

She stifled a smile and looked down. "Once or twice," she admitted. She scratched the nape of her neck with her forefinger and looked over at me. "The last time was a mess. Turns out the lady I, uh, spent time with, was married."

I shot a look at her.

She put her hands up and shook them as if waving my suspicions away. "I didn't know she was married," she said quickly. "*Demo*, *saa*, it was over after a month."

"What happened?"

She inhaled and rummaged through her purse for her cigarettes. She took one out and lit it. I backed away a few inches from the smoke. She was careful to turn her head and exhale towards the street.

"She told me the truth. She was married and she figured out that she was a lesbian and wanted to separate from her husband. She told all this to me before she told him." Ami shook her head. "I can't be in a relationship that starts with a lie, especially a big lie like that." Ami looked down again. "If she lied and cheated on her husband, she could do it to me, too."

Ami made a good point. It was never good to start a relationship with dishonesty. It tainted the love that could come later. Some relationships were complicated, though.

"Maybe the husband and wife had some arrangement," I said.

"Maybe. That's too much drama for me," she said. She finished her cigarette and placed the end in her ash canister.

"What about you?" Ami asked. "Any hook-ups?"

I scoffed. "I'm no good at those," I said. "I don't like that kind of thing anyway."

"Any girlfriends?" she asked, then giggled. "Or boyfriends?"

"A boyfriend or two in school and then a girlfriend in college." I shrugged.

I didn't like to think about her. Jessalyn. I cared about her and every time I thought about her, I felt happy and then sad. She and I had been together for over a year. She was my first real love that I felt for another woman. I could hear our arguments, our shared crying, and our goodbye.

"It just didn't work out," I said.

Ami took my hand in hers.

"Relationships are hard," Ami said. "No matter what we do."

As we walked, I noticed some people speaking English. It was nice to hear so much English being spoken. I hadn't realized how much I missed it. I had become so accustomed to Japanese and to the intimate or purposeful English that I spoke at work that hearing the nonsensical, the informal, the slang, and the colloquialisms jarred me into a state of excitement.

I also smelled fast food. Not any fast food. The greasy hamburgers, fried food, and the spice and warm tortillas of Mexican food. How I missed some good Mexican food. Actually, it didn't even have to be good. Once I smelled it, I followed the scent to a Taco stall. There was a line, just like with every food stall, so I waited. There were too many people to count.

I had some trouble walking in the sandals so I would have to stop and readjust my toes. During one of these readjustments, I stopped in front of a kind of carnival game stall and all along the outside were inflated plastic hammers, cute characters, and some balloons. Behind the counter were all sorts of toys and prizes. On the counter were three boxes each with a hole cut in the top.

A few kids were in front, some with their parents, and I watched as one gave a coin to the stall worker and then put their hand into one of the boxes to pull out a slip of paper. The kid shouted and jumped. The worker looked at the paper and reached behind the counter to hand the boy a boxed remote controlled motorcycle. He held it over his head triumphantly.

Ami told me she would go get "*kakigori*" and I

glanced to see her stand at a stall that was selling shaved ice. I decided to try the game and gave my five hundred *yen* coin to the worker.

I chose a box and pulled out a slip of paper that had *kanji* on it. I showed it to the worker who turned to the back counter and handed me a body pillow with the image of a scantily clad anime girl on the front. I didn't know what to say other than thank the lady and walk over to meet Ami as she waited in line. When Ami saw me with the pillow, her eyes shot open wide and she laughed.

"*Nani sore*?" she said.

"*Kawaii, deshyou*?" I said in a high pitched voice, doing my best to mimic an anime character.

I looked at the anime girl's face which was pulled into an expression that was between sleepy and aroused. "I don't know what to do with this."

"Put a cover over it and you have a nice new pillow," she said.

Chapter 16

I was thankful for the summer break when it finally came. Mostly, I was tired of commuting in such extreme humidity. Ami did not get such a long break, but we would meet on her days off.

On my first day of summer break, I received a message from Hannah, the Australian ALT I had met earlier in the year. She was going camping and asked if I would join. I hadn't seen her in some time and the mention of camping excited me.

When Memorial Day hit in Minot, my family would rent a large camper and go to Lake Metigoshe to enjoy the warm weather and relax by the pristine lake. Mom would go fishing and I spent the time swimming.

The thought of cool lake water soaking into my skin was too enticing to refuse. I messaged Ami to see if she could go. Since I didn't receive a reply right away, I accepted Hannah's offer. If Ami wanted to come, I'd just let Hannah know. They said would leave the next day and offered to pick me up, since she and her husband owned a car. I gave them my address.

If I was going to a lake, I'd need a swimsuit. I walked to the mall. I hadn't been to the department store area so I looked there. A section displaying summer clothing and swimsuits stood next to the women's section. The swim outfit that was on display was a long-sleeved swim top and a pair of shorts. It seemed overly modest to me.

When looking, the sizes seemed to me to be on the smaller side. I wasn't worried about the bottoms, but the tops. I wanted to make sure I had enough space to cover my chest. I took a few to try on, along with some one-piece swimsuits, all in the largest size.

I went into one of the dressing rooms and tried them on. For most, I had small coverage over my breasts. If I jumped or turned sharply, one of my breasts would slip out. I tried the one-piece but it stretched out so thin that I could barely fit it over my shoulders.

I thought about the swimming outfit on display and thought maybe a long shirt was a better alternative than potentially flashing someone. I exited, returned the swimsuits, and chose a long sleeve shirt with shorts. When I tried it on, it was tight on top, but at least it covered my chest. I checked out. As I walked out of the store, my phone buzzed. Ami replied:

—ああ！—

Tara—はい—

While it was disappointing that Ami couldn't come with me, I looked forward to seeing her when I came back. It would give me a chance to be on my own without her and share something new with her. I cared about Ami and loved to be with her, but I also tended to rely on her to help me understand Japanese. It would be good to be on my own for a little and do things for myself.

I stopped to get sunblock, which was a feat of having to first find the vocabulary for the word and then asking where it might be. The patient store worker led me to the beauty section and pointed to a few different packaged bottles. They were so small I thought they were for makeup. I thanked the store worker and picked one that

I was sure would be sunblock since it had "SPF" written on it.

The last thing I bought was a pair of cheap flip-flops at the one hundred *yen* store. I stopped at the *conbini* to pick up a quick dish for dinner and went back home. It was getting dark and the ravens were swooping the sky. The air was warm and the cicadas were singing.

****

In the morning, I woke up, dressed, and waited outside with all my things. After about fifteen minutes of waiting, a boxy white van pulled up to the curb.

When I saw Hannah, I waved. On her lap was an excited black French Bulldog who had its nose touching the window. Next to her, driving, was her husband, a tall man with glasses whose head seemed to nearly touch the car ceiling. Even from my view, the inside of the van was noticeably full of camping supplies that it looked like there was no space for me. She rolled down the window. Her dog poked its head out and she held onto its collar and leaned her head out, "The seat behind me is clear." She kept trying to roll up the window, though her dog was insisting on keeping its head out.

I was doubtful, but went to that side and opened the door. The dog snuffled at me as I took my seat. A space had been cleared so that nothing touched the seat while the seat next to me held boxes, sleeping bags, blankets, and pillows. As soon as I got in, I shut the door, and I put my bag at my feet and looked up to see the dog's face just in front of me, sniffing the air, and trying to wriggle out of Hannah's arms to jump in the back with me.

Her husband started driving, causing whatever was in the far back to shift.

"This is Clovis," she said. "Do you mind dogs?"

177

I wondered if it would have mattered if I didn't. "No. My parents have one back home."

"Oh, good."

I held out my hand so Clovis could sniff it. He licked my finger with the tip of his tongue and sneezed. I wiped my hand with the towel from my pocket. Satisfied, he settled onto Hannah's lap.

"It's about an hour or two until we get to the lake, but we'll stop at the *conbini*. Did you eat?"

"A little."

"I'm going to need another coffee," Hannah said. She lifted a plastic cup that had a mountain logo on it. "Have you tried these yet?"

"No."

"This one's a hazelnut latte. They always make such good flavors. Anyhow," she gestured an open palm to her husband. "This is Tom."

"Hi," I said.

"Nice to meet you. So, my name is Tomu," he began to explain, "the *kanji* is for '*kanau*' for 'come true' and '*yumei*' for dream. But, everyone calls me Tom. It's cooler."

"I'd never had someone describe the name 'Tom' as cool before."

"Isn't it?"

"I guess I never thought about it."

"How have your students been?" Hannah asked.

"It's alright. The same as usual. Actually, it's nice to be away from the school for awhile. So, what lake are we going to?"

"Saiko Lake,"

I chuckled. "It sounds like 'psycho'."

"I never thought about that. I'll be careful if I take a

shower there."

"Do you go here every year?"

"Not every year," Hannah said.

"I would like to," Tom said, "but my work is so busy."

Hannah pointed a thumb at him. "Don't get me started. He works at K2, the snowboarding company. Always busy. But, we get free passes to Naeba ski resort every year. Oh, you should come, too!" Hannah tapped Tom on the shoulder. "Don't let me forget."

The thought of seeing snow was at the bottom of my priorities. "I'd be happy never seeing snow again," I said.

"But you're from North Dakota!"

"That's why! I see freezing wind and snow for half the year and every time I've tried skiing, I fall on my ass."

"Try snowboarding," Tom suggested.

"Somehow I don't think that's a better option. Plus, my idea of a good time isn't hanging out in the cold weather."

"Yes, so you and I can relax at the spa."

"Really?" I asked.

"Of course! It's not like I have many friends here to ask."

I didn't know how true that was. Hannah was friendly and fun. But, it could be that her personality didn't fit in with where she was. I wasn't always the best at making friends. The combination of work and life made it difficult to carve out time for anything else.

"I'll make sure to remind you," I said.

"Deal."

I had always enjoyed a road trip. It meant going somewhere, leaving all the stress of the usual life behind, and having fun. Sitting for too long wasn't great, but the anticipation of something new, talking with other people, seeing and being someplace that wasn't ordinary, was worth it.

I had been on a few road trips in my life, most of them were to Minnesota, the closest big city to us outside of Canada, but a few were school trips to other North Dakotan towns. I liked to stare out the window watching the scenery pass. In the Midwest, the scenery would change so little that it was like one long unending road with the same prairie fields and farmlands.

Occasionally, along the Japanese road there was a bicyclist. One we passed an elderly woman who had her back hunched over and her legs pushing the pedals with determination. No small feat, as the basket behind her seat was filled with two boxes of peaches that were tied to the wire basket by some blue plastic string. As she rode, the boxes tipped back and forth, as if they were going to topple over and spill across the road.

"Aren't there any good bars there?" Hannah asked.

"There are bars. I don't know if they're good or not. The first time I went to a bar when I was twenty-one, my friends took me to this place called 'Sports on Tap' and so we got there, got drinks, and talked. I think mine was some draft beer that tasted like watery dirt and was awful. So, we were there and this older guy at the bar kept raving on and on about," I paused. What the old man had really said was of a prejudiced and racist nature and not something I wanted to repeat out loud. "Well, he was saying these crazy things while he kept drinking. He had about five or six empty bottles in front of him and kept waving around the one he was holding in his hand, spilling it all over the place. He kept on talking and then he stood up, well, as best as he could stand up, wobbling around, then pulled down his pants and shit on the floor."

Tom laughed. Hannah pulled her face into a frown.

"Then he pulled his pants back up, stepped through the mess, and left like nothing happened, tracking the shit on the floor." I sighed. "So, that was my first time at a bar. Since then, I try to avoid places like that, which is not so easy to do when there are just a few bars in a small town."

"What happened to the old man? Did you see him again?" Tom asked.

"He was elected to be a city council member."

Tom laughed again.

"Isn't that something?" Hannah said.

"That's one way to put it."

I was tired of talking about my hometown. It brought up all kinds of memories that made me feel homesick. Why should I feel homesick? That felt silly. I was the one who'd decided to leave the States and I had decided to stay here. What was I feeling homesick *for*? I closed my eyes and put my head back. I couldn't decide why it was I felt that way. Maybe I missed the food, or the familiarity. I wasn't sure.

That moment of emptiness was struck out of me with four swift paws to my stomach. I snapped my eyelids open to see the snub-nosed dog sitting on my lap, smiling happily with its pink tongue sticking out.

"Clovis!" Hannah shouted.

I petted him on the head.

"I'm so sorry," she said, trying to reach back with her seatbelt on to grab him.

"It's okay."

"Are you sure?"

I thought it was a better idea to leave him on my lap than to have her try to finagle her way to picking him up while the car was still moving.

"Yeah, it's not a problem," I said, even though his pink tongue was producing saliva that looked like it might soon drip on my clothes. In general, I didn't care much about dog drool but since I packed just a few clothes with me, I wanted to keep what I had on as clean as I could manage.

Well, I considered, *I could always rinse it out*.

Tom pulled the car into a *conbini* parking lot. Before I could try to get out, Hannah said, "Do you mind staying with Clovis? He gets so spun up if he's left alone."

"Uh," I started. I would have liked the chance to stretch out my legs, which were going somewhat numb from the dog sitting on me.

"I'll get you whatever you want, don't worry about paying."

"Oh, so, a coffee and some snacks would be good."

"Great. We'll be right back."

She and Tom got out of the car.

As soon as they did, Clovis jumped up to the front and propped his front paws on the dashboard. He whined a little at watching them go, but when I shushed him gently, he looked back at me, and then sat on the passenger seat, waiting patiently. I wiped my pants where the few spots of drool had dripped.

Having nothing much to occupy my time, I fiddled with my fingernails, trying to smooth out the ends with my right forefinger nail. Then, I pushed on the cuticles to even them out.

Clovis barked and I looked up to see the couple returning, both of them carrying two full plastic bags.

Hannah went towards the driver's side and Tom to the passenger's.

When Hannah opened the door, Clovis hopped on the driver's seat. She handed me one of the bag, saying, "Here, I wasn't sure what exactly to get, so I just got a bunch." And then picked up Clovis with the other one. She sat in the driver's seat, placing her bag on Tom's lap, and closing the door.

I looked in the bag. There were three different kinds of coffee, small bags of chocolate, crackers, a packaged anpan, a fruit bar, and a thin container of mints. I took out money to give her, but when she saw it she put her hand up. "No. I won't take it."

Hannah put her seatbelt on, asked for the keys, and turned the engine over. Tom was rummaging through the bags and then I heard the sound of a bottle being opened. Hannah then flipped the visor down where there was a CD holder. She removed one and put it in the player. The song "Let's Get Loud" by Jennifer Lopez played at a low volume. Hannah turned the dial up, flipped the visor up, and pulled out of the *conbini*.

She started singing during certain portions. I drank one of the coffees and ate some of the crackers that she got. We passed about half an hour that way, with all of us content with listening to the music and keeping to ourselves, until Tom broke the silence, to my surprise.

"It's nice getting away," he said. "Have you traveled often?" he turned and asked me.

I was eating, so I swallowed, and passed my tongue over my teeth to clean any particles out before I opened my mouth.

"The most I traveled was to Las Vegas. I went once with a few of my friends. We all wanted to gamble and have one of those memorable Las Vegas holidays. Instead, I got food poisoning and stayed in the hotel half the time watching movies while my friends had fun."

"Oh, Vegas. I went before."

"Oh, yeah," Hannah said without mirth. "That time you lost five hundred dollars and ended up with a prostitute."

Tom laughed. "That's not exactly the way it happened," he said.

Now I was curious. "Well, what happened?"

"He went to Vegas after college," Hannah started.

"*Chotto*, I can tell it," he protested.

Hannah shrugged and focused on driving with Clovis laying down and napping on her lap.

"Like she said, I graduated university. So, my parents gave me graduation money and I went to Las Vegas with my friend."

"That's generous," I said. "All I got after graduation was dinner at Olive Garden."

"Oh, I like their breadsticks," Hannah commented.

"So, we get out at the airport and they had those gambling machines. We were there for two hours," he held up two fingers. "And I won at first one hundred fifty dollars. I thought I had such good luck so after we went to the Rio hotel to check in we went to the casino downstairs.

"You know, they make it so there are no clocks or windows so I never knew what time it was. I had good luck so I tried more and more to win. My friend was doing the card tables. I was bad at cards and didn't speak such good English at that time so I didn't go, but he won about fifty dollars. I would lose and win, and a waitress came by often to give me free drinks.

"I thought, 'Wow, such great service.' And kept playing. I did win a little, but I started getting drunk from all the alcohol the waitress was giving me. I went to find my friend to try to go back to the room, and he insisted I play some cards, too, Blackjack. So, I did." He paused to drink from his water bottle. "At first, I won once or twice. I thought I must be good after all, so I kept playing. Ah, unfortunately I was too bold and kept bidding too much.

"I thought that I could show the Americans how good I was. I was stupid. When it came time to show the cards, I lost. Five hundred dollars gone in a few minutes. It was crazy. That was most of the money I needed to buy food and anything else I wanted to get.

"Anyway, so I kept arguing with the dealer until my friend pulled me away. He said we should go for a walk and he would buy dinner. We went outside, walked around, and had some good steak and beer. I think when we left, we were both drunk. Since our hotel was nearby and the sign was so bright, it was easy to walk back.

"Then, there was a woman who was talking to us. I don't know how, but she came with us to our room. We were trying to talk to her and then some staff people from the hotel opened our room door. We tried to tell them that we didn't want her there, but, like I said to you, we didn't speak very good English. I tried to use my Dictionary but they didn't understand anything I was saying. So, the staff took our luggage downstairs and two big security men led us out of the hotel. I still don't know if they put us out because we were noisy or if it was bad to have a prostitute in a room."

I sat quietly, absorbing the story he had just told me. "So, then where did you go after that?"

"Ah, this is the embarrassing part. I didn't have much money and my friend had some but not enough for a hotel room. So, we took a bus to the airport and stayed there for two days before our flight back to Japan."

"Uff da," I said.

"That was my first time in America. So crazy. I couldn't explain it well to my parents when I came back. They asked me why I didn't take pictures. I told them we were too busy. My father still complains that I didn't bring back any souvenirs."

I smiled.

"Here we are!" Hannah said.

She pulled into a dirt driveway and parked in a full area. As there were no open spots, she pulled into a space on the grass next to another car which had done the same. Tom got out of the car and walked to a wooden house which had a giant fish tank that could be seen from the dusty window. Hannah took the keys out and put them in her pocket. She opened the door, startling Clovis, who jumped to the ground. I worried that he would run away, but he stayed near Hannah, even as she walked to the trunk and opened it to remove all the items.

I got out as well, thankful to be able to stand up and stretch. I had to use the bathroom and asked Hannah where they were.

She said, "There," and pointed to a long white building next to the car with entrances on the far ends. I noticed a man coming out the right entrance, so the woman's bathroom must have been on the left. I sprinted to it. I half-expected a porta-potty or a camper's type of bathroom smell, but it was thankfully freshened with air fresheners that hung on each stall door. I opened one of the doors but instead of a standing toilet, there was something else.

There was a porcelain oval with foot ridges on either side affixed to the ground. I had some experience with squatting to pee. On long car rides where there were no rest stops, it had been necessary to stop on the side of the road and squat in the ditch. I approached the toilet in the same way. The difficulty was in making sure I didn't get anything on my clothing and I wasn't sure how successful I had been.

The area we would stay in was a short walk from the lakeshore. We pulled up in front of a small wooden house.

"It's a bungalow," Hannah said. "One year we came here and it poured down rain, flooding our tent. After that, we always rent the bungalows. It also keeps the bugs out."

I put my bag down inside and then walked around the campsite that overlooked the lake. What surprised me most was how green everything was. Everywhere there were trees, bushes, flowers, plants, and other greenery whose names I couldn't guess at. Even in a Midwestern summer, I'd never seen so much green. And in that green were little insects and butterflies. The smell was all fresh like moist leaves after a light rain. I stood there touching the leaves of one of the spear-leaved trees, feeling the soft fibers.

When I was a kid, I used to find the tallest tree and see how high I could jump from one of the branches. This tree was what I would have called a, "good climber": a tall, strong, tree with lots of thick winding branches.

I had the impulsive childish notion to climb the tree. I took one brand in hand and lifted my legs, hoisting myself up to a lower branch and then up farther until I guess I was about three feet from the ground. I sat on a branch at a spot near the trunk and looked out over the lake surface.

The one thing missing from the beauty of the lake and the greenery was Ami. If she were sitting next to me on the branch, I wondered what she would say. Actually. She might not say anything. That didn't matter. It was the being with her that was important. Sitting next to each other quietly, in each other's company, without having to say anything but still knowing how the other felt was the most important. I could do that with Ami. We could be together and not say a word to each other. Nothing was expected of me except to be myself and I felt the same about her. That seemed like love to me.

I took out my phone and sent her a message:

—*I miss you*—

I hesitated to send it. It was something a lovesick teenager would say. Still, I pressed "send".

A few seconds later, the tiny light on my phone flashed to indicate a message.

Ami—あたしも(*^^*)♡—

It said, "Me too". I smiled.

I felt a pointy object poke me on the bottom of my foot. When I looked down to see what it was, I saw two young boys, both holding a long, thick stick, and using its jagged tip to poke me.

They shouted and laughed so I kicked the stick with my heel and unintentionally made that into a game for them. Now, they were following my foot as I moved it, more determined than before to hit their target. I stood up on the branch and moved to another side, only for them to follow me. Their laughter summoned other children who picked up sticks of all lengths. The kids with the shorter sticks climbed up the lower branches and tapped my ankles.

In a swift action, I grasped one of the longer sticks and was able to wriggle it from the two young boys, who shouted "*Abu-nai*!" as they looked up at me. I laughed triumphantly.

I had another message from Ami asking which lake and campsite we were staying at. I answered the text and then snuck away from the playful children. I changed my clothes and waded into the lake, watching the small fish dart around the rocks. I walked farther and submerged into the water. The brisk water caused my skin to prickle. I swam in the shallow water, watching the fish dart between the rocks.

I regretted not buying a fishing rod. All I would have to do would be to cast a line out a ways and I was sure I'd catch a fish in no time. When I would go fishing with my mom at one of the many lakes around North Dakota, it was never assured if we caught anything.

I was never much for fishing. Being so far from my family made me miss it. I never thought I'd want to see a fishing rod again or smell the pungent stink bait or the wet dirt smell when mom opened the container of live worms.

I thought about her standing next to me, casting a line out, staring out at the line, waiting, willing, for it to move, for the bobber to dip below the surface. We would spend hours standing or sitting by the shore, sometimes moving to a different spot, hoping that a fish would bite or that my mom would eventually give up and we could leave. I looked up to see a boat some distance away and a person sitting in it, holding a fishing rod, sitting, waiting. Maybe fishing was always like that no matter where someone went.

I spent the rest of the afternoon swimming on my own and then joining Hannah and her husband for a campfire dinner. An American camping dinner would largely consist of canned stew or baked potatoes. This one, however, had some brown noodles with bits of cabbage and carrots that Hannah told me was "*yakisoba*" cooked on a flat pan over the fire, fried fish, and rice. We finished off with some small cups of *sake,* which Tom was eager to share. We sat quietly by the fire with Clovis sitting on Hannah's lap, occasionally barking when a person happened to walk past. It was Hannah who broke the silence.

"Let's go to the *onsen,*" she said. Hannah reached over to tap me on my shoulder. "Have you been yet?"

I shook my head.

"Then we have to." She stood up and handed Clovis to Tom who was drifting off to sleep sitting in his chair.

"Should you drive?" I asked, thinking about the alcohol we drank.

Hannah shrugged her shoulder. "I didn't have that much."

I wasn't convinced that she was sober enough to drive, but before I could refuse, I was in the passenger seat. We drove to the *onsen* on a dark and winding road with barely any light except for a few dim streetlamps that looked like they were at least thirty years old. I held on tightly to the seat cushion as we drove, convinced that Hannah would miss a curve in the road and we would drift into the lake.

"So, what's an *onsen* exactly?" I asked.

"Like a spa," she answered. "You have to be naked. But don't worry, no one will care."

I doubted that and asked, "I *have* to be naked?"

She nodded. "Those are the rules but they give you a towel so you can cover up."

"I guess that's slightly reassuring."

Hannah laughed. She turned the car into a parking lot next to a dimly lit white building with a large blue fabric flag hanging in front with a white symbol in the center that looked like a flat circle with three vertical wavy lines in the center.

It may have been the influence of the *sake* or the steam from the baths, but the process of entering the building, getting a ticket for the *onsen*, undressing in front of strangers, and placing the narrow towel strategically over my chest and front, went by in blurred confusion. Hannah on the other hand, folded the towel neatly on the top of her head and walked confidently into the bathing area. I followed her while keeping my gaze towards the marble floor.

One tiled area had a line of faucets before foggy mirrors. In each area there was a plastic seat and a short shelf which had shampoo, conditioner, and soap dispensers. Most of the seats were occupied so I waited until an older woman was finished before taking my turn. I sat next to a mother washing her young daughter's hair. All the while, the daughter wailed, shouting "*Mama, yada!*", to which the mother was unresponsive and dutiful in her task of cleaning her daughter. I washed myself quickly and went to find where Hannah had gone. Beyond the washing area was a set of glass doors leading outside.

In the night the water looked black. If I stepped in, I wondered if I would fall through the center. When I took a step, the water was hot, just enough to be comfortable and not to burn. I folded the small towel and placed it atop my head as I had seen Hannah and the other women do. I submerged comfortably in the water.

The waterfall nearby trickled and the low cicada hums reverberated across the water. I looked up into the starry sky. It reminded me of my old home where, if I stayed up late into the early morning, I could look up and see Mars or Venus amongst the stars.

Was Ami looking up at those same stars? I missed her, but I also enjoyed spending time alone.

A blue and red flash caught my attention and I turned to see fireworks some distance away. I folded my arms on top of the warm rock barrier and watched the colorful sky. I wanted to remember how it looked, how I felt in that one moment, have it seared into my memory, that I was happy.

Chapter 17

I woke in the morning to the noises of calling birds and clonking boats. Hannah and Tom were already up. Clovis sat at the open door to the bungalow, his eyes closed and his mouth open as he basked in the sun.

Tom was lighting the cooking stove and had some fish, a carton of eggs, and a loaf of bread set out which he intended to cook. Hannah stood next to him, opening the package of bread as she held a small glass jar in her hand.

When she saw me, she said, "Come here," and lifted her hand to show me the jar which was filled with a pale yellow substance. "Try my honey," she said. She took out a slice of bread and a knife and spread a thin serving of the honey onto it. "I know it's not much, but it's the first year that I actually got a decent amount." She gave herself a serving.

I ate it eagerly, both because I was hungry and because I wanted to taste it. The spongy, soft bread soaked up the smooth honey, letting it melt on my tongue. The taste of the honey had a light sweetness that could easily be missed if I wasn't searching for it; it reminded me of a long-ago memory of when I would pluck the white petals from a clover and suck on the moist end.

"*Oishii*," I complimented.

That seemed to please Hannah, who gave a nod and

a smile, as if she had succeeded in what she set out to do.

After breakfast, I helped clean up while Clovis rustled around my feet snapping up any food scraps that landed on the ground. Hannah and Tom chatted in half-English, half-Japanese about work and gossip while I listened and then retired to the bungalow.

Clovis barked sharply and I turned to see who he was complaining about.

It was Ami. She smiled, though her eyes were puffy, and her face seemed pale. I rushed up and hugged her.

"What are you doing here?" I asked. "I thought you had work."

"I did. I stayed late so I could have the day off. I wanted to surprise you."

I hugged her tighter.

"Mm. You smell good."

"How'd you get here?"

"Dad let me borrow the car. And," she lowered her voice, "I have a surprise for us."

She took her wallet out of her bag and showed me two tickets to Summer Sonic for the 14th. That was two days from now.

"Do you know it?"

I looked at the tickets more closely. "Some concert?"

Ami nodded with a wide grin on her face. "I can't believe I got them, but my co-worker was going to go and changed his mind, well, he and his girlfriend broke up, so he sold them to me for cheap."

"I haven't been to a concert in a long time," I said. I tried to remember the last time I saw a famous musician perform in concert. That would have been seeing Keith Urban play at the state fair.

"Good!" She put her wallet back. "*Sa*, so how's the vacation? It's been a long time since I've been camping."

I showed her to the bungalow where Hannah and Tom were now sitting, she with a crochet hook in one hand and a ball of yarn in another and he reading a baseball themed manga. Clovis barked and Hannah looked up, glancing from our clasped hands to my face. Clovis hopped down from her side and trotted over to sniff at our shoes and then trotted back again, satisfied.

Hannah smiled. "Is this your girl?" she asked me.

That wouldn't have been my choice phrasing, but it was close enough. "Yes, this is Ami," she said.

At the sound of conversation, Tom glanced over and then turned his sights back to his reading.

"So happy you could make it after all," Hannah said, but the way she said it made me wonder if that was the entire truth. "I don't know if there's enough room…" she started.

"*Daijyoubu*," Ami said hastily. "I'll sleep in my car."

Hannah looked relieved. "Oh, well, no worries, then."

I moved my sleeping bag and other things from the bungalow into the car. When I returned, Ami had pulled the seats down so that there was a flat surface. She had brought comforters and several smooshy animal pillows and had arranged it so that I probably didn't need my sleeping bag at all. She insisted that I use it anyway.

"Even in the summer it gets cold at night," she said. "I went to softball summer camp one year around here and I was stupid and only brought one blanket. I thought my toes would freeze."

"You didn't bring a sleeping bag this time, either."

I pointed out.

She sighed. "No. But I did bring more than one blanket."

Before getting ready to sleep, we both went to the bathroom to brush our teeth.

"So what did you do yesterday?" Ami asked as we walked to the bathrooms.

"Hung around the lake. Oh, and I went to an *onsen*."

"*Hontou*? *Dou desu ka*?"

"It was fine," I answered. Then I recalled the nakedness. "Well, it was a little different. It was weird being completely naked around so many people. The water was so nice, though, and there were fireworks."

"*Sugoi, ne*." Ami sighed. "I should have gone with you."

"Then you wouldn't have gotten the tickets," I said.

"This is true."

When we returned, Ami nestled under the blankets and played a game on her phone. I went in and snuggled under the covers next to her. The doors locked automatically, which startled me. Ami turned over on her back and I nestled on her shoulder to watch her play a type of puzzle game.

As much as I wanted to stay awake, my eyelids kept drooping closed until I fell asleep. I woke up during the night to rain pattering on the windows. The inside of the windows were thick with condensation. I reached my hand out of the covers, getting goosebumps from the cool air, and wiped some of it away so I could see clearly.

"*Ame fute masu ka?*" Ami mumbled.

"What?"

She cleared her throat and rolled over to me, her eyes still closed. "Is it rain?"

"Yes."

"Mm. Good. I love rain."

She put her arm around my waist. I settled back down and looked out at the rain until I fell asleep again. It must have been early when I woke up since few other campers were awake. Ami was still sleeping.

I slunk out of the blankets and climbed over the front seat to exit the car and use the bathroom. Since the doors locked automatically, I left the front door slightly open so I wouldn't be locked out. The ground was moist as I walked but the air smelled heavy with moisture and wet leaves. As I walked back from the bathrooms, I saw that at the shoreline there were a few men taking their boats out.

I would have liked to have gotten on one of those boats myself, but I was more interested in going back home with Ami to the concert. Once Ami was awake, we packed up and I said my apologies, thanks, and goodbyes to Hannah and Tom.

On the drive back, Ami and I planned out our trip to the concert and I practiced speaking Japanese with her. My understanding of the language was gradually improving, so that if I listened I could grasp the general meaning, but my speaking skills were lacking. I constantly tripped over my tongue when pronouncing some words and mixing up the prepositions or word order. Though Ami said my Japanese was fine for a beginner, I was determined to study harder.

****

Back at home, I went on my computer. I checked the Summer Sonic lineup and I became instantly excited. Looking at it read like the soundtrack of my teenage years. Panic! at the Disco, Avril Lavigne, Red Hot Chili

Peppers, The Strokes, James Blunt. The only other bands that were missing were Fallout Boy and System of a Down. I took out my portable MP3 player and scrolled to Panic! at the Disco to listen to their first album. I couldn't believe that I would listen to them in person.

I went through the rest of the afternoon at the coin laundry. Once I was done, I spent the night at Ami's apartment so that we could catch the train together to Makuhari where the concert would be. We shared her bed, which was much more comfortable than my futon. Her place was also quieter, with the night sounds coming from the electronic hum of her lights and the misting of her humidifier. I snuggled up next to her and fell asleep with my head on her chest.

Chapter 18

In the morning, we dressed, and I cooked scrambled eggs. Ami looked up the train schedule and after washing the dishes and a trip to the *conbini*, we went to the station. The weather was comfortably warm; the cicadas were already chirping.

The train ride was soothing. I thought about my parents, the flood, and the people in Japan who were still displaced because of the earthquake. I began to feel guilty that I was having fun when so many struggled.

"It's weird," I said.

"Hm. What do you mean?"

"Well, the earthquake and then my family dealing with the flood. It's weird that I'm having a good time when they aren't."

Ami stopped playing her game, tilted her head and looked at me. "I don't think you need to feel like that. *Shouganai.* You should enjoy yourself."

"You think so?"

"Why not? We can't stop such things from happening. Think of it like this: would your parents want you to feel bad or would they want you to enjoy your life?"

She made a good point.

I smiled. "Maybe it's my old Catholic upbringing that's still affecting me."

She reached out to hold my hand. "I think especially

because so many bad things happened this year, we should have fun."

"Maybe you're right."

So, I would not focus on anything other than the day and spending time with Ami.

The train pulled to a stop and we exited to walk along the pathway towards the venue. The venue itself was nothing less than astounding. The gargantuan concert area stood out in front of the blue Tokyo Bay. I didn't know where to begin with what to look at first. Whether to focus on the shimmering sea waves, the giant architecture, or the groups of concert-goers dressed in an array of styles from punk to formal. We lined up at the entrance along with all the others who were chatting excitedly. There was a ruckus at one point and shouting ahead of us. Two security guards rushed up and escorted a man away.

"Fake tickets," Ami explained.

We had our tickets scanned without issue and after they were accepted, the attendant wrapped a plastic bracelet around both our wrists and gave us each a program.

Then, we were in.

We stopped at the merchandise tents. As we waited in line, we both looked over the program with the line-ups. When it was our turn in line, I bought a concert t-shirt that listed all the bands on the back with, "Summer Sonic 2011," spread across the front. Ami bought a long sports towel that had the Summer Sonic logo and hung it around her neck.

We went from stage to stage over the next few hours, jumping and dancing to Japanese bands that I'd never heard of, as well as famous American bands like

The Red Hot Chili Peppers and Korn.

I made sure that we slipped our way closer to the front for the next band. We were jammed in a crowd of people who were all as hot and sweaty as we were. I generally was uncomfortable with crowds, but I had become accustomed to them in the time I had been living here. And since Ami was with me, I felt safer as I held her hand. Then the music started with the intro to "But It's Better If You Do". I screamed for the sixteen-year-old me who listened to the same song when I made out with my first serious girlfriend. I screamed for the happiness at my good luck that I could stand where I was with a woman I loved as we both pressed our bodies together and let the music move our bodies to the rhythm. Ami stopped between the set and prompted me to turn around so she could take a picture of us together with the band in the background. Then, we danced and jumped along, sweating and singing as the music played.

We eventually broke away, pushing past the crowds and the immovable people to get some food and water. Ami stepped away for a few minutes to smoke while I used the bathroom. My ears warbled and buzzed from the exposure to the loud music and crowds. When I looked in the mirror as I washed my hands, I splashed water on my flushed cheeks and my sweaty chest. I went out and waited nearby for Ami to finish smoking.

Another young woman with long hair who wore a flower headband came to stand near me and took out a makeup kit in front of the mirror to touch up her makeup. Another woman with her face painted with fluorescent colors to look like a cat joined her and gave her a hug and kissed her cheek.

The cat woman said, "*Atsui da ne*?" and tied a knot

in the front of her pink tank top so that her stomach showed. She took out a pack of Lark cigarettes and stuck one in her mouth. But what she put in her mouth looked very different than a cigarette. I smiled at the ingenuity. That was the kind of clever trick that I imagined one of my students would do, though they were more concerned with getting cigarettes or alcohol into school without being noticed, usually by hiding a single cigarette in a hollowed out sharpie marker or vodka in a water bottle.

The cat woman offered one to the makeup woman who took it and put it between her lips. She looked at me in between stroking her eyelid with purple glitter eyeshadow. She turned to her friend, said something, and then passed me one of their cigarettes.

I thought of taking it, out of politeness and curiosity. I'd had one experience with drugs when I was in middle school, as most girls did, and despite the many tv specials which always showed those things happening in school bathrooms or in hallways, mine was in the classroom in front of the teacher as he was on a computer behind his desk. It was in science class and we were supposed to be using thirty minutes to work on our packet assignment material. Instead, a classmate sitting near me who I knew had a crush on me passed me a pill labeled "Xanax". I took it, afraid that someone else might see it, and threw it in the trash in the hallway during passing period. I was too scared to try it. Drinking some alcohol was one thing, I could control how much and how long I wanted to drink, but with medication or cigarettes, I was never sure how potent or how much it would affect me.

I declined the mystery cigarette that the makeup woman gave me. She nodded once and returned it to her friend.

Ami came to find me, smelling of smoke. I told her about the offer from the two women.

"We are at a concert," she said. "Drugs happen. Did you take it?"

"No."

"That's probably a good idea. I think it's illegal. It might have been a little, uhm, interesting."

"Have you…" I started, but then decided that I didn't need to know. "Never mind."

The food was what I would call, "beer food", the kind that would fill the stomach without the risk of vomiting, or that would be the hope. We both had ramen served in Styrofoam bowls and bought overpriced water bottles. I hadn't planned on drinking, but Ami bought a cocktail that we ended up sharing.

Another show started near the food court. Listening to it, it seemed like a Japanese rock band. Conversation was impossible while they played, so we finished our food and then brought the water with us to find the next venue.

I felt a little buzz from the alcohol. I was also hot, so I took off my sweat moistened shirt and tucked it into my back pocket. That left me to walk around in my black lace bra. If I could've taken that off without getting into trouble, I would have. Buzzed or not, I knew that going topless was probably ill-advised. We went to a smaller stage inside a different section where crowds were leaving and others were taking their places in the front.

"Let's sit down," Ami said loudly. "It's a while before the next one."

She found an empty spot a ways from the stage and in a corner next to one of the arching pillars where we could rest our heads. There were others doing the same as us, with one group at a far end all in different states of relaxation. I sat down and stretched my legs in front of me. My calves were a little sore. I leaned back and drank some water. Ami sat next to me.

I had Ami sit in front of me with my legs astride on either side. The music started. At first, I had my arms around her waist and rested my head on her shoulder. I kissed her earlobe and then her neck. Without thinking, I slipped my hand down the front of her pants. She turned her head.

"I'm sweaty," she said.

I shrugged. "So am I."

She smiled and I felt her laugh. She took the neck towel and put it over her lap then placed her hand over mine and pushed it down farther. As the music played, the sound drowned out her moans but I could feel her breathing against my chest that smelled of breath mint and alcohol. She relaxed her head against my shoulder and pressed her face against my neck so I could feel her hot breath on my skin.

Chapter 19

The fun from the festival and the buzzing in my ears remained fresh as I took a shower the next afternoon as soon as I woke up. I stayed at Ami's again as the trains were closed by the time we arrived in Tachikawa.

As I was drying off, my phone rang. It was Haruyo. Strange of her to call.

"Hello?" I asked.

"Ah, Tara-*sensei*, I apologize for calling you so late."

"It's alright."

"There had been an incident with Okabe Natsumi."

"Is she alright?"

"I am sorry, but she has died."

"What?" I asked. I heard her words but didn't understand them.

"There was an accident with a train," she said. "I am sorry. I will give you information about the *tsuya*...uhm. The *funeral*. Please take care."

"Yes, you too."

The call ended.

I sat on the damp tile floor. I couldn't think. I had seen Natsumi just before summer break. She drew me a picture of a frog. She had signed it on the bottom with her name in *kanji* and drew a small heart underneath and when I got home I taped it to my wall with the others.

I called Ami who rushed into the bathroom. I told

her what happened.

"Oh, Tara, I'm so sorry." she said sleepily.

I kept pacing the single bathroom, mulling over and over in my head that a student was dead. Ami hugged me and helped me to walk to her bedroom. She put one of her soft, minky blankets over my shoulders. My dripping wet hair made dark spots on the flower pattern. She walked away and then came back with two silver cans that had *kanji* I couldn't read, a picture of a sliced lemon, and 8% written on the bottom.

"It's *chu-hai."* *Ami* said and gave me one. "*Kampai*," she added and tapped her can against mine.

We drank. The taste of the alcohol was light compared to its sweet lemon flavor. I drank again and told her what Haruyo told me, repeating it without emotion since I was still in shock.

"It sounds like suicide," she said.

"What?" I asked. "No. Haruyo said it was an accident."

"That's the polite thing to say," she said. "I remember that when I was in Junior High, there were a few classmates who did it the same way. They'd fall in front of a moving train. The Chuo line was the most popular place."

"Why?"

She shrugged.

"There isn't one reason. Maybe they failed their entrance exam, maybe they were depressed, maybe they were bullied." I inhaled sharply when she mentioned bullying. I thought of that day when the three girls were cornering Natsumi in the school hallway. "Why does anyone decide to kill themselves?"

I scoffed. I didn't need Ami's direct analysis of the

situation. I needed...I didn't know what I needed. I shook my head. I could still see Natsumi's face, her smile, how she practiced her English with me.

"I just saw her," I said. I started crying.

Ami hugged me and we sat there together until I had cried every tear I could manage. Exhausted, I fell asleep on her lap and didn't wake up until the next morning. When I woke up it was to the smell of savory broth. I spotted Ami in the kitchen standing over the single gas grill. I didn't want to get up, but my full bladder convinced me otherwise.

I went to the toilet and decided that a shower might help. I felt sweaty. I took a shower, cleaned up, but I couldn't stop thinking about Natusmi. When I looked at my phone, the light was blinking to show a missed call. All of them were from Haruyo. There was also a text message that gave me the information for the funeral that would take place the next day.

****

I didn't want to go. I had an *obligation* to go. Ami had to work and I wanted to go back to my apartment to be alone, though Ami insisted that she come over after work. I spent the entire day in my apartment with the blinds drawn playing video games, and only taking breaks to snack and use the bathroom. By the time I was ready to fall asleep, I had finished *Chrono Trigger.* There were twelve or thirteen possible endings to get in the game and I got one of the good endings, meaning I would soon replay the game so I could get the best one. Ami was there sleeping next to me as I watched the credits and listened to the music.

My motions of the day were automatic: from waking up, getting dressed, to riding the train to the funeral location. Ami walked to the station with me before she went to work. I was glad that she was there but I could barely speak. If I did, I was sure that I would cry.

I stood on the train listening to music and staring out the window. I didn't want to look at anyone. I wanted to zone out and stop thinking about Natsumi. That proved impossible as soon as I arrived at the location. Haruyo waited outside a wooden shrine for me. She talked and I nodded as she did, but I failed to comprehend what she was saying. Settled at the front of the dais was a type of decorative house and set before it was a formal picture of Natsumi. Surrounding the picture and descending in the space before it were colorful flowers whose types I did not know.

Amongst the family members and friends, I saw Jyumi, Fuuka, and Miu and their parents and grandfather. Jyumi was sitting and crying silently. Fuuka kept her head down. When Miu's parents saw me, they said something to her. She walked up to me, keeping her head tilted downwards, and then stood in front of me.

She shook her head once and said, "*Hontou gomen nasai. Atashi wa machigai deshita.*" I knew most of what she was saying. I heard the apology. I didn't know how sincere she was.

I told myself that kids made mistakes all the time. Peer pressure was a real phenomenon. It was powerful to be part of a group, especially if that group was made up of friends or the admired. Had that happened with Miu? Did it matter? Someone had made the decision to tease and harass Natsumi and others followed when they didn't have to. It was hard for me to feel sympathy for those three, knowing that their bullying may have pushed Natsumi to her decision.

I didn't have anything to say to Miu. I couldn't tell her that it was okay because I didn't know if it was. All I could tell her was that I was sorry. And I was. I was sorry that the whole thing happened in the first place. That seemed to placate her. She bowed and returned to her family.

Haruyo touched my shoulder. I turned and she was standing with two adults, a man and a woman, and a younger woman, all dressed in formal black attire. The younger woman held a plastic animal container with plant matter on the bottom and a small rock cave. Inside was an orange and white snake. It must have been Natsumi's pet snake. What did she call it? I tried to remember our conversation but for some reason I couldn't.

"This is Okabe-*san's* family," Haryuo said gently.

The parents bowed a little but it was the young woman who spoke first, and quickly, in a shaky tone. When she was done talking, Haruyo said, "This is Okabe-*san's* sister. She said that Natsumi loved learning about English. It was her favorite class. Ehm," Haruyo paused. "She said that there was a note."

A suicide note? I suppose that was common for people to do, to give their reasons why. I wanted to know why. It probably wasn't polite of me.

"Did she say why she…" I started to ask Haruyo.

Haruyo shook her head.

"It will be rude to ask," she answered.

She was probably right. Still, I wish I knew more Japanese to ask for myself. At least Natsumi left a farewell letter. The snake moved in its container, distracting me. I stared at it.

"Rio-*chan*," I said suddenly, remembering.

"*Hai*," the sister said excitedly.

"*Kawaii*," I said. The parents smiled in a sad way, as if their solemn mouths flinched for a moment, forgetting that they were mourning. I didn't think the snake was particularly cute, but it had a charm and I wanted to give the family something nice to think about, something outside of their daughter's death. That was probably impossible, but I could try. It was a distraction for me. I'd rather think about a snake slithering around inside its plastic house than about a dead girl.

"Do you want to tell them something about Okabe-*san?*" Haruyo asked me.

I looked from Haruyo to the parents. What could I say? I had no idea. It was pointless. Her death was pointless. She didn't need to kill herself. I didn't see a reason for that. I had studied about juvenile depression as a student teacher. I knew the academics of it, the data, the ways to help a student dealing with depression. But reading about it and seeing the reality of it was different. What was worse was that none of us could do anything to have stopped it. I'd tried to help her, to stop the bullying, to be a friend, and that didn't keep her alive. What could I tell them? I kept seeing the picture that she drew for me.

"Natsumi was always kind," I started while Haruyo translated. "She was a good artist. She would always sit with me at lunch…" I trailed off, feeling my throat swell. I shook my head. "I'm sorry."

I looked down at the snake who had slithered under a tree branch.

"It's understandable," Haruyo said. "It is time to sit."

Haruyo bowed to the parents and said something. I

bowed as well and said nothing. We dispersed and went to our seats, which I assume were assigned since Haruyo led me to a specific section in the far back while Natsumi's parents went to the front.

The Buddhist monks entered and all was quiet. They called their prayers. They lit incense. I hoped Natsumi was happy where she was. I began to cry quietly. I wished she were alive.

****

After the funeral, I took three days off. I probably could have done what I'd done so many times before when I felt unable to teach; I'd toughen up and push through it. But I'd never had a student die.

The thought of going into the class and not seeing her there or her not sitting near me and sharing her pictures and drawings at lunch while she tried her best to practice English, hurt me. I didn't want to go anywhere or see anyone. I didn't even want to talk to my family. I downloaded more games to distract me. Then, I wouldn't have to think about everything that was wrong.

Ami would send me messages often to check on me and most of the time I would answer them. Somehow it was hard for me to type an answer. I knew what I would have wanted to type and could visualize it, but when it came to actually responding, I didn't.

I didn't want to talk to anyone, not even Ami. I needed to be alone. It was a fault of mine that I recognized. When I was stressed or upset, I would "shut down." It was one reason why I had very few friends or general hobbies while I was a teacher. I couldn't be distant from my students, parents, or co-workers, so once I was home for the day, I wanted to be alone. It wasn't the best coping strategy, but it was what I did.

After shutting myself inside for much too long, I had run out of food and needed to go shopping. It was such a normal thing to do, but for some reason I didn't want to go alone. I texted Ami to see if she would go with me later and she said she would.

When Ami came over, she hugged me. "I'm so sorry. Are you okay?"

I started by trying to say "Yes", but it came out as a broken weep.

"Let's get delivery," Ami said.

She made a quick phone call and sat with me, silently, as I laid down on her lap and held her hand. She only let go when there was a knock on the door. The smell of food grabbed my attention and I realized how hungry I was. She'd ordered pizza. Domino's pizza. I ate four slices.

"I forgot how much I missed American pizza," I said.

Having a full belly helped my mood. I took a deep breath and relaxed.

"I want to give you this," Ami said. She took out a tiny white bag with flower designs and handed it to me.

I took it and pulled open the strings. Inside was a small, freshly cut, silver key.

"It's for my place," she said.

I looked at it. We'd been together for…I had to think about it…six months almost. Was it that long already? I then felt guilty. I had been so upset and self-isolated that I had forgotten. And now, she gave me a key to her apartment. That was a big step. But it was one that I was excited about.

I smiled. "You're sure?"

"Of course, yes. I want you to come over whenever

you want. I told the front desk so they will know who you are." She scratched the back of her ear. "If you're sad, I know you like to be alone, but you can always come to my home."

"Home," I murmured.

This was my home now, with Ami. I hugged her and she kissed me on the cheek.

"Sorry I'm so moody," I said.

She held my hand. "Of course I understand. Your student died. It's okay to be upset. You don't have to be upset alone, though."

"Thank you."

She rested her head on my shoulder. "Sorry to talk about death some more, but next weekend I have to go to visit my mother's grave for *ohaka mairi*," she said. "It's *Obon*."

She said it like I knew what it was.

"Oh, yes, *Obon* is like a festival to remember people who died. We also clean the family's graves. You can come, if you want."

"A festival for the dead?" I asked. "Like *Dia de Los Muertos*?"

"*Tabun*."

"When will you go?"

"I think, on Sunday? We'll meet at my father's house and drive. Then, after, we go to the festival. So, maybe my brother will come, too, but I'm not sure."

I thought about it. I wanted to be with Ami but I was also tired of thinking about death. If I was sad anyway, I decided I might as well be with her and her family. I was tired after eating so much and being so emotional so I got ready for bed. Ami stayed the night with me and we snuggled in my small futon together, wrapped up in the blankets like we were inside a cocoon.

Chapter 20

The rest of the work week went better. On my way home each day I would pick up something from the Daiso or the *conbini* that I thought Ami would like and drop it off at her apartment.

On Friday evening, I picked up dinner so she would have something when she came home from work since she often didn't come home until after seven in the evening. Then, we went to bed. We got into a couples routine that was comforting and safe. I usually stayed at my apartment during the week and at the end of the week I'd stay with Ami or she would stay with me.

The weekend came to go to Ome for *Obon*. Ami smoked before we left and then put on a nicotine patch. Like last time, her father met us at the station. The car was still as messy as before but the outside of it had recently had a car wash. In the back seat of the car was a bouquet of wisteria blossoms that had been buckled in.

"I'm sorry," he said. "Ami told me about your student who passed away."

"Oh," I said. "Yes. It was a surprise."

"*Shouganai, ne?*" he said.

It can't be helped. Was that really true? She could have easily decided not to kill herself.

"So," he said. "We'll go up here," he pointed towards a hill, "Where Jenny's stone is."

"Was she Buddhist?" I asked.

He tilted his head.

"*Chotto*," he said and laughed. "She believed about a lot of things."

"Mom didn't follow one religion. I think she was more of a, uhm, what did she used to say? Something about faith being a buffet."

"Mmn," he said and nodded once. "She said she believed in 'Buffet-ism', like taking each good part from different religions."

"Huh."

"It was a little weird sometimes," Ami said with a smile, "Because some days I would come home from school and find out about a new holiday because Mom would decorate the house or make some new food. Do you know about Holi, from India?"

"It sounds familiar."

"I remember a day when we all went into the yard and started throwing colored paint dust at each other. The neighbors must have thought we were crazy."

"She seems like she was fun."

"She was," Ami said. "But also so strict."

Ami's father nodded his head. "She had to be. You and your brother could get into mischief so easily."

Ami smiled to herself.

"That's true. I felt bad about it when I got older. I think it was hard for her with all of us and she was also working."

"*Saa*, you were children," he said.

We parked at the cemetery on the hill. There were other families doing the same as we were. As we got out, I saw a cleaning station set up just outside the entrance with buckets, sponges, and a faucet with running water. Her father took the flowers from the backseat and Ami had me go with her to fill a bucket with water and take some sponges.

"This way," she said.

She led me through the gravesite and to a particular stone column. There, she prayed, and then started brushing some fallen leaves away. She took one of the sponges and said, "We can start cleaning."

I took a sponge and cleaned the bottom, scrubbing off dust and dirt.

"*Papa, doko da?*" Ami mumbled and then looked back at the car. "Ah, my brother is here," she said.

I turned to look at the car and saw a young man in a suit talking to her father. "Should we go over?" I asked.

"No," she said gruffly. "We're busy."

Even though she said that, I stood up to shake his hand when he came nearer as he held a bucket and sponge in one hand.

"Tara. It's nice to meet you," he said in perfect English. "I'm Junsei."

"*Osoi*," Ami chastised.

"*Dakara. Kuruma ga ippai*," he said to her. "I'll help."

He put the bucket and sponge down and rolled up his sleeves. Then, he started cleaning the gravestone as well. We all were silent as we worked. Her father helped also and when the cleaning was done her father gave us each a wisteria blossom to place in the vase affixed to the stone. They each prayed and I did too. Not to God but to thank her mother.

I wished I could have met you.

We all returned to her family house with Junsei following behind in his hybrid Toyota Prius. No one said much in the car. We didn't stay at the house long. Junsei got into the car with us, and we drove back to the train station. There, we got out and there was a short argument between Junsei and his father about who would pay for the parking. Eventually, Ami pushed through the two of them and paid for it herself, calling them both, "*Baka,*" in the process.

We all walked together towards the town center. It began to get cloudy.

"*Kasa ga wasaretta*," Junsei said.

"I hope it doesn't rain," I murmured. After a silence where no one spoke, I asked, "So, Junsei, was it a long drive?"

"Oh, a little long. It gave me time to study some English."

"Study? Your English sounds good to me."

"It's for a test. I want to pass the EIKEN level one test. I finished pre-one before college but now I want to finish the rest. It'll be good for my work."

"What work is that?"

"Salaryman," Ami said.

Junsei laughed. "That's right. It's an office job. It's boring. The salary is good and I get vacation and a pension. And my hours aren't as long as some other workers."

"That's good."

"Mm. I have a family so I want to spend time with them."

"Why didn't they come up?" Ami asked.

"Yes, you should have brought Sayu and Lilly," her father said.

"Ah, Lilly didn't feel well and Sayu has trouble with long car rides," he said. "She's still little."

"How old?"

"Three," he said. "This year was her *shichi-go-san*." He pulled his wallet from his inside blazer pocket and flipped it to show a picture of a bi-racial little girl in a brightly colored *kimono* smiling in front of a shrine. She was cute, like all kids were when they are that young.

"You should have come to her *shichi-go-san*," Junsei said to Ami.

"*Jikan ga nai*," she said. "My work is busy."

"So is mine!"

Ami scoffed. "You're not studying to cure diseases."

Ami seemed irritable and I wondered if it was the nicotine withdrawal. I held her hand to give her some support and I hoped it would help in easing her temper.

Junsei laughed. "No, I'm not." He turned to me. "Ah, it's because I'm boring. I don't like to do so much."

"You should come to my hometown," I said. "You'd love it there; nothing to do."

"One day, maybe," he said.

As we got closer to the center of the town, the smell of fried food drew me in.

"Oh, that smells good," I said.

"It's *okonomiyaki*, I think," her father said. "Like a pancake."

"*Ii ni-o-i*," Junsei said.

That was the first stand we stopped at. The cook took batter and mixed in bacon, vegetables, and other seasonings on a large frying pan. I couldn't eat it fast enough, and burned my mouth by being too eager.

"*Umai*," Junsei said as he ate.

We found an empty space off to the side to eat. I looked around a little more, at the red lanterns hanging above the stalls. Drums and bells came from down the street. Ladies in *yukata* and wearing curved straw hats started dancing through the street. The dance consisted of a few repeated movements, and, as they approached, some of the other people around the festival joined in behind.

"Let's try," I said, wanting to join them.

Ami was reluctant.

I stepped in and mimicked the dance along with them as I enjoyed the colors and the music and how we all moved together in unison, remembering those who died. I thought of Natsumi and hoped that she could see me, dancing for her, celebrating her peace and her life.

Chapter 21

September 2011

The season changed as quickly as it had begun. There were the hot and humid last days of August and then the first waves of fall came with cool air, a welcome break from the humidity.

I felt more comfortable in my apartment when I could open the window and get the fresh cool air in the morning as I got ready for work. Inevitably, by the afternoon it would be warm again and I would be sweaty.

On my regular walk to the train station one day, I caught a sweet scent in the air that came from a large tree with spear-shaped olive colored leaves and tiny blossoms the color of ripe persimmon. I plucked a tiny branch of one and kept it.

When I went to work, I asked Haruyo about it. It was a tree called *Kinmokusei.* On the way home from work, I gathered more of the branches to keep. I got home and realized that I didn't have a vase so I rinsed out an empty plastic tea bottle in my recycle bin and used that.

I settled back into a routine. At first it was difficult to go into class and see the empty seat where Natsumi used to sit. Gradually, I was able to ignore that empty chair. Miu began to become more interested in me. Somewhere between the funeral and summer break, she had broken her friendship with Jyumi. Rather than arguing or speaking to each other, they ignored one another. I thought that might be for the best. Some discretions couldn't be forgiven.

She sat across from me at lunch. She didn't often speak to me, but would write down text on her *keitai* and show me. In class, her spoken English was not the best and I guessed that she was shy about her ability to speak. Her written English, however, was very good.

On a warm day in September, the school's fans were running and the windows were open, but nothing could stop us from sweating. On a break between classes, I stood outside in the hallway. Miu came up to me to ask me how my weekend had gone. When I answered her, her eyes widened.

"*Sensei, Nihongo shabette yo,*" she admonished. *Teacher, you're speaking Japanese.*

I wanted to tell her that I wasn't, but as I thought, I realized that my answer to her had not been in English. I had thoughtlessly spoken to her in Japanese. I had done it without thinking, without having to consider the sentence or the word order. It tumbled out of my mouth as easily as if it had been my native language. Something had clicked in my mind. All the months I had been in Japan, listening, absorbing, studying, speaking, in that moment I suddenly understood. I smiled at my success.

"*Gomen,*" I said with a smile. "I will remember to speak English."

"*Onaji, sensei.*" She wrote, "Why do girls have to menstruation?"

"Uhm," I started, not really knowing how to answer. I'd had young girls ask for sanitary pads or tampons during breaks, but that was as far as my involvement went. No girl had ever asked me why they "had" to have a period. It was understood. There were options for not having a period, though I felt that explaining birth control might not be appropriate over a lunch table.

"It's just life," I said. I then typed the sentence into my dictionary, hoping my meaning would come across. I showed it to her and she nodded.

"Boys don't have like that?" she typed into her phone.

"No," I answered.

"*Sore ga fukuheida*," she mumbled.

I didn't recognize the word so I asked for the *hiragana* spelling and typed it into my *jisho*. *Fukuheida*: unfair.

Yes, I thought. It was unfair. It was all new to Miu, so the experience of dealing with all that came with puberty could be unsettling. I recalled being excited to finally get my period because then I was "grown." I was like the other, older girls who were part of something that connected them.

"*Shoganai*," I said.

"*Ne, sensei*."

****

At the end of the week, I had something planned for myself and Ami. I had been researching about places where we could go for a date and I found a place I thought she would like. On a cool Sunday morning, we met at Akishima and got on the Ome line. Ami looked tired; her puffy and half-opened eyes stared downward and she didn't say much as she sipped from a carton of coffee.

"Is everything okay?" I asked.

She nodded once and sighed. "Late night. Do you know about *nomikai*?"

The word was familiar and I vaguely remembered Ami explaining it to me once.

"Not really."

"It's like going out to drinks after work, but we are expected to do it. Normally, my work doesn't do it but we had a visit from one of the directors. So, we had to go to an izakaya after." She finished her coffee.

"Oh. We could have stayed home," I offered.

Ami shook her head and then smiled at me. "I wanted to see what you had planned."

We rode the train in silence. At one of the stops, passengers got off so we could both sit. Ami fell asleep, still holding her empty coffee carton. At our stop, I nudged her awake and we got off, with Ami ensuring that she put her carton in the trash. I had a picture of the map route on my phone so I started walking. Outside of the station was a normal looking Japanese neighborhood.

"I don't think I've been here before," Ami said. "Where are we going?"

"To a park," I answered.

I hoped I wouldn't get us lost. At several points, I was convinced I had since the sidewalks continue to curve around and there were blocks of houses with no sign of what I was looking for. I was beginning to lose confidence that I could manage guiding us there on my own but I didn't want to ask Ami for help.

Too often I relied on her or let her be the one to guide me in the right direction. I was determined to prove that I could be just as useful. I looked at the map again and realized my mistake. I had turned too soon on one of the streets. I apologized to Ami and then circled back, finding the correct street that led up a sloped dirt road and a little wooden sign with *kanji* that read "野山北・

六道山公園". I matched that *kanji* with what was on my map. I sighed in relief.

"Here we are," I said.

"Ah, then I can take a break." Ami leaned against the sign. She crossed her arms. "Sorry," she said. "I am trying to convince myself not to smoke."

"Really?"

She pulled her sleeve up to reveal a white square nicotine patch on her shoulder.

"*Ganbatte*," I said.

Ami smiled sardonically.

I knew what could get her mind off smoking. I pointed at the sign. "This place is also called Totoro park," I explained. "I read that this was where the creator got the idea for Totoro. There are rice patties here that are in the movie."

I watched to see her eyes widen.

"*Sugoi ne*, Tara." She stood up and embraced me in a tight hug. She released me and held my hand. "*Iko*?"

Up the dirt path, the scenery became clearer to me as I saw the lush hillsides crowded with all kinds of trees whose leaves were tinged with yellows and oranges alongside the evergreens. Past tall beige grass was a wooden gate that led inside a courtyard. A giant thatched-roof raised house stood in the center of the bleached dirt courtyard. The *shoji* doors were opened and some children were playing inside.

One of the kids ran onto the outside porch and jumped down to put on their blue shoes that lay disorganized on the smooth rocks under the porch and ran around the back of the house. The other kid emerged from the side of the house, shouting, and ran around a red water to look for the first child. Smoke came in a long stream out of the rooftop that smelled of wood and reeds.

Ami let go of my hand and went to the open door. She turned and waved me towards her, taking me out of my awe at the surrounding nature that had been hidden within a neighborhood. I joined Ami inside the house. Where I stood was on the dirt floor. Above me were rafters and shelves for storage. On the shelves were bags of grain and a few crates. On this level I saw a large round object that looked like a kiln. Towards another door was a table with brochures and heavy rocks atop them so they wouldn't blow away.

"It's an old *satoyama*," she said. "Like a…"

"A farmhouse?" I guessed after looking around.

"Yes, like a farmhouse."

Ami wandered to a shelf that had a small fish tank and peered at the content.

There was a large wooden ledge that separated the lower ground from the house interior and its tatami floors. In this spot I saw the fire and a metal pot hanging from a giant hook which had a large fish ornament in cast iron. The fire crackled and popped as I removed my shoes to stepped inside the interior.

Inside it was bright from the sunlight coming from the open doors. The only decorations were one old clock that was ticking on the wall above a dresser and a wall scroll inside an alcove. I heard the children playing outside and looked to see them walking around on pieces of cut bamboo that had rope attached on either side, like short stilts. It looked challenging since they would often fall and then try again, clomping around the courtyard and laughing. On a table inside the main room there were wooden toy spinner tops, some string, a worn out deck of cards, and wooden tiles with *kanji* written on them.

I sat at the table and spun the tops. I turned at the sound of Ami's footsteps shuffling on the *tatami*. She sat next to me and put her arm around my waist.

"This was a great idea," she said.

I spun one of the wide wooden tops painted with red stripes.

"Like this," Ami said. She took one of the tops and a piece of string. She wrapped the string around the base of the handle then pulled it towards the base of the bottom needle and wrapped the string around so that it covered the entire underside. She leaned back a ways. "*Ichi, ni, san*," she said and released the top so that it spun across the table and wobbled onto the floor.

"Ah, well, I'm a little out of practice," she said, and went to pick up the toy from the floor and put it back on the table.

Looking out the open doors to the nearby forest made me restless. "Should we go walk?" I suggested.

"Hm?"

"I bet there are mushrooms," I said.

Ami leaned her head back. "*Chotto matte*," she said. "It's nice and quiet now."

She must have really been tired. I'd never known her *not* to be enthusiastic about mushroom hunting. Instead, she sat in the corner of the room and fell into a quiet sleep with her head against the inner wall and her legs crisscrossed. I let her sleep and went about exploring the house and the surrounding courtyard.

Other than the main house, there was a smaller one that served as a store room, the red water pump, and a building in the back which had bathrooms, a vending machine, a locked office, and a set of faucets. Walking around it took me to a small garden with green growing plants, and then a pathway to a vast green field and long wooden racks with long dried grass hanging from it. The children from earlier were bending over in certain areas of the field. One of them held a long-poled net. One shouted and a man who I assumed was the father walked over. to see what the child had in their hands. Seeing them made me homesick.

I went back to the vending machine and bought two cans of milk coffee and went to the house to where Ami was still sleeping and sat next to her. Either the smell of the sound of opening the can woke her. I handed her the other can.

"*Arigatou*," she said. "Was I asleep for long?"

"I don't think so."

We sat and finished our drinks. Ami stood up and stretched her legs.

"There were some kids catching bugs or something."

"Oh? Where?"

"I'll show you."

When we got to the fields and passed the rows of dried grass, I looked at them more closely and saw the small nodules on each end. "Are these seeds?"

Ami looked as well. "It must be rice," she said.

"How do you know?" I asked.

"In elementary school, I had to do this project about rice cultivation. We had to grow some rice at home and report about it. I was so terrible at it that just one of my stalks grew and at the end I had ten grains of rice."

"I didn't know it was so difficult," I said.

"*Totoro mitai ne*," she said. "Those are similar to the ones in the movie. The family drives past on the way to their new home."

We walked on the narrow trail through the grass and the moist raised pathways around the empty and mucky rice paddies. On the outer trail, the ground was covered with acorns and as we walked, a gust of wind would rattle the trees and cause more to fall. We turned up on a path up a hill.

I noticed a few mushroom caps sprouting from a fallen tree branch. "Ami," I said. "Do you know these ones?"

She came to where I was and squatted to look at the mushrooms. She stroked the cap and then peered underneath. "It looks like *maitake*."

"How can you tell?" I asked.

"Mm. So, you can look at the shape first, then see the texture, then check to see if you can see the gills, and if there is a veil around the stalk. Some mushrooms are so difficult because the poisonous ones look almost the same to the ones you can eat."

"Is this one poisonous?"

Ami shook her head. "No, this one you can eat. It's good in *miso* soup."

We continued walking up the pathway and then she stopped to point out a slimy orange mushroom.

"This looks like the one I got poisoned by once. It was when I very first started learning about mushrooms. I was maybe a little too confident and was sure I had a *buri* mushroom but it wasn't. I ate a little piece of it and had such stomach aches that I went to the hospital. It was good I didn't die."

"I think so." With her sweat moist on her neck and forehead, her mouth open in a smile, I thought she looked so beautiful. I kissed her on her cheek.

She startled.

Then she looked around and waited until a pair of hikers passed by. "Over here," she said.

We climbed up a small ledge in an area that was off the trail. She walked a few feet and stopped, then looked around again to make sure no one was around. Knowing exactly what she was up to, I took off my backpack, set it on the ground, and helped her to do the same. She stifled a giggle.

"I've always wanted to do it outside," she whispered in my ear.

"What would happen if someone found us?" I asked quietly.

She chuckled. "They would tell us politely not to do it," she said. "Most people here don't like direct confrontation."

I took her hand and guided her to an old ginkgo tree so that she would have a place to stand comfortably. I licked my fingers and slipped them into her pants where she was already warm and wet. She kissed me and played with my breasts over my shirt.

She began to moan softly and placed her hand over her mouth to keep from being too loud. With her other free hand, she wriggled her fingers into my shorts and rubbed the most sensitive part around my clit.

I stroked her faster.

She rested her forehead on my shoulder and moaned into my chest, muffling her screams. I felt my own climax as she circled her finger slowly around. I raised my head and groaned as softly as I could.

We stood there together in silence with only our haggard breathing and the sound of singing birds in the air.

That night, we watched *Tonari no Totoro* while we

snuggled together under a soft blanket and ate our dinner.

Chapter 22

October 2011

Some of the school lessons had me explain Halloween to the students. The holiday existed in Japan, but it was focused on aesthetics. Most of the students wanted to know why it was celebrated in the first place. How much they understood of my explanation and Haruyo's translation was questionable.

I searched through websites that shared things to do in Tokyo. It seemed that there was always something exciting happening in one of the wards. That was a sharp contrast to how I was used to things in my hometown where the biggest events took place twice a year and consisted of the state fair and a Scandinavian festival.

Scanning through webpages but not able to decide, I asked Hannah if she would want to do something. I hadn't seen her more than a few times after our camping trip since we were both busy, so it seemed a good time to invite her out. We agreed to meet on Friday evening in Kunitachi.

I texted Ami to see if she wanted to come. Since she did, I wrote to Hannah that she would join.

****

At a little after seven on Friday, Ami and I met Hannah at Kunitachi station. Hannah was dressed unlike I'd ever seen her. The form-fitting black dress she wore with silver glittery kitten heads decorated around the fluffy skirt and tall red high heels was far from her usual casual wear. She was also wearing makeup with red lipstick and had her hair curled.

"Did we need to dress up?" I asked, glancing down at my jeans and sweater.

"I thought I'd get fancy tonight," she said. "It's super *kawaii*, right?"

Ami and I glanced at each other.

"*Ne, kawaii deshyou*," Ami said in a tone that almost sounded sarcastic.

We got on the train together.

"So," I asked, "where exactly are we going?"

Hannah put her finger up to her lips. "You'll see."

The train was so crowded with late-night prowlers that it was hard to jostle to find any space. We three were smooshed together. I was used to the closeness in the train so that I didn't get as panicked as before. But it still bothered me at times, like the elbows that would shove into my back or my shoulders when others around me were also trying to find a comfortable position.

Hannah kept whisper-talking while on the train, asking Ami or I questions about our relationship or about work in general. I was more worried about where it was that we were going that Hannah felt the need to dress up as she was.

She led us to a building that I thought was for office workers. The building was normal, nondescript, with the only identifier being the sign that showed "Dionyusus." It seemed like a misspelling of the Greek god known for his drinking.

When we entered it was into a hallway and a white corridor. On one side was a brown door with gold accents and the sign on the wall next to it had a lit sign with the bar's name and bat wings on either side.

I opened the door and the inside was a large room with a long leather couch that was occupied by five women that spanned one wall, curving around the corner. Above the center of the couch was a large wall cross. Other than the ropes, whips, and handcuffs hanging from the wire frames on the walls and the bamboo bars hanging from the ceiling in a stage area, the interior was modern. It reminded me so much of when Ami and I went to the Maid Café and how it was hidden in a normal-looking building that I wouldn't take a second glance at. Japan seemed to hide their kinks behind a bland wall or a trim suit.

We were greeted by a well-dressed young woman that said, "*Sashin dekimasen.*" Or, no photographs were not allowed. She then explained the pricing, which she also showed to us on a brochure she was holding.

"*Majide,*" Ami said and laughed.

"Is this what I think it is?" I asked Hannah.

She shrugged.

"Do you think we could just leave?" I whispered to Ami.

Ami tapped her cheek with a fingertip. "Hm. I don't think so. It would be rude to leave when she went through this trouble."

"It's fun, right?" asked Hannah. I looked at her for a while, noting she was possibly scowling. "Well, you wouldn't have come if I said what it was!"

She was probably right. I generally tried to avoid the night life or even going out after dark if I could help it.

"How do you know a place like this?"

"I happen to know the owner."

That was enough explanation for me. I didn't care to know the details of how or why she knew someone who owned a bondage bar.

Ami, on the other hand, did ask. "How?"

Hannah's eyebrows raised and she smiled widely.

"Oh, it's mundane," she said. "I used to teach at an *eikaiwa* on weekends and there was a man in my class who wanted to learn more English. He was stylish, always, and actually his English was fantastic, but anyway, I taught him for two years before he would tell me what he did for work. 'I own a club,' he said, and invited me to go with him. So, I tell Tom and we come here."

"I wondered how you knew about it. It's not a common thing to know about. I didn't even know there was a bar like that here," Ami said.

"Your husband came with you?" I asked.

"Why not? It's a good place to relax."

I looked around the room, at the ropes, whips, and restraints. "Relax?" I asked.

"It's called *Shibari*. A kind of rope-tying," Hannah explained. "Come on,"

We paid for an hour in the room, which included drinks. The maître d' gave us both a sheet of paper, which Ami explained was a questionnaire. Since it was in Japanese, the only parts I could read with any fluency were the *katakana*. Ami helped me with it. The questionnaire contained questions about level of comfort. I told Ami to write down "beginner" for me on all of them. She wrote mine quickly and then answered her own questionnaire. I wished I knew how to read more Japanese so I knew what Ami was writing. It seemed to be more involved than the simple answers she wrote for me.

We were led to a seat and asked what we wanted to drink. I chose a sweet looking drink.

"What did you answer?" I asked.

Ami gave a little half smile. "Ah, maybe I'll tell you later."

Hannah peeked at her answers and smirked.

The woman came back with our drinks. A svelte older man in a black suit who was sitting with the ladies stood up. There were some murmurings from a table in front of us and then a middle-aged woman stood up, bashfully. The man spoke to her gently and removed a skein of tan rope from the back wall. The man removed his blazer and rolled up his white shirtsleeves. He then began to confidently and professionally wrap and tie the rope around the woman's chest and breasts. He spoke softly as he did it. Though the woman laughed nervously at first, she calmed as he spoke.

"What's he saying?" I asked Ami.

"He's explaining what he's doing. The rope is soft, and the knots are tight. Now he's telling her to relax and breathe."

Ami drank and then stopped. "He says that the person tying the rope is the 'rigger' and the person being tied is the 'bunny.'"

"Have you ever been a bunny?" I teased Hannah.

She smiled. "Once or twice. It's really not at all bad. He has very gentle hands."

We sat together and watched as the woman was tied up and allowed to hang. At some point, her face became a little flushed, and she told him to, "*Sutopu.*" The man stopped immediately, let her body down on the floor, and began to slowly untie her. When she was unbound, he placed a hand on her back and helped her to her seat. When he coiled the rope again, he replaced it on the wall and then came towards us.

"Hannah-*chan*," he said. He touched her on the shoulder and whispered something to her. She laughed.

"These are my friends," Hannah said and gestured to us.

"Ah, *hajimemashite*," he said in a softly spoken, confident tone and bowed slightly. "I am Ryosuke. *Yoroshiku-onegaishimasu*."

He sat down next to Hannah, relaxing against the couch and crossing his legs, holding his hands on his knee.

"How do you know these beautiful ladies?" he asked.

I wondered if that line worked to flatter straight women. It seemed to since Hannah was smiling.

"Tara and I work together," she said while touching my arm and she then pointed at Ami, "and Ami is her girlfriend."

"Girlfriend?" he asked. "Oh! Welcome, please, we are friendly here. You know, many of the people who come here are women," he gestured to the room which did not have one other man in it, "you see?"

"He told me when I first came here that it's mostly women," Hannah said. "Isn't that funny?"

"I wouldn't call it 'funny'," I said.

"*Nande, onna?*" Ami asked.

The man sucked air in through his teeth and crossed his arms while tilting his head. "*Nande, saa*," he said. "So, it must be control, *wakarimasuka*? I can tie them, but the submissive can control what happens; she says 'go' or 'stop' and I must listen to what she says."

"I can see how a woman would enjoy that," Hannah said.

The maître d' came by to ask if we wanted more drinks and Hannah ordered for us. The drink of mine was sweet and fruity so I couldn't taste the alcohol. I didn't usually drink so much but I started feeling relaxed and woozy.

"How come you started this?" I asked.

He nodded, causing his glasses to fall a little and he pushed them back into place using a well-placed finger on the left edge of the rim.

"About twenty years ago, I started. I became interested in shibari as a kind of play. Actually, it was the lady I was dating at the time who introduced it to me." He nodded to himself.

"Your wife?" Hannah teased.

"*Iie*," he said. "This was," he tilted his head. "*Ano*, about three years before I was married. This lady was Russian. So, I don't know how she knew about *shibari*. But she wanted me to try it."

"How have I never heard this story before?" Hannah asked.

He looked at her in surprise. "I'm sure I told you. *Saa*, maybe we were both drunk and forgot."

Hannah laughed and in response took a drink from her glass.

"After that, I became a fan of *shibari*. Over time, I went to some conferences in France and America to learn more about it. France is very interesting about this because they started to use it as a kind of therapy, like yoga, *to ka*."

"Like yoga?" I asked, looking at the ropes and hooks. "Really?"

"The relaxation is similar," he explained.

"*Dou*? How can it be relaxing?" Ami asked.

"*Yarou*?"

"*Ii-ya, daijoubu desu.*"

The man looked at me and asked, "Want to try?"

"I thought he might ask you," Hannah said in a dry tone.

"Why?"

Her eyebrows shot up and her eyes widened. "Would it surprise you that many Japanese guys I know have a fetish for white-skinned, blonde-haired girls?"

"I'm not blonde," I said.

"Close enough."

I wondered if the man had a similar fetish or if he was just doing his job. In either case, I was curious to experience it and agreeable from my drunkenness. It was something new and the man had been gentle and considerate with the other woman. Plus, he listened to her when she told him to stop. I turned to Ami.

"I kind of want to try it," I whispered.

"*Hontou*?"

"Yeah, what about you?"

Ami shook her head. "No, but if you want to…" She gestured towards the room with an open hand. She then turned to the man. When she answered him, he nodded once and stood up. I did the same. As he spoke, Ami helped by translating.

"He's going to use the *gote-shibari*," Ami said, "it's a type of knot for beginners."

The man passed the rope over my chest, then wrapped, tied, wrapped, tied so that soon my hands and arms were behind my back. He passed the rope around my thighs and my pelvis. As he was working, he was speaking and Ami translated for me, but I was so focused on the feeling of the tension on my body. There was pressure but no pain. He passed the ends of the rope through a pulley and pulled, lifting my body so I was suspended sideways. I felt relief as I hung there, a culmination of the alcohol relaxing my nerves and of the odd comfort of restraint.

The man asked me "Okay, *desu-ka*?"

"*Hai*," I answered.

I breathed slowly, deeply, and let my muscles relax. I became increasingly aware of how the pressure on my pelvis gave me a slow-rising arousal. I hung there for a few minutes until I was let down on the floor and my arms were released. When I looked out, Ami was staring at me intently. She took a cigarette out of her purse and started smoking.

The blood rushed to my limbs immediately as a tingling sensation rushed through them. The man began untying the knots, relieving me of the tension, and as he did, blood flowed to the most sensitive parts of my body, making me dizzy. I thanked the man and returned to my seat to finish my drink. Ami didn't say anything to me. She had finished her cigarette and then put a mint in her mouth. She must have been upset and I didn't want to say anything that would start an argument.

"I don't know how you could let a man touch you," Ami said.

"He was professional," I answered.

"He is," Hannah chimed in. "Don't worry; he's just doing his job."

I crossed my arms. I didn't like the insinuation that what I did was wrong. I wasn't attracted to the man; I was satisfied at the experience he shared with me. Ami looked at me. She bit the inside of her lip as if she was holding a confession.

"*What*?" I asked. "Just say what you mean."

Ami shook her head once. "You're drunk," she said.

To Hannah's credit, she broke the tension.

"It *is* getting a little late," Hannah said. "I won't be insulted if you want to go home."

Ami stood up. "*Gomen*," she said, "Thank you for the drinks."

Hannah waved her hand. "No worries. Just take her home safe."

I wanted to stay for a little longer but I also began to feel sleepy from the alcohol. Ami held my hand as I swayed while walking. The city lights were bright and I heard cars and a train but other than that I was unaware of exactly where I was beyond knowing that Ami was holding my hand.

I was sleepy and when I felt a soft cushion underneath me I slipped into unconsciousness. I woke up at some time during the early morning when it was still dark. The soft blankets and soft plushies told me that I was at Ami's apartment but she wasn't in bed with me.

I got up to use the bathroom and saw her asleep on her couch, wrapped in a comforter, while the television chattered in the corner. I turned the television off and went to the bathroom. Glancing in the mirror as I washed my hands, I noticed I looked awful. My eyes were tired and my skin seemed pale. I remembered bits and pieces of the bondage club and I definitely remembered the sweet alcoholic drinks that must have sent me into a stupor. My head was still a little dizzy and I went back to sleep.

When I woke up again it was later in the morning

241

and I smelled food. My stomach growled.

On the kitchen counter were shopping bags and ready-made dishes. I looked for Ami, who was on the patio checking on her mushrooms. She had her hair tied back messily and was still in her pajamas. I noticed the nicotine patch on her left arm just poking out under her sleeve.

"*Ohayo*," I said to Ami.

"*Ohayo*," she said, not looking up from the top of the mushroom. I felt that there was some tension since she wasn't looking at me and especially since she didn't share the bed with me.

"Thanks for bringing me here," I said, then tried to lighten the mood with some humor. "I had a weird dream that I was tied up by some lanky guy. That was a dream, wasn't it?"

"*Nandemonai*," she said. She said it factually with no inclination that she was angry. I couldn't tell if she was being nonplussed or if this was more of her "shouganai" attitude.

"That was kind of a weird night, right?"

"Hm. A little. I didn't know about a place like that. It's not really my taste."

"Well, that's the last time I let Hannah choose a place to go, that's for sure."

Ami stood up straight. "Would you like breakfast? The *conbini* had *oden*. That's the best if you have a hangover."

Ami went past me to the kitchen and so I followed her. She took out two large circular containers from the bags. Steam came out of a pre-cut hole in the center of a clear top. It smelled savory. She slid one of the containers to me along with a pair of chopsticks. When I opened the lid, there was glistening brown broth, a boiled egg, cabbage, a large sausage, and a round white puffy ball. I ate without talking and so did Ami.

"So good," I said when I finished drinking the broth.

"Mmn," she mumbled.

I noticed that she hadn't eaten much of hers. I thought about her distant demeanor. I wasn't sure if I should say something or ignore it. But, I never thought it was good to ignore problems. It was too easy to let small problems become bigger and turn into resentment. I didn't want that to become me and Ami. Better to say something than to wonder.

"I feel like you're upset," I said.

She sighed. She tensed her lips and tapped her finger on the rim of the bowl as she stared at the broth. "Yes, I am. And it's stupid,"

"What?" I asked, preparing for a recount of something I must have done the night before.

"Last night," she started, "I don't know why but I felt a little…jealous."

"Jealous? About what?"

Ami leaned back and folded her arms over her chest as she turned to look out the kitchen window. "About someone else touching you," she said.

"Oh," I said.

"It's stupid. I know. It's not like you liked him and he was being a good host. *Dakara…*"

"I'm sorry," I said at once. "I'm the stupid one. I wasn't thinking. I should have been more considerate."

Ami turned to look at me. "No. It's me. I have a problem with jealousy. I try to work on it but it's still hard for me."

"I think it's normal to feel like that," I said.

"But I don't want my jealousy to push you away. That's how some of my past relationships ended, because I was too jealous. So, I don't want that to happen with us."

Ami reached over and took my hand in hers. "I think I really like you," she said.

I brought her hand up to my lips and kissed her fingertips. "I really like you, too." I was happy, absolutely happy to be with Ami.

****

All through the fall, I taught classes as usual. What I enjoyed but also found stifling at the same time was the regimentation of lessons or daily life in general. Haruyo told me that there was a special day in November called *Bunka no Hi*, or Culture Day.

"On that day," she said, "we will have a school festival. Would you be able to join?"

"Yes!" I said a little too loudly as we were in the teacher's room and others looked at me when I raised my voice. I lowered my voice. "I mean, yes, that sounds like fun."

"So, it will be on Sunday and some students will perform music and dances. Would you be able to help with something?"

"I think so."

"Ah, so, thank you. We need some help with the *yakisoba* stand."

"Er, I don't know how to make *yakisoba*."

"You do not have to make it. You can take the money and give the food."

"Oh, that doesn't sound too bad."

She nodded. "Good, so I will tell Kurobe-*sensei*, the gym teacher, that you will help."

I had seen the gym teacher a few times when passing through the gym to get to another classroom, but I couldn't recall her face. "Maybe we can go to a café after?" I suggested.

"Ah, I think it will be late when we finish."

"That's okay."

"*Ano*," she said, "before the festival is maybe better. Ah. There is a café called '*Nonbiri*' in the neighborhood. So, is that okay?"

"Yes."

"So, I think at eight thirty we can do it and then go to the festival after."

"That's great."

I finished my day on Friday and stopped at the mall before going home to get dinner.

On Sunday, I woke up early to meet Haruyo. I wore my casual clothes there. Haruyo met me at the café. I noticed her standing out front of a small café with a brown and white banner with the café's name, her smart phone in one hand. She usually dressed formally at work, like I did, so seeing her in blue jeans, a flowery blouse, and a long khaki colored cardigan with a purple and black plaid scarf was refreshing. She also wore a set of pearl earrings, which I had never seen her do before. Hanging from her shoulder was a black tote bag with a kind of hippo character that looked familiar to me but I couldn't place it.

"Oh, you look so American," she said when she saw me.

"I am American."

"*Seikai, deshyou.* You are right."

"I've seen that character before," I said, pointing at her bag.

"Oh, *hai*, it's Moomin. I love Moomin. The story is from Finland."

I then remembered going to the Heritage Park gift shop in Minot and seeing the character on the books for sale, and then again at the Scandinavian Host Fest. I smiled to myself at the connection. "I think I've seen that hippo in my hometown."

"*Hontou*? Ah, but he is not a hippo. Moomin is a fairy." She put her phone in her bag. "Shall we go in?"

The inside looked less like a café and more like someone's home kitchen. But, there were three small round wooden tables, just large enough to rest two cups on, and round seated stools set up underneath each one. The entire café was about the same size as my apartment. The floor was hardwood that was so shiny that it reflected the hanging ceiling lights which I had to duck my head under to avoid. There were a few small windows, one which was a circle of stained glass that left a colorful kaleidoscope pattern on the floor when the light came through it. On the kitchen counter was a menu. It was short, listing six items: coffee, latte, hot tea, bread, cake, and *onigiri*.

"*Irasshaimase*," came an aged voice from the kitchen. I couldn't see who it was at first until I peered over the counter to see a small, elderly lady, with her white hair pulled back by an indigo kerchief. She wore a padded orange cotton house coat with an apron over it. Haruyo ordered first and then asked what I wanted, and ordered for me. I wanted to do it myself since I liked to use Japanese as much as I could but I thought she was trying to be polite.

"*Kashikomarimashita*," the old woman said.

We both went to sit down and wait to be served as

clinking and preparatory sounds came from the small kitchen.

"This is a cute little place," I said as I looked at the framed pictures of dried flowers and fauna on the walls.

Haruyo removed her scarf and put it in her bag. Doing so revealed a locket necklace hanging from her neck. I thought to ask about it as I wondered who's picture she might have in the frame, but thought again. It was too personal to ask her.

"*Hai*. I sometimes come here if I have the time. Uchida-*san* opens early so I can come before school. She also makes good, robust coffee."

The older woman, Uchida-*san*, stepped her way towards us carrying a tray with two cups of coffee and two pieces of steaming homemade bread buns. I jerked to help her but soon saw that she needed no help as she held the tray firmly in both her hands so that it barely moved.

"*Douzo*," she said and placed each item on the table.

The space was so confined that she stood very near me. I could smell her fresh, clean laundered clothing and another smell that was very similar to menthol. The older lady turned to me and asked me a question but because of her pronunciation or my untrained ear, I wasn't sure what she asked.

"Do you know what '*nonbiri*' means?" Haruyo translated.

"No."

The old lady explained in her crackly, heavy voice.

"It can mean 'happiness'," Haruyo said. "So, when you drink and you eat, you can be full of happiness."

"*Ne?*" she asked and she tapped my shoulder and smiled.

The woman went back to the kitchen to sit on a stool and look through a magazine. I sipped the coffee. Haruyo was right. The coffee was strong and with a little sweetness to offset the bitter taste. I tried the bread next. It was soft, fluffy, and lightly buttered. I ate the entire thing in a few bites.

"Did you eat breakfast?" Haruyo asked.

"Yes," I said.

"Oh, you seem hungry."

"I just like food," I stated.

"Seems so." Haruyo sipped from her cup.

"It's good that we could finally get coffee together," I said. "We've been working together almost a year and I only see you at work."

Haruyo nodded. "Yes, we teachers are always busy," she said.

"That's true," I said. "It was a hard year."

Haruyo nodded again.

"I can't believe all that happened."

"Yes. *Shouganai*. But, it seems it is getting better now."

I was quiet for a little as I finished my coffee. That word, *shouganai*, was used so often. I knew its definition, but its meaning seemed to range from a dismissive "whatever" to a close approximation of "this too shall pass."

"I hear that word a lot," I said.

"Which word?"

"*Shouganai*."

"Ah, yes. It means like 'it cannot be helped.'"

"Like the earthquake," I said.

"Yes, like that. We cannot control disasters."

"Hm," I said. "That's true." I folded my arms across

my chest. "Did I tell you that there was a flood in my hometown this year?" I couldn't remember if I told her. I know I talked to Ami but everything around that time was a little blurry.

"*Majide*? Was it bad?"

I nodded.

"I'm sorry," she said.

I told her briefly about the flood, how my parents had to stay with friends, and that they still couldn't move back home.

"Still, it is good they had help," Haruyo said. "A house is just a 'thing'; it can be built again."

"I think you're wiser than I am," I said and I meant it.

She lowered her head and shook it. She checked her watch. "I think it is time to go," she said. "Did you like the coffee?"

Was it time to go already? I would have liked to have talked more. "Oh, yes. It was very good."

I followed Haruyo's lead in picking up the empty dishes and placing them on the counter. The old woman, Uchida-*san*, had stopped reading the magazine and was hand sewing a quilted fabric bag with some anime characters on it. I had seen small children carry bags like that while I was on the train. Maybe the old woman had a grandchild.

"*Arigatou gozaimashita*," the old woman crooned at the sound of the plates on the counter. As we walked, I felt the caffeine begin to wake me up.

"*Souyu koto ne*," she said. "I will show you to Kurobe-*sensei*."

We walked to the school and towards the back where the playground was. As we walked, students passed by in their street clothes, laughing. The playground that was usually a dirt lot was set up like a small festival. There were some students helping teachers set up stalls, others placing instruments by a foldable stage.

Haruyo showed me to one of the stands which was being assembled. Miu was helping to put it together and I said hello to her. She looked different to me. It could have been that she was wearing casual clothes that showed her individuality more; her rainbow stockings, jean shorts, and a baggy hot pink sweater with some cute animals on it showed a completely different style than her usual monochrome uniform.

"*Eigo-no-sensei!*" I heard.

I looked over to who I assumed must be Kurobe-*sensei*. She was a short, lean woman who wore the school's track uniform: a blue sweatsuit with the school's name in white lettering. First, she greeted Haruyo with a bow and a good morning, then she took my hand and shook it vigorously.

"San-kyu. Today we make *yakisoba*. So, when it is about four o'clock, we will clean up and you can go home." Four o'clock? I hadn't expected it to last so long. I couldn't refuse to help, though, since I'd already agreed.

I nodded. "Okay."

Haruyo said, "*Yoroshiku-onegaishimasu,*" to Kurobe-*sensei* and walked back inside the school. I'm sure she had her own busy schedule.

The next hour was one spent hurrying back and forth around the yard and going where Kurobe-*sensei* pointed me. I helped put up the stalls, hung banners, fetched plastic containers from inside the school, and did anything else that I was asked to do.

At one point I knew the festival would begin soon because Kurobe told me to stand behind the stall counter. It was my job to take the containers filled with *yakisoba*, put two rubber bands around it, slip a set of chopsticks under the rubber bands and hand it to the customer. It was Miu's job to take their money, then give them any change. Kurobe would be behind the flat cooking tray making the *yakisoba* and putting the food inside an empty container.

People started arriving and I focused on what I was supposed to do. Every once in a while someone would see me and say, "America-*jin*," in a tone of casual surprise before paying for their food. Music came from the stage and I got to listen to some of the students show off their talents.

At one point, Miu tapped me on the shoulder, handed me a container of *yakisoba*, and told me to, "Go to take a rest. *San-jyu-pun.*" A thirty minute break.

Normally I would refuse but I had to go to the bathroom and I wanted to eat. When I was done I perused the other stalls and tried one of the games. It was a pop-gun game where I had to shoot cork bullets at the prize I wanted to knock it off the shelf. Mostly there were snacks but there were a few small toys that I aimed for. In the end, I didn't hit any of them down but my consolation prize was a small bag of fruit gummy snacks, which I took and ate.

I took a chance to sit down in front of the stage and watch the students perform a dance while dressed in *kimono*. One of the teachers was sitting offside the stage playing a long, stringed instrument while the students danced to the thronged rhythm.

At the end of the song, my break was finished and I went back to handing out *yakisoba*. By the end of the day, the coffee had long worn off and I was ready to go. Kurobe turned off the gas burner and put the last of the *yakisoba* into empty containers. She patted me on the back, reached down under the counter and handed me a *chu-hai*.

"*Kyou wa jyouzu!*" she said.

She grabbed one for herself, wiped the sweat from her forehead, opened it, and drank.

"*Kampai*," she said.

I opened mine, tapped my can to hers, and drank.

"*Sensei*," Miu said as she was rubber-banding the remaining containers, "*Atashi mo nomu.*"

"Ah! *Go-nen-mai kara.*"

"*Daijyoubu, sensei. Himitsu ga.*"

"*Dame*," Kurobe said. She exhaled. "Ah, *tsukaretta.*"

"Tara-*sensei*," came Haruyo's voice.

I turned around and there was Haruyo looking frazzled. I swallowed the drink and said, "Oh, yes?"

"Thank you for today. It's finished, so you can go."

"Okay," I said.

"I will see you tomorrow."

I finished the *chu-hai* and put it in the recycle as I left.

Thanksgiving was soon and I wanted to be sure to call my parents. I hadn't heard from them much except for some emails here or there to tell me how things were going. It had been months since the flood and they were finally able to start renovating the house. They promised to call so I could see it.

Chapter 23

December 2011

I opened the window. Although it was December, it felt like early Spring to me. I was used to a Midwestern winter with harsh winds, blizzards that could leave feet of snow, temperatures that dipped to the frigid negatives, with arctic winds so cold that they often left my skin red, and a sky with barely any sunlight. Here, the worst that happened were the typhoons and some mild snowfall.

I also felt better physically. I suffered from terrible seasonal depression when winter came every year in North Dakota. I'd often become irritable and would have rolling headaches for months because of the cold and the lack of sunlight. Although I took extra vitamins during the season, I never seemed to feel like myself until the warmer temperatures arrived in the spring. Feeling like my whole self all year long made me reconsider if I ever wanted to go back to my hometown.

It was cool enough for me to wear a light down jacket and a scarf. I was still use to North Dakotan winters so the weather outside was a cool comfort. At about forty degrees Fahrenheit, that felt like spring to me. This was in contrast to the others who were heading to the train for their commute who were bundled up in hats, and wrapped scarves around their necks and over their nose and mouth.

When I sat at my desk, Haruyo had placed the lesson plans for the day as usual. And when she noticed me, she walked over holding some clear file folders and sat next to me.

"Good morning," she said in that hushed tone she used in the teacher's office. "This is your renewal paperwork," she said. She put one of the clear files on my desk that had paperwork all in Japanese.

"My renewal? Like for teaching?"

"Of course."

"So," I said, feeling elation come to me. "You want me to keep teaching here?"

Haruyo furrowed her eyebrows and nodded. "Of course, yes. You are a good teacher."

I smiled but I also felt like I might cry so I bit the inside of my cheek. How quickly had I been dismissed from my last teaching job? How often had I been scolded there and shunned? How often had they focused on my personality and not on learning or what was best for the students? And here, at this school in Tokyo, there was no question that I was a teacher and, as Haruyo said, a good one.

"So, the principal already signed, and here are your hours for next year. Also, there is a bonus for returning teachers which you will receive after the paperwork is processed by the Department of Education. If you agree, you can sign, and your work visa will also be renewed for three years."

I signed it eagerly.

On my break before class, I sent Ami a message about the good news. For the next three years at least, I'd keep my home in Japan. Ami sent an image of a party hat and streamers. I wanted to celebrate so on my way home, I bought some ready-made dishes and a strawberry shortcake at the Cozy Corner cake shop and stopped at Ami's place. I took a shower and washed the dirty dishes that were in her sink while I listened to a talk show.

The door clicked open and Ami shouted excitedly for me.

"Three more years!" she said as she came in. I met her in the hallway and saw that she was holding a cake box. I laughed and gave her a quick hug and kiss.

"I got a cake, too."

"*Hontou*? What kind?"

"Strawberry."

"*Ii-yo-u.* I got cheesecake from this place called 'Pablo.' It was the last one, too."

"Let's eat."

"I'll wash first. The train was so busy."

I took the cake and set it next to the one I bought. I had an idea. I wanted to emulate something I'd seen in television shows and surprise Ami in the shower. In those shows or movies, one of the partners would go into the steamy shower and kiss their lover and soon there would be passionate, shower sex.

When I tried it, Ami was rinsing off the shampoo in her hair and when I stepped in, I slipped on the soap bubbles and bumped into her. She laughed and kissed me. After a few minutes, it turned out that a steamy, wet, shower wasn't the best way to have sex. We tiptoed to the bedroom, dripping water on the carpet, and nestled under the covers together. When both our stomachs started rumbling, we ate dinner and for dessert had a slice of each cake, although I ate nearly half of each.

That night, I sent Hannah and my parents the news

that I'd be staying in Tokyo for a few more years. My parents were less than pleased. My mom wrote a long email about why I should come back. I didn't read the entire email. I was in too good of a mood to be brought down by the same complaints and arguments that she'd made when I decided to move in the first place. Hannah messaged me back to invite me to her Christmas party.

Ami was checking on the mushrooms she was growing inside. When I told Ami, she said, "She's not going to bring any *shibari* fans is she?"

"What?" I asked, and had to think about the word. *Shibari* was the rope tying. "Oh, I don't think so. Not at a Christmas party, anyway."

Ami raised her eyebrows. "I wouldn't be surprised."

I chuckled, imagining a Japanese woman dressed in a Santa Claus costume being tied up. "It could be fun."

"*Shibari?*"

"A Christmas party."

Ami scrunched her face. "*Tabun*. I don't know."

"It might be fun to go together."

"*Kangaemasu.*"

I was too excited to sleep and I stayed up even after Ami went to sleep. I was staying in Japan. And I was staying with Ami.

All through the next week, Haruyo wanted me to teach the classes about Christmas. More specifically, about how Christmas was celebrated in America. I told them about some of the things I did in my hometown and I explained that some people went to church. There were a lot of questions when I mentioned church. For as long as I'd been in Tokyo, I hadn't yet seen a single church, but then I also wasn't looking for one. One of the students, Jyumi did share that she was Christian.

"*Christo*," she said and made a cross with her fingers. I almost didn't believe it but Haruyo confirmed that she was. Of all people, I hadn't expected Jyumi to be Christian.

With Hannah's Christmas party on the weekend, I thought I should get in the mood. As with Halloween, there were Christmas decorations, but they were superficial. They were pretty and festive but without much meaning except to spark some joy. It was an appropriation of the western secular holiday; it was gifts, decorations, food, parties, and music, without the thorough understanding of the meaning behind it.

In a way, it was refreshing as it was free from being overtly religious and was more inclusive. It had nothing to do with Christianity but everything to do with comfort, kindness, and generosity. There was no one here who would care if I went to mass or not or would comment and gossip about my absence. I liked that kind of anonymity and non-judgement. It was interesting to be in a place where any type of Christianity was in the minority, especially coming from a place where there was a church on every corner.

I missed seeing Christmas decorations, though, so I thought that I could buy some items to make my apartment more festive. Christmas in America tended to last from the end of Halloween until well beyond Christmas day. There were January days when I would drive to school and still see houses with decorations.

One house on the corner would often keep them up until Valentine's day. I would see the waving Santa Clause each morning when I made the turn into the staff parking lot. One day the wind had been so strong that his arm was lost and I saw it on the main road two days later, crushed by hundreds of cars passing over it.

I wondered how the weather was back home. It was mid-December, so there would already be snow and negative temperatures. I got chilled thinking about it. I stopped at a café for a warm cup of coffee.

I went to the one hundred *yen* store to buy some cheap Christmas things. Everything was noted as being "X'Mas," and they had most of the normal decorations that I was used to except with slightly different designs. Instead of a wizened or chubby Santa Clause, theirs looked like a cute cartoon character. I bought a cheap tiny plastic tree, a string of lights, window stickers, and some battery powered tea lights. While I was there, I also picked up some pencils with chubby cats on them and a pair of fuzzy socks. I thought that I should get some present for Haruyo since she was my co-worker and since she worked so hard. I didn't know what she might like, so I erred on the side of caution and bought her chocolates.

After buying the decor, I walked around the rest of the mall looking around the windows and seeing the new items on display, deciding that I would have to get Ami a present. We'd been together for almost a year. We'd given each other small gifts before. I placed my hand in my pocket and absentmindedly fiddled with the cell phone charms. Jewelry was too committal. I didn't want to put undue pressure on either of us. I knew she liked mushrooms, so I went around to each shop looking for something that might appeal to her. I finally found a gift in a stationary store and had it wrapped. I tucked it in my backpack.

The days went by as usual. Students were growing ever more excited as we came closer to the winter break holiday. Though I found some of the lessons boring and repetitive and my role in the understanding of English as small, I mostly enjoyed it.

Our next class talked about how to ask questions and how to form questions. Haruyo asked an interesting question during the lesson after she heard me pronounce the question phrases: "Why does your intonation change?" I wasn't aware of any change as I was reading the phrases. Then, I looked again at the sentences written on the board. I had to think for a few seconds to find a reason why the intonation changed. Then, I remembered about closed-ended and open-ended questions.

"So, the first question can only have set responses, like 'yes' or 'no', so you'd raise your intonation." I drew an upwards arrow at the end of the question mark. "But, the next question can have many answers, so you lower your intonation." I drew a downward arrow.

Haruyo translated as I spoke. Some of the students mumbled sounds of understanding.

"That was interesting," Haruyo said. "I did not know that was why."

As the few days before winter break went on, the students would give me presents sporadically. A card with holiday greeting, a small bag of candy, a hand-drawn picture.

It was the hand-drawn picture, from Miu, that made me say a quick thank you and leave the room. The picture was inoffensive at face-value. It was a drawing of a little cartoon rabbit in a Santa hat standing in front of a decorated Christmas tree.

It was too much like the presents Natsumi used to give me. I didn't cry, there, in the bathroom with the door shut and locked. I stared at the picture. Was Miu trying to be nice? I didn't know. All I could think about was that Natsumi was missing Christmas. I thought I recovered to a place of normalcy but seeing the picture was too much.

I stayed in the bathroom for several minutes until I heard the bell tone for the next class. I had to get myself together. There were other students who needed me to help them learn. I folded the picture and slipped it in my pocket. Then, I splashed my face with some cold water and returned to the next class.

Haruyo was in the hall waiting for me. She said something to me in a tone that sounded concerned. I shook my head, telling her I was fine. I would be fine. The predictability of the lessons made it easy to focus on teaching and not on myself. Over the next few hours, I felt better. Once the day was finished, I gave my gift to Haruyo.

"For me?" she asked in her soft, surprised voice.

"Yes. I wanted to thank you for everything this year," I said.

"Of course, but I didn't get anything for you," she said as she took the box of chocolates.

"It's okay," I said. "You did so much already."

"Eh? What do you mean?"

"Well, I learned some ideas from you and you've been so helpful. Actually, I don't know how I'd get here without your help." I gave her a hug, which she mildly returned. When I let go, she bowed a little and said, "Thank you. Please have a good holiday."

I left. All the walk to the station and home I thought about Natsumi. I knew that her death was over, that maybe I shouldn't keep thinking about it, but it wasn't just her, it was everything.

I fixated on the bad things again. All that was wrong. I thought of what Ami would say to me. She said that bad things always happened but that I should enjoy myself. Ami would know. Her mother died. What was I complaining about? She knew a greater kind of loss than I did. And she found a way to keep living and to keep loving. I could, too.

Chapter 24

It was the night of the Christmas party. Ami decided to come with me on the term that she could leave whenever she wanted, which I thought was understandable. The party was at the Grand Hyatt in Roppongi. Ami dressed up in a sleek black dress, red heels, and a fluffy black coat that looked like imitation fur. I was wearing a pair of black trousers and a white blouse.

"I look like your butler," I said.

Ami laughed.

"You look fine."

"I didn't expect you to be so dressed up."

"*Saa*, I usually don't care but my dad said I should look nice and take pictures."

"Good idea."

We rode a crowded train to Roppongi. When we exited, Ami said, "Since we have time, we should look at the illuminations before we go."

I figured that she meant, "Christmas lights," and hadn't heard it referred to in that way. I agreed and we walked a winding path past the station, down a tunnel, and then to a line where other dressed-up couples or families were waiting.

The area was a plaza. With the evening lights, the decorations were dim but as the sun set, the scenery became a little more magical. The pathway through the gardens showed trimmed trees covered in blue and white twinkling lights. Vaguely holiday themed music played from unseen speakers. Ami held my hand. The hem of her coat sleeve tickled my wrist. We walked around, viewing the lights.

****

The hotel was easily the most exquisite place I had been to. The floors were polished marble that reflected the dimly lit crystal chandeliers hanging from a high ceiling. Everything inside looked expensive. Even the front desk concierge wore a formal suit.

"Wow," I said.

"It's nice, isn't it?" Ami asked.

I nodded.

"Isn't there a place like this at your hometown?"

"Uhm," I started as I thought about the one hotel in Minot called The Grand, a hotel that peaked twenty years ago and hadn't had a renovation since. It was a place where the smell of the indoor pool had soaked into the carpet and there was always a hint of cigarette smoke. "Not like this," I answered.

"Oh," Ami said. "So, let's see."

"I should have dressed nicer," I said.

"I don't think anyone will care," Ami said.

We walked through the hall to the conference area where a gigantic ballroom was decorated in a way that it looked like a Thomas Kinkade snow globe exploded. It was like a skewed, vaguely country style decor.

In the center of the room was a giant Christmas tree that was easily over eight feet tall with hundreds of tiny square shaped wrapped gifts piled under the tree. Some jazz music played over the speakers. There were already other people there.

Hannah stuck out easily in her platinum dress with a form fitting top and a flared skirt that was decorated at the collar with white and blue sequins that caught the light. She wore a pair of glittery red shoes that reminded me of Dorothy from the Wizard of Oz.

When she saw me and Ami, she waved enthusiastically and summoned us over with a flip of her hand. She was talking to three people, two men and one woman.

The woman was dressed in a way that made her look like a cute doll. Her hair, which I assumed was a wig, was blonde and curled and decorated with bright pink hair clips with diamond accents and cursive lettering that read, "Baby the Stars Shine Bright." Her dress was the same bright pink as her hair clips with a puffy skirt and a petticoat underneath. The dress had a pattern print of teddy bears at a tea party around the bottom skirt. She wore white stockings with the matching pattern on the dress and a pair of pink platform shoes with ribbons on the straps.

"Oh, she's a lolita," Ami said.

The term, "lolita," was one that I associated with Vladamir Nabokov in the book of the same name where an older man creeped on a young girl.

"Is that a joke?" I asked, thinking that she was pointing out how the woman was with some older men.

"No. It's because of the way she's dressed. The style is lolita style."

That served as something of an explanation but it didn't seem enough for me. Was it supposed to be ironic that a cute, doll-like way of dressing was named after a character in a novel about pedophilia?

"Tara!" Hannah said in a sprightly tone. "Merry

Christmas." She proceeded to hug me. I held my breath against the bombarding smell of her floral perfume.

She gave Ami a hug as well, which Ami reluctantly accepted.

Hannah backed away and was about to introduce the people she was talking to, given her hand gesture towards them, but was interrupted by the lolita. The young woman looked directly at me to show her blue colored contact lenses with her eyes wide and said in a high-pitched voice that must have been for show, "Oh! So white!"

"Uh," I stammered, not knowing whether it was a compliment or a criticism. Ami stifled a laugh.

The lolita then touched my hair and I pulled back.

"*Eh! Iro ga sugoi da nya. Atashi no kaminoke wa totemo seijou.*"

I understood a little of what she was saying, that there was something wrong with her hair.

"I didn't get that last part," I said. "*kaminoke wa totemo seijo.*" I repeated.

The lolita covered her mouth when she giggled. "*Demo, arigatou.*"

"Did I say something wrong?" I asked.

"Not really," Hannah said. "You just called her hair a 'saint'."

"Oh."

"I thought it was cute," Ami said, and she held my hand.

"*Rezu desu ka?*" the lolita asked.

Ami nodded.

The woman smiled.

"*Ii, ne?*" she said, then she scooched closer to us and whispered, "Men is so headache."

Before I could answer, there was a shout coming from a table by the Christmas tree.

"Oh, come on," Hannah said. "We got a *kagami-biraki*, so you'll have to drink." Hannah paused. "It's like a beer keg, but with *sake*."

The lolita clapped her hands together and jumped up and down. It looked like an act to me, but her male friends seemed to find it entertaining.

"*Iko?*" she asked and slung her arm through mine. "*Ne, Onee-chan,*" she said, turning to Ami, "*honyaku kudasai you nya.*"

"I think she wants to talk to you," Ami said.

"Oh."

"*Wasaretta, ja, Atashi no namae wa Saya-chan desu,*" she said as we walked towards the table with the *sake* barrel and stood in a long line.

"She says her name is Saya," Ami said in a monotone voice.

"I got that much," I said.

"*Anata wa?*"

That I knew. She was asking for my name. "I'm Tara,"

"Tara?" she giggled. "*Sakana kono kanji ka nya?*

I knew the word "*Sakana*" for "fish" and sighed. "*Hai,*" I answered.

"*Omoshiroii,*" Saya said. "*O-shigoto wa?*" she asked.

She was asking about what I did for work.

"*Eigo no sensei desu.*"

"*Ah, sono koto ne. Eigo wa natsukashii.*"

"*Anata wa?*" I asked to see what her occupation was.

"Ah, maybe you don't need me," Ami said proudly. "You're doing well."

Saya covered her mouth and giggled. "*Eto, ne, tokidoki wa*," she lowered her voice to a whisper, "*hosutesu desu.*"

I could grasp everything she was saying, that she was sometimes something but I didn't know exactly.

"She's a hostess," Ami said.

"*Tokidoki ga*," Saya added.

"Sometimes," Ami explained. "Maybe that's why she's with those guys."

Ami spoke some quick Japanese to Saya, who replied in just as quick of Japanese and exclaimed.

"What?" I asked.

"*Ano*," Ami started, "She's not working right now."

I felt like there was more to what was said but didn't press it.

"I like her dress," I said to change the subject.

We waited in the line as Saya and Ami kept talking. I picked up some pieces of the conversation but it was difficult to figure out what Saya was saying because her tone was so high and she used terms that I didn't catch, plus she sounded an awful lot like a kitten asking for milk. When we came to the *sake* barrel, there were wooden square cups with *kanji* burned into the front. We each took one and took a cup-full of warm *sake* then went off to a clear area to drink. Hannah joined us, all smiles.

"What a year, huh?" Hannah said. "Here's to it being over," and tapped each of our cups with the edge of hers. "*Kampai!*" We all drank. The *sake* was strong and stung my sinuses but it was warm against my throat.

"You betcha," I said.

"How do you know Saya?" Ami asked Hannah.

"Oh, she was another one of my students about six or seven years ago." Hannah said some quip in Japanese, which Saya smiled at.

"Actually, a lot of my students come to my Christmas party. We do it every year. My husband's co-workers and clients, too," Hannah lowered her head, "Some are *yakuza*, you know. So, don't start trouble."

"I don't plan on it," I said.

"*Yakuza ga yo-i shiharai da nya*," Saya said.

"Really?" Hannah said to Saya. "They were so helpful this year with giving money to the disaster."

"Oh?" I asked.

Hannah nodded. "Yes, they used a lot of their money to help the families in Fukushima."

"Seems like even the gangsters here are kinder than most."

Hannah nodded. "It's expected. I think they're lovely people, when it comes down to it."

"Apart from the crime," Ami said flatly.

Hannah laughed. Her stomach then grumbled and she poked her belly. "Time to eat soon," she said. "I have to tell the kitchen."

Hannah walked away, leaving us three women together. It was awkward. I didn't know what to say at all so I looked around the room. I recognized Ryosuke from the *shibari* club although he was dressed in a bright pink suit with his hair coiffed.

"Oh, look," I said and pointed. "It's Ryosuke,"

"Eh, *Shibata-san ga shiteru yo*?" Saya asked.

From what Saya said, it looked like his last name was Shibata and she was asking if I knew him.

"*Shikoshi*," I answered.

Saya nodded. "Mm. *Atashi mo. Shibata-san no yubi ga sugoi yasashii desu yo ne*."

Ami's eyebrows shot up at what Saya said. There

must have been some implication in what Saya said that was lost on me.

"*Sa, mo hitotsu ga,*" Saya said while lifting her *sake* cup. She bounced over to the *sake* barrel just as Hannah took a microphone and spoke in her Australian-accented Japanese to announce that the food was ready. Some white uniformed staff brought out silver platters to lay on long tables, buffet style.

Without needing prompting, everyone began to line up. There was so much food, I ended up filling three plates, taking turns going back and forth after finding an empty table. During one of the food trips, I noticed Ryosuke and waved to him. He reciprocated with a slight nod and smile. I also refilled my *sake* cup and got one for Ami as well. We sat and ate together at the same table. Soon, the music changed from light jazz to more obvious Christmas themed music.

Ami sat at the table and played on her smartphone. She did this often but for some reason I was irritated that she was doing it at the party. She had been doing the same thing when we were at the *shibari* club.

Hannah found us, holding a tiny plate with a slice of strawberry cream cake and a red macaron. She sat down. As she did, I noticed that her neck was moist with sweat.

"I hope the food is good," she said. "Oh." She stopped to look behind us and wave. "The Harada's made it. Kaori had a baby, oh, maybe six months ago. I haven't seen her in all that time. I guess that's what happens when you have a baby." Hannah looked at both of us. She took a bite of the macaron, which left some red speckles on her lips that she brushed off with a finger. "What about you two?"

"What about us?" Ami asked, not looking up.

Catori Sarmiento

"Well, a baby? One day, maybe?"

Ami scoffed and I said nothing from surprise. We'd hardly been dating for more than a year. The question of having a kid was a long way off.

"And you?" Ami asked.

Hannah leaned back and looked up in thought. "Nah, I work with kids enough to know that I don't want any. It takes so much of your time. I wouldn't be able to do what I want, would I?" She shook her head.

"I don't know," I said, thinking of how many siblings I'd had and how my mother seemed to find her own time for her hobbies or odd jobs. "I guess you just figure it out."

"Lucky for me that my husband's the younger son, so there's not much expectation."

"Maybe we can stop talking about having kids?" Ami murmured.

Hannah ate some of her cake. She then waved at someone else and stood up, leaving her plate on the table. "Sorry, I'll be right back," she said and walked away.

"Ami?" I asked. I looked over to Ami who was still looking at her phone. "I feel like I'm talking to the side of your face," I said.

She put her phone down and looked at me. "Yes?"

"What's wrong? You seem irritated."

"*Sono tori*. It's because I am."

"Why?"

Ami sighed. "She just bothers me. Kind of *nechi-nechi*." Ami sighed. "I also want a smoke."

"Do you want to just get out of here?" I offered.

Ami shrugged. "I'll just get a coffee," she said.

I finished most of my food but became so full that the sight and smell of the buffet table made me nauseous.

Ami drank her coffee. I was having a good time just watching all the people interact, and listening to the Japanese being spoken, trying to pick up what I could.

Hannah started speaking with a microphone again and soon after, several people took turns going up to the Christmas tree and taking one small present each.

"I'll go," I offered, so that Ami could sit and drink her coffee.

I waited my turn and took two small boxes, each wrapped in the same red and green paper decorated with white snowflakes. I handed one to Ami.

"I wonder what it is?"

I opened the wrapper and the white box and inside was a small silver circle on a red ribbon that was stamped with *kanji*.

"It's the year," Ami said. She leaned over to view the gift. "It's nice."

Ami rested her head on my shoulder. I wanted to stay at the party but not if she wasn't feeling well. "Let's go," I said.

"No," Ami said. "You wanted to be here."

"It's okay," I said and stood up to leave. "I'll tell Hannah."

I found Hannah with Saya as they were talking a picture together in front of the tree. I caught her attention and told her that we were leaving. She wasn't upset, but smiled and gave me a hug, thanking me for coming.

"You should take a picture before you leave," Hannah said. "Go get your girl and I'll take your picture."

I went back to the table to tell Ami. Although I noticed that her eyes were bloodshot, she said, "That's a good idea."

Since I had a basic phone, we decided that Ami's would be the best to take a picture with. We stood in front of the Christmas tree, standing next to each other as we held hands. Hannah held Ami's smartphone to take the picture. As she counted down, I decided to do the cheesy thing and kiss Ami on the cheek. That caused Hannah to say, "Aww."

She gave Ami back her phone and we both looked at the picture.

"It looks better than the one from the maid café," I said.

Ami chuckled.

"You went to a maid café?" Hannah asked. "Oh, you'll have to tell me about that next time."

"Or not. It was embarrassing."

"That's even better!" Hannah hugged me. "Thanks for coming." Hannah also hugged Ami, who was a little more open to it than she had been before.

We left the party. As we did, Ami sent the picture to her father and we walked quietly together. The quiet was nice after being in a crowded room with music playing. Once we got on the train, we were lucky to find two open seats.

"Oh, *atama ga*," Ami said.

"Put your head down," I offered, tapping at my shoulder. She did. I rested my head on hers and stared out the window as the train passed by the city towers and the neon lights. At one of the stops, the passengers that were standing departed and I saw our reflection in the window. Ami was sleeping and had her hands on her lap. Her hair that had been tucked behind her head had come loose and hung over her cheek. My head rested on top of hers and in that reflection we seemed to look like two kittens snuggling together, seeking each other's warmth.

****

Ami and I spent the Winter Holiday together. On Christmas Eve night we couldn't decide what to eat for dinner until she declared, "Yama-*chan's*. They have the best chicken there. It'll be crowded, but it's worth it."

So, we took a very crowded train to Hachioji and exited to a brightly lit sidewalk. There was a game center near the train station which I noted for the way back and followed Ami to a narrow street and a two-story building with a long line of people waiting outside continuing outside the stairwell and onto the street.

At the top of the second floor were some windows showing the crowded patronage within. The sign above had the name of the restaurant in *kanji* and what looked like the hand-drawn image of a man with an overly large head, a tiny blue shirt, and what seemed to be chicken legs and wings but with human hands. His face had a bland expression as he held up his left hand in a peace sign while he held a red flag in his right.

The line moved quickly as a large party of people descended the steps.

We finally approached the front counter. The woman asked what I imagined to be how many people were in our group. Ami answered in quick Japanese. She turned with a smile.

"We're lucky! They have a good spot for us!"

Past the counter was a room packed with tables and people. Tables full of food and drinks. Rising in the air amongst the smoke was bouncing conversation and laughter. The petite lady led us along the side where the cooks were visible behind a tall counter and opaque steam until we were in a corner of the restaurant next to a window overlooking the street and the Lawson's on the corner.

We sat down. There were menus on the table. The woman explained how to order, but all I understood was when she said, "Welcome" and "Thank you."

Ami tapped her fingers on the table.

"I'm so excited," she said. "I haven't eaten here in a long time."

"It seems popular."

"I told you, right? It has the best chicken."

The waitress returned with a plate stacked with chicken wings and an empty stainless-steel bowl.

"So, there's a special way to eat them," she explained, "The Yama-*chan* way." She picked up a chicken wing. "You hold it like this and then you put the whole thing in your mouth and let it slide off inside, then you pull out the bones. Watch," She took off the end piece and placed the chicken wing in her mouth, then she pulled the end to show only the remaining bones, which she placed in the empty bowl.

I did the same. What I tasted was the juiciest, most savory, spiced chicken I had ever eaten. I let out a satisfied groan, the type that came when I ate something especially delicious. I immediately ate three more, all the while thinking that I had been lied to my whole life that America had the best chicken.

"I think we should order another plate," I said.

We ordered another plate of chicken, along with drinks that Ami chose.

"I'm getting full," I said. "But I know that if I don't eat at least five more of these, I'm going to regret it."

Ami laughed. She put her hand in front of her mouth as she did.

We split the bill. She took two packs of the complimentary matches. We walked down the steps and she handed me one of the packs, saying, "A souvenir."

I put it in my pocket and she put hers in her purse. When we went back to my decorated apartment, we both showered and changed. I brought the wrapped box into the sitting room and placed it on the table. I told her to open her eyes. Sitting across from her, I watched her untie the ribbon and lift the top. She held the top where it was for a little and when she finally put it to the side, I saw her wide smile.

Inside the box was a puzzle. Not just any puzzle, but one with all different kinds of realistic mushrooms. She kept smiling as she picked up the box and put her hand on the top. She kissed me and then took out her own present from her bag.

Ami passed the wrapped gift to me. "It took a long time to find," she said.

I opened it. Inside was a plastic wrapped book. On the cover were the characters from *Chrono Trigger*. I was speechless at the thoughtfulness. We spent the rest of the night doing the puzzle together while listening to Christmas music

Chapter 25

New Years Eve was when Ami and I stepped onto the Fifth Station at Mt. Fuji. There were others there, doing the same as we were: preparing for the night climb so that we could see the first sunrise of the new year.

"Oh, mushrooms," Ami said. She stopped and crouched down to investigate a few mushrooms that sprung out from the tree.

No amount of practice would have prepared me for what I saw. I was already breathing hard and sweating and then came face to face with the actual climb. It was one thing to have looked at it from afar, but another to see the hikers at various points on the height of the mountain, and to see what I still had to accomplish. A group of elderly hikers walked up together being motivated by a younger man carrying a pole with a small Japanese flag hanging tied to the top. He would shout *"Ganbatte!"* every few minutes and a few of the hikers would repeat it back.

From where I stood, I couldn't see the peak, just an uneven path snaking up the side of the mountain. How would I manage that? Ami must have noticed that I was daunted.

"Daijyoubu?" Ami asked.

"Ehm, I guess I'll find out."

Ami held my hand. "We'll go as far as we can," she said and kissed my cheek.

Her encouragement was what I needed to start. I kept walking, even when my calves burned. When I stopped to rest, to drink water, to just catch my breath, I looked down to see how much progress I'd made. I couldn't see where we started from anymore. There were treetops and the slope of the mountainside. I made it that far. I could go farther. I looked over at Ami who was leaning on her hiking pole. A little more and we'd be at the next station.

I handed my pole to the man who branded it. I was determined to get all of the stamps, to make it to the top.

A man next to me stopped, bent over, and vomited all over the volcanic rocks.

I could see the edge of the summit. I was a few hundred feet away. Just a few steps and I was breathless. An older man a few feet above me sat on a rock and breathed in from an oxygen tank. It took all my strength and will to continue up at a tiring pace.

But, then, we were at the top.

The sky was overcast and it began sprinkling. I was fatigued. My muscles quivered from overwork and I was still catching my breath. But I had done it. I turned to Ami and hugged her. I had been through a lot, we had been through a lot the past year, and we'd now climbed the tallest mountain in Japan together. It made me reflect on the turn in my life.

There were little things that were different, which was something that happened no matter where I would be, but so much was the same. There were basic understandings that all of us had about relationships, in general, that we should care about each other and care for each other. That was true with Natsumi and with her death. That was what I saw with the support that came in the Fukushima Disaster and the Souris Flood. Before I left for Tokyo a year ago, I was apoplectic about my situation, disgruntled with my experience of being ostracized and dismissed from teaching. But, by and large, I saw that most people would help when it came to it.

Ami had once talked about fate. I was never sure about where fate or predestination fit in with my life. Had I not been let go from my teaching position, I would have stayed in Minot and would have been homeless and may have been out of a job anyway if the school flooded. Because I left, I was spared that. Because of that, I met Ami at the exact time when we would both be having dinner at a hotel in Tokyo.

It could be that Ami was right about fate. If she was right about that, she was also right that we were meant to meet. *Koi no Yokan*. That we were predestined to fall in love. Or the heart string that connected our hearts. That was encouraging to think about, that there was a string that tied us together that I never wanted to break.

In my moment of absolute happiness, I hugged her.

"I love you," I said.

She smiled.

"I love you," she answered.

And when we kissed, I knew that with her was where I was meant to be.

A word about the author...

Catori Sarmiento is an author, artist, poet, and educator. She has written several books, including two award-winning titles *The Fortune Follies* and *Carnival Panic*. Although she began writing at an early age, it was not until she began writing poetry during her time as a University of Maryland student that she decided to seriously pursue professional writing. She went on to study writing in a graduate program at National University of San Diego while also living in Tokyo, Japan. When We Were Flowers is her first romance novel inspired by her time living in the Kanto area of Japan during the 2010s. She hopes all readers will enjoy her stories! www.catorisarmiento.com

Thank you for purchasing
this publication of The Wild Rose Press, Inc.

For questions or more information
contact us at
info@thewildrosepress.com.

The Wild Rose Press, Inc.
www.thewildrosepress.com